IN FOR A PENNY

A CLEOPATRA JONES MYSTERY

In for a Penny

Maggie Toussaint

FIVE STAR
A part of Gale, Cengage Learning

GALE
CENGAGE Learning™

Detroit • New York • San Francisco • New Haven, Conn • Waterville, Maine • London

GALE
CENGAGE Learning™

Copyright © 2008 by Maggie Toussaint.
Five Star Publishing, a part of Gale, Cengage Learning.

Set in 11 pt. Plantin.
Printed on permanent paper.

LIBRARY OF CONGRESS CATALOGING-IN-PUBLICATION DATA

Toussaint, Maggie.
    In for a penny : a Cleopatra Jones mystery / Maggie Toussaint. — 1st ed.
        p. cm.
    ISBN-13: 978-1-59414-646-6 (alk. paper)
    ISBN-10: 1-59414-646-2 (alk. paper)
    1. Single mothers—Fiction. 2. Women accountants—Fiction. 3. Bankers—Crimes against—Fiction. 4. Maryland—Fiction. I. Title.
PS3620.08915 2008
813'.6—dc22   2008000701

... and Ed Gorman.

Prir
1 2

This book is dedicated to the fabulous lady golfers of Glade Valley Golf Club in Walkersville, Maryland. For your patience and friendship, you have my undying gratitude. Those halcyon days of camaraderie in the ladies nine-hole league are a cherished memory.

ACKNOWLEDGMENTS

Many hands make light work and that's certainly true with this book. First, I need to thank my agent, Janet Benrey, for liking this story. Mystery writer Peter Abresch helped polish the opening. Accountant Carol Ann Greenwood graciously shared the ins and outs of her profession. My very own professional golfer, Craig Toussaint, helped with my "course management." Granddog Missie provided the inspiration for the short-haired Saint Bernard in the story. For her rowdy partner in crime, I used the personality of my other granddog, Leroy. (You know you can't just mention one grandbaby, you have to praise them equally.) Suzanne Phillips and Michelle Adams gave me a lifetime of material on daughterly interactions. Marianna Hagan and Suzanne Forsyth taught me the true value of friendship with their trust and devotion for all these many years. My mother read every story I ever wrote, not just the good ones; thanks for your unflagging belief in my ability to tell a story. Last, but not least, the Gray Beast in the story, our trusty Volvo sedan, provided many years of service.

CHAPTER 1

The golf course is one of the few places I don't have to pretend. Oh, I still give the socially correct answer of "fine" when asked how I am, but I am not fine. There's enough anger churning through my gut to fuel a volcano.

Golf therapy is how I'm relieving my stress. I imagine my ex-husband's face on every ball I hit, and when I'm done, I'm almost fine.

My name is Cleopatra Jones, Cleo for short. Self-employment allows me to spend my Wednesday mornings playing golf in the Ladies Nine Hole Golf League. So far in today's round, I hadn't experienced any signs of rebirth into a nicer, perkier thirty-five-year-old, but I hadn't given up hope.

Sunbeams danced around me on the number six ladies tee of the Hogan's Glen Golf Club as I aimed my shoulders at the distant flag. I swung hard. My tee shot hooked left into the trees lining the fairway.

I whacked my driver against the ground. Exorcising Charlie through golf was therapeutic to my mental health, but it was hell on my golf score.

"Provisional ball," Jonette Moore suggested. People thought of Mutt and Jeff from the comics when they saw us together because I was tall and slender while she was short and stacked. I'd known Jonette since forever, a fact she never let me forget.

Jonette's tee shot taunted me with its perfect lie in the middle of the fairway. By mutual agreement we'd decided that the winner of the previous round got to drive the golf cart. I can't remember when I last drove Jonette around the course.

I dropped my provisional ball on the tee box. Hitting this second ball would speed our play if I couldn't find my first ball. Unfortunately, my provisional ball curved along the same evil trajectory into the woods.

Drat. I stomped back to the cart.

"Looks like you'll be buying more golf balls," Jonette said with a smirk.

I'd used up my late father's lifetime accumulation of golf balls during the first year of my golf therapy. If I didn't find either of my tee shots, I'd only have one ball left for the remaining three holes. Not good. "I've been over there before. The underbrush isn't too thick."

"Have you given any more thought to going out with that lawyer friend of Dean's?" Jonette asked as we zipped towards the woods. Dean was the current man in Jonette's life. He was also her boss at the tavern where she waited tables.

The thought of dating twisted my stomach in knots. "Sure I've thought about it. And the answer's no."

"Damn you, Cleo." Jonette waggled her finger at me. "Don't let Charlie win."

My ex hadn't won. I was being cautious. I wasn't giving up. Who said I had to jump back in the dating pool right away? The view from the high dive was terrifying. "I'm not ready."

"Maybe some hot guys will move into White Rock. I wouldn't mind checking them out for you."

"That development is wishful thinking and you know it." The much-hyped new subdivision on the old Wingate farm had stalled in the bulldozer phase of construction.

"You need to get out of that house."

"If I wanted to get out of the house, I should take a golf lesson so I don't spend half my round scouring the woods for my balls."

"There's an idea." Jonette beamed her approval. "The golf pro is definitely hot."

I sure wished Jonette would get off this dating kick. "Don't go getting any ideas. I'm not interested in dating."

"You may be right about Rafe Golden," Jonette said. "He's supposedly slept his way through the women of the club. But, he's a such a hunk."

"I don't want a man that reeks of sex appeal. If I ever dated again, I'd want someone like me. Hardworking, loyal, trustworthy, family oriented, and obedient."

Jonette's mouth gaped. "Where's the excitement in that? You need someone to sweep you off your feet."

I leveled my sternest gaze at her. "Forget it."

Jonette rolled her eyes and huffed her disapproval.

Too bad. If I could erase Charlie from my life, I would, but his weekend visitations with our two daughters put him on my schedule every week.

Shedding Charlie was more difficult than getting fungus out from under a toenail. Just when you thought you had the problem solved, there it was again.

Jonette stopped the cart near where my balls had disappeared into the woods. "Should I help you look?"

"Stay put." I waved her back in her seat. "I won't be responsible for you getting poison ivy again."

I marched into the thicket alone, kicking through last year's musty leaves as I searched for my golf balls. A gleam of white beckoned in the honeysuckle-scented shade ahead.

Both balls lay adjacent to each other. That brought a fleeting smile to my face. Hell, if I couldn't hit straight I'd settle for consistent. "Got 'em," I called to Jonette as I pocketed my provisional ball.

A massive maple stood between me and the number six green, blocking forward progress. I had no choice but to chip out of the rough and hope for distance on my next shot. Of course if I missed and hit the slender trunks of the myriad of smaller obstacles between me and the fairway I'd quite possibly lobotomize myself. Fair enough.

I marched back to the cart and selected my pitching wedge. "You might want to back up the cart while I hit."

"Won't do it." Jonette smoothed her flirty little red golf skirt. "But you hit me and you are one dead dog."

Back in the woods, I took aim at Jonette and whaled away. My ball skimmed over the top of her head and landed in the center of the fairway.

Success tasted sweet in my mouth. "Hot damn! I'm on a roll." I jogged back to the cart and noticed Jonette had a death grip on the steering wheel. Served her right. I thumped her on her back.

She choked in a breath of air. "Didn't think you had it in you, Cleo. Nice shot."

I was still furthest from the hole, so I exchanged my wedge for a seven iron. In truth, I didn't see the point of having so many clubs in my bag when my trusty seven worked well for any occasion. I took a deep breath and swung easy.

My ball landed twenty yards ahead of Jonette's. Counting all my strokes, I lay three to her one, but that was beside the point. If the world ended right this minute, my ball would still be closest to the pin. That was worth a lot.

The golf gods must have taken a lunch break because my next shot zoomed over the green and down a steep embankment. I grabbed a club and started down the hill.

Jonette followed, sniffing tentatively. "Do you smell something?"

I did. My eyes watered at the latrine-like stench. It wasn't unusual to smell something ripe this time of year in Maryland. The odor could be anything from farmers manuring their fields to the groundskeeper's natural fertilizers. "No telling what that is."

Using my golf club as a cane, I crabbed sideways down the hill, scoping the terrain near my feet for my ball. At the base of the hill, I saw something that resembled a bundle of clothes. A huge lump formed in my throat. "What is that?"

"I've got a real bad feeling about this," Jonette said.

"You and me both." The closer I came, the more certain details stood out in my mind. I saw that the bundle of clothes was actually an expensive business suit. Pinstriped trouser legs were rolled up to reveal dark crew socks and black-and-white golf shoes.

The man lay on his back staring straight up at the cloudless sky. Between his slate-gray eyes was a dark circular wound. Bloodstained grass framed his lifeless head in a grotesque abstract shape, as if some wicked cartoonist had thought to ink in the conversation.

Only there was no conversation coming from this person. He was dead. Very dead.

My personal problems receded in a heartbeat. I fought down dizzying nausea as I felt my blood charge through me like a speeding freight train. I wanted to run and get far away from this grisly scene, but my feet weren't listening.

I knew this man. He was my ex's best friend and coworker down at the Hogan's Glen Bank. His name tumbled from my lips. "Dudley Doright."

CHAPTER 2

"Donny Davis," Jonette said. She bared her arms across her chest as if that would keep the death cooties at bay.

Technically she was right about the dead man's name. Donny Davis was Dudley's real name. Charlie had nicknamed Donny "Dudley Doright" in first grade and the name had stuck.

Jonette pointed to Dudley's crotch. "What are you going to do about that?"

Nestled in the narrowest vee of his inseam was my ball. I knew it was my ball because I could clearly see the initials I'd hastily scribbled on the brand new ball this morning. Those initials radiated from the dimpled surface like a search beacon in a midnight sky. I grimaced.

"How many penalty strokes do you get for hitting a dead man? What club has the correct loft for an inseam lie?" Jonette asked.

From the high-pitched tone of her voice, I knew Jonette was about to crack. The best thing would be to get her out of here, away from Dudley. I had to come up with a plan, fast.

"Don't be ridiculous. I wouldn't dream of playing that ball." I drew up a mental to do list. We needed help. An ambulance. The police.

I pointed up the incline. "Go back to the cart and call nine-one-one on your cell phone."

Jonette stomped her foot. "Damn him. Why is he dead? Why did *we* have to find him? Why couldn't Alveeta or Christine stumble across him?"

"I don't know, Jonette. This is a police matter. That's why you need to go call them."

"I can't. Folks know I have a history with Dudley. They're going to think I had something to do with his death. Let's get out of here. We can call the cops from the pro shop."

Dudley had stolen Jonette's virginity as a teen, foreclosed on her house in her twenties. They'd spent the next fifteen years ignoring each other. Not easy to do in a small town like Hogan's Glen.

"We can't just leave him here," I said.

Jonette's face turned as red as her golf skirt. "Are you choosing him over me?"

Of all times for their old rivalry to crop up. Here I was trying to help her save face, and she was giving me a hard time. I didn't have a cast-iron stomach either. I was, however, cursed with a strong streak of responsibility.

"This isn't a competition, Jonette," I said. "Dudley was a screwup, that's for sure, but he's also my daughters' godparent and honorary uncle. I thought you'd want to go back to the cart, but if you want to stay here, fine. I'll go make the call."

"No, wait. Don't leave me down here with him. Are you sure he's dead?"

"For God's sake, Jonette. There's a hole in his head and the ground is saturated with more blood than I've ever seen. How can he possibly be alive?"

"Would you check? Please?"

If Jonette wasn't my best friend in the whole world, I would have said hell no. But she was my friend and if she wanted me to check I would.

Acting like there was nothing to it, I nudged Dudley with the toe of my scuffed Foot Joys. I might as well have kicked a wooden bridge. A smelly wooden bridge. I fanned fresh air

15

towards my face. "Definitely dead."

Jonette's face turned green. "I'll make the call."

While Jonette scrambled back up the hill, I stood watch over Dudley. It didn't seem right that the sky should be so blue when something terrible had just happened. It should be dark and overcast and nasty. Sleeting even.

I'm an organized person and I like information to be arranged in tidy piles. To escape the nauseating terror clawing at my stomach, I imagined the scene before me was a disassembled jigsaw puzzle. The first piece of the puzzle was that Dudley had been shot. There were no guns lying about, so his wound was most likely not suicide. That meant someone else had been involved.

I glanced through the wire fence separating the out of bounds area from the nearby fallow farm field. Not a soul was in sight. Who did this? The better question was who *didn't* want to kill Dudley. We'd all wanted to from time to time, myself included. He had a talent for pissing people off. In addition to thinking he was the ultimate Casanova, Dudley liked to play God in the bank loan department.

He didn't look very godly now. I glanced down again, trying to be clinical and unfeeling. Not easy when my breakfast was looking for the emergency exit.

Dudley still wore his signature onyx ring and his watch. I wasn't about to search his pants for his billfold, but a robber would have taken the watch and ring. So, his demise probably wasn't a robbery.

And it wasn't like he had been in the wrong place at the wrong time. The golf course wasn't in a high crime area, not that there were many of those in Hogan's Glen.

That left murder. Sadly, I couldn't say Dudley didn't have any enemies. When it came to life, Dudley wasn't a nice guy. There was a long list of folks he'd hurt because of his attitude about money coming first. I'd turned a blind eye to Dudley's machinations because he was Charlie's friend. Now, with the clarity of a single mom trying to make ends meet, it was apparent that Dudley was a financial and emotional black hole, sucking the life out of anything he touched.

It was a Wednesday morning, for Pete's sake. Why wasn't Dudley in his office at the bank? I couldn't believe that he was dead, that his blood stained the ground at my feet.

Jonette climbed back down the hill. "The police are on their way. I also called the clubhouse and told them not to wait for us to finish today."

I nodded. With all the gurgling in my stomach, speaking didn't seem like such a good idea.

"You don't look so good, Clee." Jonette put her arm around my shoulder and steered me back up the side of the hill. We sat on the side of the green. With distance, I gained some needed perspective and my head cleared.

"You're no tower of strength, either," I said. "You're trembling like a leaf and your face is bile green."

"I can think of a hundred things I'd rather be doing right now. Wednesday mornings are supposed to be our fun time. This isn't fun and after we get done with all this mess, I've got to work tonight at the Tavern. My life sucks."

Sirens wailed in the distance. The police would be here soon. "Not as much as Dudley's. I wonder who killed him."

"I didn't do it. Though I can't say I never thought about it."

"I can't believe he's dead. Pinch me so I'll wake up from this bad dream."

Jonette pinched me.

I jerked away from her and rubbed my arm. "Ouch. That hurt."

"You said to pinch you."

"It was a figure of speech. Why aren't the police here yet?"

The sun went behind a cloud and the air temperature dropped several degrees. Goosebumps covered my arms and legs.

"I can forget about having a life now," Jonette said. "It's public record that Dudley screwed me every way possible. I'll probably spend the rest of my miserable existence doing time for a crime I didn't commit. Will you visit me in prison?"

"You're not going to prison. I won't let anyone railroad you for Dudley's murder."

Jonette shoved her hands in her skirt pockets. "I'm gonna hold you to that."

"We'll tell the cops what happened, and they'll let us go. You've got nothing to worry about."

Jonette started to say something, but the closing of a car door preempted whatever she was about to say.

"Cleo?"

I groaned aloud at the sound of that very familiar male voice. Of all the cops in the world, why did it have to be this one that responded to the call?

Detective Britt Radcliff had been the first on the scene when my screams of adultery had rent our peaceful neighborhood. He'd also been my fifth-grade Sunday School teacher. You might say, he'd spent his life looking out for me, as if he were my big brother.

Britt seemed fated to turn up at my most embarrassing moments. Wishing wouldn't make him go away. I'd tried that last time and it hadn't helped one bit.

Two uniformed officers scrambled down the hill to inspect the body, but Britt stayed with us. His thunderstorm gray eyes narrowed with suspicion. All of a sudden I felt like I was eleven years old again and guilty of coloring happy faces on the Sunday School walls with Jonette.

"This is not our fault, Britt." My face flushed with sudden heat. "We were playing through and found Dudley like this."

"It's okay, Cleo," Britt said, his voice softening. "No one is accusing you of anything. You and Jonette wait in a squad car while we secure the scene. I want statements from both of you."

Jonette turned white. "I need to move our golf cart. We're in the way of anyone else who'd want to play through."

"Don't worry about that," Britt said as he shepherded us towards the nearest squad car. "I've closed the course for the day. No other golfers will be coming through."

I had no doubt that the hand he had on each of our backs could just as easily snatch us up by our collars if we didn't do as he said. The dark suit he wore did little to hide the thick muscles of Britt's beefy frame.

I shivered. Sitting in a warm car, which had been driven right across the golf course in clear violation of every course rule, seemed like a wonderful idea to me. "Don't you need to separate us like they do on TV cop shows? How do you know that we won't be rehearsing our stories?"

"This isn't TV," Britt said harshly, then his tone softened. "I thought you'd be more comfortable in each other's company. Do I need to separate you two?"

"No," Jonette said. "Shut up, Clee. You're going to get us in trouble."

Britt opened the car door for us. "Give me a few minutes at the crime scene, then I'll be back to question you."

Jonette slid in next to me in the backseat. "Are you trying to get us arrested? We're not involved in this. We're innocent bystanders, remember? This is all Dudley's fault. Trust him to screw me over in death too."

It was hard to put Dudley's death out of my mind. His ghostly image and that dark, crowning bloodstain had been permanently imprinted on my retinas.

Dudley, what happened to you?

Dudley and Bitsy had double-dated with Charlie and me in

high school. They'd married while Dudley studied banking in college. It hadn't been long before he'd produced two boys to match our two girls. Sons that would now grow up without a father.

Charlie and Dudley. I had a zillion memories of the two of them together, laughing at the world. I shivered as another thought occurred to me. Were Dudley's extramarital affairs the reason behind Charlie's affair and subsequent marriage to Denise?

If it was, my ex was a damn fool. Charlie should have remembered how Dudley crumbled when Bitsy moved out and took his boys over to her mom's in Virginia. But then, Charlie had never been one to think long and hard with his brain.

Charlie's affair pushed me the closest I'd ever come to domestic violence. That damning credit card statement had exploded into my world, sending me into a screaming fit Hogan's Glen had never seen the like of. My Lexy had saved me from a career of making license plates. She'd called the cops before I killed her father.

I couldn't stop shivering. No wonder. Britt left the door open. "Close the door, Jonette. I'm freezing."

Jonette pulled the door closed. After a moment, she squeezed her balled fists against her crossed legs and gazed expectantly out the window. "I've got to pee. I hope this won't take long."

"Hell." Jonette had a thimble-sized bladder. If she had to pee, she had about five minutes until she'd pee anyway.

Thanks to Jonette, I knew the location of every bathroom within a forty-mile radius of Hogan's Glen. "Forget waiting for someone to take our statements. Let's make a dash for the clubhouse restroom and come right back. No one will even know we were gone."

Nodding, Jonette fumbled with the door for a minute. I shivered again. Once we made it to the clubhouse, I'd get some coffee and maybe buy myself a wind-shirt or a jacket. I couldn't believe how cold I was.

"Uh, slight problem here, Clee." Jonette's voice sounded oddly flat.

"Deal with it." For the first time I noticed the metal grate separating the front- and backseat. I couldn't wait to exit this tight little box. My chest hurt with the effort it took to breathe in this confined space. "Let's get out of here."

Jonette slumped back in the seat. "Can't. No door knob."

I clawed at my door and found the same thing. Nausea swirled up my throat like a plugged toilet. I held my hand over my mouth. If I didn't get out of here immediately, I was going to throw up all over this car. I looked at Jonette and she looked at me.

With one accord, our mouths opened. "Help!"

CHAPTER 3

After an eternity of ear-splitting screams, the door opened. Jonette bolted out of the car so fast you'd have thought her skirt was on fire. Britt reached for her, but she'd had years of practice overcoming obstacles, first as a star on our high school track team and second as a veteran of divorce courts. Jonette streaked towards freedom and indoor plumbing.

Fresh air wafted in my face, helping to quell my nausea. I stumbled out of the car in Jonette's wake. "She'll be right back." I lowered my voice. "She has to use the facilities."

Unfortunately, I'd moved too quickly, and a sudden spell of dizziness caused me to go temporarily blind. This is a thing that happens to me occasionally because of my low blood pressure. If I get up too quickly, often I see little floaters in my vision. Other times the world goes black for a few seconds.

Our club's golf professional, Rafe Golden, stood beside Britt. Thick strawberry-blonde hair crowned his head and eyebrows. This I knew from memory, but I couldn't tell you what clothes he had on right at this moment because I couldn't see a darn thing.

Manly aftershave filled my nostrils as someone reached to steady me. It wasn't Britt's spicy scent. It was the woodsy smell that permeated the pro shop. I was slick with nervous perspiration and slid right through the golf pro's hands. Just before my head clunked on the ground, Britt caught me as if I were a wayward football.

I prayed the ground would open up and swallow me whole. I was mortified. Absolutely humiliated. As the world brightened from black to gray to brilliant sunlight, I struggled to right myself.

Britt held me fast in a headlock. "For God's sake, Cleo. Be still. I'll get someone over here to check you out."

My hands fisted in the warm grass and my shirt clung to me like shrink wrap. "I'm okay. I just need a minute for my head to clear."

"You're not pregnant or anything, are you?" Britt asked. "My wife used to get light-headed when she was pregnant."

Not unless I was the victim of some heavenly prank, and I didn't think God would be that stupid. Heat poured off my face. "Absolutely not. Let go of me so that I can sit up."

Britt peered briefly at my pupils, then shoved my sun visor back in my hair and allowed me to sit up. "Only if you'll tell me what was going on in the squad car. What's with all the screaming?"

I stared at my trembling hands. Britt already knew I had lunatic tendencies, but I'd hoped my screaming fit wasn't common knowledge. If I had to tell the truth right now, my cover with the golf pro would be forever blown. "This is embarrassing."

Changing the subject is what my girls always did when they wanted to skirt the truth. Directly below me was the crime scene. I couldn't help but take in the beehive of activity down there.

When I saw an officer bag my golf ball, my heart skipped a beat. I pointed at the evidence bag. "My fingerprints are all over that golf ball. I didn't kill Dudley. I just found him. Make sure they know that, Britt. My golf ball is not evidence."

"Take it easy, Cleo," Britt said in a soothing voice. "You've had something of a shock here today. Should I call your mom to come when we finish up here?"

That did it. I didn't need anyone taking care of me. And I resented the fact that Britt thought I couldn't handle this. The world was in perfect Technicolor again, so I assumed my equilibrium was back. I struggled to my feet. "I'm fine. This happens to me sometimes. It's a blood pressure thing."

Rafe Golden gathered me up by my armpits and effortlessly lifted me to my feet. Horrors. I was wet all over, but wet arm pits implied that I didn't recognize the importance of deodorant.

Mine had obviously worn off and now my arm pit sweat was on the hands of the sexiest man in town. Well, at least now I wouldn't have to worry about any date anxiety with this man. No way would he want to have anything to do with me after this.

I studied Rafe out of the corner of my eye. Jonette was right about his being hot. His six-foot-tall athletic frame weighed something in the vicinity of one hundred eighty pounds. His thickly lashed bedroom eyes seemed to be riveted on me.

Why now? Was he amused by my helplessness? Was he gathering information to entertain the guys around the clubhouse bar?

"Dammit, Cleo, what went wrong in the car?" Britt asked. "Did Jonette tell you something about the murder that alarmed you?"

I tried to shrug off Rafe's grip around my torso, but I might as well have been back in Britt's headlock. Typical male response. Whenever there was a problem, a man answered with his physical strength, while a woman used her head.

It was about time I started using mine.

From Britt's question about Jonette, I surmised that she was already a suspect. It was time for me to do a little damage control for my best friend. "No. I already told you. She had to go to the bathroom. That's why she was hollering. I was yelling because I didn't want to throw up all over the car. There. Are you satisfied?"

I was uncomfortably aware that Rafe's fingertips were still under the minor swell of my size thirty-four b's. If he had any thoughts of dating me, he would be checking out the merchandise. As it was, I wasn't even sure he realized I was female.

"Easy there, Red."

Rafe's sexy growl brought to mind things best done on satin sheets. I shivered in response, then as his supple fingers tightened around my torso I had a rewarding feminine experience. All on my own.

The unfamiliar thrill raced through my body at the speed of light and rendered me speechless. I savored the extrasensory burst of sensation like a dieter sneaking a forbidden slice of chocolate cake.

If this man had this effect on all women, maybe the stories about him weren't exaggerated. Maybe the word was out—why was I always the last to know these things—and the entire female contingent of the club had demands on his hands.

I'd spoken to Rafe Golden probably a dozen or so times as I signed in for the Ladies League, and I'd never gotten so much as a hint of any unusual sensory powers. Now I was feeling like slipping him in my golf bag and taking him home with me. I already knew he had great hands. I glanced down and was thrilled to see his feet were larger than Charlie's size tens.

The old adage about the correlation between long fingers, big feet, and a certain male body part came to mind. In recent years, I had been paying more attention to those old sayings.

Rafe Golden was looking better and better. But, there would be the problem of sharing him with the rest of the world. That wasn't going to happen.

I wasn't about to be made a fool of twice. I'd just have to worship Rafe Golden from afar and settle for the odd thrill whenever he touched me.

"Thank you for your help, Rafe." I squeezed out a thin smile. "I'm fine now." I wrenched myself sideways out of his grip and levered myself up on the warm hood of the squad car.

I'd just discovered a dead man, learned of a friend's murder, and melted because of a man's touch. As mornings went, this one was an emotional roller coaster.

Britt flipped open a notepad. "I'll take your statement now, Cleo. Tell me exactly what happened."

I obliged him, leaving out the part where Jonette was sure she was going to jail for Dudley's murder. By the time I finished, Jonette returned with the ladies from our league. I almost wept when I saw that she'd brought me a can of ginger ale. "God bless you," I said as I took the can from her and opened it.

Britt took Jonette's statement. While Jonette spoke, I noticed the other ladies mobbing Rafe. Through narrowed lashes, I studied them covertly, wondering if they were all undergoing rewarding feminine experiences. I couldn't tell a blasted thing. All I knew was that it annoyed me that they were hovering around him.

Good thing he wasn't mine. I'd have to constantly worry about sex-crazed women throwing themselves at him.

Mental head slap. I didn't want another man, particularly not one as sexy as Rafe. If I couldn't hold onto Charlie, who had been the love of my life before he fell from grace, why would I want to put myself through the agony of wondering if I could trust another man?

For kicks I tried our names together. Rafe and Cleo. Laughable, really. We didn't sound like a couple.

That was the downside of fantasies. When you took the next step and tried them on in real life, there were all sorts of problems. Things happened for a reason and you just had to go on to the next thing.

Or at least that's what I told myself every morning as I woke up alone. Then I made myself get out of bed, even though I'd love to spend the next twenty years lounging in my pajamas, but that would be taking the coward's way out. I was made of stronger stuff than that, according to Mama, who at this very moment was charging across the fairway.

I'd gotten Mama's height and slender frame, Daddy's red hair and green eyes. Today Mama wore her usual triple-stranded Barbara Bush pearls, along with a double-breasted navy-blue blazer, matching slacks, and sensible pumps. Her soft feminine disguise didn't fool me. She'd be ordering everyone around in a matter of seconds.

"Thanks a lot, Jonette," I grumbled.

Jonette shot me a thick grin. "You're welcome."

"Oh, do, Jesus! Cleo, my precious baby, tell me that you aren't warped for life and that I'm not going to be stuck with those two hellions to raise," Mama said as she swept me off the car and into her trembling arms.

I rolled my eyes at Jonette. This was classic Mama. She managed to take any event and make it all about her. When I was undergoing the double trauma of adultery and divorce, she had the entire family hovering in a holding pattern outside her cubicle in the hospital's Intensive Care Unit for days. "I'm fine, Mama. Dudley's not. He's dead as a door knob."

Mama released me and looked me over, worrying at my collar, adjusting my hunter-green golf shorts which weren't hanging straight after my squeaky slide off the car. "Better him than me, baby girl," Mama said. "I've got a lot of living to do yet." She pried the ginger ale from my hand and took a swig. "How'd he die?"

I glanced over at the body, which now rested in a black body bag, and realized that contrary to popular opinion, Mama did not have X-ray vision. "Gun shot wound. Right between the eyes."

Mama nodded in affirmation. "Serves him right. Bitsy should've shot him as soon as he started fooling around on her. This is what comes from amoral behavior. I swear, the whole damn country needs a refresher course on morals."

Bitsy was my other best friend. I couldn't imagine her killing anyone. She had the patience of Job and the disposition of a saint. Both of which had been necessary while she was married to Dudley.

I felt the color drain from my face. "Mama! Nobody thinks Bitsy shot him. She doesn't even live here anymore."

Mama nodded again. "Even better. If no one thinks she murdered him, then she'll get away with it. Although, I would have shot the man in his privates if he cheated on me."

I made a quick mental note to sell all of Daddy's guns on eBay before Mama took a notion to fix Charlie when he came over to pick up the girls this weekend. In the meantime, I hoped she didn't look under my bed, which is where I had all three of Daddy's guns squirreled away.

I fixed Mama with a grim glare. "If you don't behave, Britt is going to arrest you for slander. I'll tell him to throw away the key until you keep your thoughts to yourself."

"Hell will freeze over first," Mama muttered. "What's the point of having an opinion if you don't express it?"

What was the point indeed? The girls and I had moved in with Mama when my marriage disintegrated and we'd been regretting it ever since.

Twice I'd found us a nice three-bedroom apartment to move into. Twice we'd had health scares with Mama that turned out to be false alarms.

I had a feeling that not even the Third World War would get us out of her clutches. She was very passionate about having us around, whether we wanted to be there or not.

I strongly suspected her shenanigans were the result of having too much time on her hands. She stayed busy during tax time, of course, as January through April fifteenth was our busy season at Sampson Accounting. But after that, our business revolved around minor matters that didn't keep the two of us occupied full-time.

Not that I was complaining. If I worked more hours, I wouldn't be able to golf in the Ladies League. Priorities were important. And I was my number-one priority these days.

"Did you close the office?" I asked Mama.

"Sure did. A trauma of this magnitude calls for at least one pair of new shoes."

I shook my head in denial. "Mama, I'm a tight-fisted accountant. I don't believe in new shoes."

Mama humpfed. "You might as well spend your money, Cleo. The government takes such a big chunk that what's left over never seems like much. I say we hit every shoe store in Frederick. Lunch will be my treat." She turned to Jonette. "You're welcome to come along too, Johnsy."

Jonette's eyes crossed from the effort it took not to throttle Mama for calling her that. Husband number three had dubbed her Johnsy and Mama had picked it up. So far, Jonette's nickname had lasted five years longer than Roger Dalton. "No thanks. I've made other plans for the afternoon."

Mama stomped on Jonette's foot. "Don't be ridiculous. You can't desert Cleo in her hour of need."

Jonette howled and jumped around on one foot. "Dammit. That was my *good* foot. Why the hell did you do that?"

"Allow me." Rafe Golden scooped Jonette up into his arms.

Jonette wasn't in the mood to be soothed. "Put me down, you muscle-bound oaf."

Rafe took the hint and put her down.

I searched Jonette's face to see if she was in the thrall of a rewarding feminine experience after his touch. I didn't see the slightest indication of ecstasy or bliss, so I decided not to murder Jonette in front of witnesses. But I did need to get Mama out of here before she started ordering the entire police force around.

From a nearby treetop a bird sang out, purty-purty-purty. I most definitely didn't feel pretty. I felt like I needed a shower and a new life. I gripped Mama's elbow and tugged her forwards. "Come on now, Mama. It's not good for your heart to be getting so stirred up."

Mama sniffed copiously and dabbed at her dry eyes. She allowed herself to be steered towards the club parking lot. When Britt made no move to stop us, I assumed our leaving wasn't a problem. After all, he knew where we lived.

I led the parade back to my indestructible Volvo. I refused to ride in Jonette's death trap and Mama's ancient Oldsmobile navigated like a small ocean liner. It was the Gray Beast or nothing.

So much for my hour of need.

CHAPTER 4

I nibbled at my free lunch. Mama had insisted on going to a discount store, and she'd sprung for hot dogs. Not my favorite comfort food, but I needed something in my empty stomach. "Sure you don't want a bite?"

Jonette snorted. "Hell no. Your Mama lured me here under false pretenses. She promised me a real lunch. Grabbing a hot dog is not my idea of comfort food. I need about two pounds of macaroni and cheese followed by a hot fudge brownie sundae. With real ice cream." She pointed at my lunch. "No telling how old that hot dog is."

I shrugged. "Who cares? It's got enough preservatives in it that it'd be safe to eat two hundred years from now."

Jonette gestured towards the industrial girders and fluorescent lights overhead. "Why are we sitting here? I don't want to go shopping and neither do you." Jonette narrowed her gaze at me. "This is all your fault anyway. I told you in fourth grade that Charlie Jones was trouble and did you listen to me?"

I arched an eyebrow. "You're going to fling that in my face again? What about all those men I warned you off of? What about Lance and Nathan and Roger and Vern and Simon? I'd go on but I've run out of fingers."

"Hey. I only married three of those losers. And it wasn't my fault they were all such duds. They were really good kissers."

My recent encounter with Rafe Golden had me feeling as if there was life in this dead wood after all. Dreams and hopes and wishes all seemed as possible as my next breath. "Speaking of kissing, have you ever kissed the golf pro?"

Jonette gazed sharply at me. A slow smile tugged at the corners of her lips. "I'll be damned. It's finally happening, isn't it? You're noticing men. Good God Almighty. I'd dance a little jig but your mother smashed my foot. And no, I've not had the pleasure."

I licked the last of the mustard from my fingers. So much for Rafe's involvement with every female golfer at our club. Hope flickered like a single candle in the darkness. "Me either. I didn't even know I wanted to until today. For some reason, I want to jump his bones. Do you think my reaction is a springtime thing like sap rising in the trees and animals mating?"

Jonette patted my shoulder. "Yeah, you're such an animal and all that. But I have to warn you. Rafe Golden isn't a training wheels kind of date. He has a reputation for getting around."

Part of me wanted to play it safe but the rest of me wanted to forget that I had good reason to be cautious. That reckless part of me was willing to pay any price to feel alive again.

A stoop-shouldered woman with a screaming kid in her shopping cart wheeled past. I waited until I could hear myself think before I spoke again. "That is a problem. How would I know if he was sincere or if I was just the flavor of the week? God, Jonette. I feel like I'm in eighth grade again. Doesn't this attraction stuff ever get any easier?"

Her eyebrows arched up under her highlighted bangs. "You're asking *me?*"

I was a mother of two and I lived in the same house as my Mama, neither of which was conducive to a freewheeling singles atmosphere. Besides, Mama, Jonette, Charla, and Lexy all had ideas about the type of man that I should acquire.

Mama wanted me to marry a billionaire, while Jonette thought anything with a Y chromosome was fine. Charla wanted me to get back together with her father, and Lexy, bless her, was trying to fix me up with the football coach at the high school. I, of course, wanted Sean Connery, but he wasn't knocking down my door.

My gaze traveled down to my feet and I realized I still had on my golf shoes. I'd been doing a good job of not thinking about the events on the golf course until then, but that one glance took me right back to the number six rough and Dudley. Sitting there in the little hot dog alcove under fluorescent lights seemed every bit as surreal as the crime scene at Hogan's Glen Golf Club.

I'd have to tell the girls that Uncle Dudley was dead as soon as they got home from school. If I hadn't left my cell phone in my golf bag, I could start making calls while we waited here. But I wasn't the only one with a mobile phone. "Gimme your phone, Jonette. I should call Charlie and tell him about Dudley."

She shook her head. "Forget it. You're not putting yourself through that. Bad idea. Very bad idea."

I knew it was a bad idea, but it needed to be done. Charlie and I maintained an amicable façade for the girls, but Dudley's death would hit him hard. He didn't have any family left to help him bear up under this strain. I owed him the common courtesy of a phone call.

"Jonette, Charlie will come unglued when he finds out," I said. "He needs to hear the news from someone he knows, not the police."

"Cleo, don't do this to yourself. How can you forget for a minute that Charlie *threw* you away for Duh-nise? You don't owe him a damned thing. The man deserves to rot in hell. If you forget that, you're going to be stuck in emotional backwash forever. Cheaters never change. They cheat, period. Don't get sucked into thinking you're doing him any favors. The man made his bed. Let him lie there."

Two gnarled old men circled the alcove, obviously annoyed with us for sitting in their spot. I shifted uneasily on the bench we occupied. There was no question I hated what Charlie had done to our family, but there had been sixteen years of good times. I couldn't erase those memories.

My head ached. Charlie's betrayal of our wedding vows had cut deep, deeper than any hurt I had ever experienced, including natural childbirth. Jonette was right. Charlie Jones and his feelings were no longer my responsibility. "Sounds like you've got an ax or two to grind. Is this how you've managed to get on with your life?"

Jonette's lower lip trembled. "I feel for you, Cleo. I know exactly what you're going through with Charlie. It feels like your guts have been ripped out and trampled. It feels like you want to curl up in a ball and check out. You start to doubt everything about yourself, from your ability to tie your shoes to how you drive a car. Being tough is the only way to survive."

In that moment I wanted to lash out at any member of the male species. I glared at the old men orbiting our bench. From the way they started at my fierce expression, you'd have thought I was the Antichrist.

I drew in a shaky breath. Did I want to go through the rest of my life scaring old men? Was that really me? "Being tough sucks. I want my old life back."

Jonette growled at the old men and they shuffled away. "Get a grip. Your old life is gone. This is your new reality. If you had your old life back, you'd be watching Charlie like a hawk, waiting for him to mess up, and he would. There's no going back. Forward is the only way to go."

I hated that she was right. I wanted to stick my head in the sand and wake up when I felt whole again. That wasn't going to happen. My marriage was past tense, and so was Dudley.

Speaking of Dudley, I wondered about Jonette's edginess around the corpse. Had Britt's suspicions about Jonette had any basis? I cleared my throat delicately. "About Dudley. Is there anything I should know?"

Jonette stared at the thronged checkout lines. "What do you mean?"

"I have a feeling there's something you're not telling me about Dudley. Do you know why he's dead?"

Except for a sudden hitch in Jonette's breath, you wouldn't have known my question bothered her. "Sure do," she said. "The man was a royal prick. It's a wonder he lived this long."

"I know you two had your differences, but I was wondering if there might be something more going on. Was there ever a time when you wanted your name linked with Dudley's?"

Jonette leaped to her feet. "One little mistake. Where's your Christian charity? It's not enough that Bitsy hates my guts, you're going to hound me about it all of my days."

I waved her down. Jonette could do mad better than anybody I knew. She didn't have to convince me she was upset. Back in high school Dudley had cheated Jonette out of her virginity. That single event had a profound effect on all of our lives. "I'm not talking about ancient history, for Pete's sake. I'm talking about right now."

The old men made another lap past. They must have thought we were vacating the bench when Jonette got up. I glared at them again and they shuffled away. One of them flipped me a finger, but I couldn't be bothered with him right now.

Jonette was hiding something. I could smell it. The problem was that Jonette and Dudley had always been like oil and vinegar. Had something changed?

She had always claimed she hated Dudley. His denying her a bank loan when she desperately needed one hadn't helped either. Love and hate were two sides of the same coin as I had

35

recently discovered. What wasn't she telling me?

Jonette grabbed my leg. "This is Dudley we're talking about. The biggest liar of all time. What makes you think I'd let him back in my pants again? I'm not a complete idiot."

I pried her fingers loose lest the old men get the wrong idea. I loved Jonette like a sister but I knew she wasn't being completely truthful. Did that make her a murderess?

"Dammit, Jonette. You can't fool me. I know you're hiding something. Is it something that can get you arrested?"

She shot me her best Queen Bee look. "That's for me to know and you to find out."

That did it. I lunged for her throat.

"You girls ready to go?" Mama asked sweetly.

Sanity returned. If I was going to manhandle Jonette into spilling her guts, I was intelligent enough to do it where there were no witnesses. "Past ready." I glanced down and saw that Mama had no shopping bags attached to her hands. "Where are the shoes you came here to buy?"

"They didn't have my size in the style I wanted. My choices were to chop off my toes and buy a smaller shoe or stuff the toes of a larger pair with tissue paper. I don't need shoes that bad. Besides, we've still got the mall to go."

Jonette and I would kill each other if we had to spend more time together. "Not today. I've gotta get home, Mama. The girls will be home from school soon, and I have things that have to be done."

"Me too," Jonette added hastily as she limped out of the discount store. "I've got to get ready for work."

Mama ignored Jonette's comment and grabbed my arm. "Things? What kind of things do you have to do today?"

I got Mama settled in the passenger seat while Jonette climbed in the back. Walking around the car, I collected my thoughts.

If I dodged Mama's question, she'd be merciless and no telling what else she'd also weasel out of me. If I said what I was going to do, I'd hurt Jonette. But Jonette had hurt me by not trusting me, so I wasn't going to spare her feelings right now.

I started the car and pulled out on the highway. "Things. Like picking up the house. Like making calls. I'll offer for Bitsy and the boys to stay with us as long as they need to. It will be easier for her to make the funeral arrangements if she can stay here."

In my rearview mirror, I saw Jonette's face tighten with anger. She'd always had trouble with my friendship with Bitsy, even aside from the Dudley thing. Jonette viewed Bitsy as a rival for my friendship.

She had nothing to worry about there, and I'd told her so repeatedly over the years, but old insecurities die hard. In the twenty years I'd known Bitsy, we'd never shared the same level of closeness that Jonette and I had. For instance, I couldn't imagine ever lunging for Bitsy's throat.

Jonette was different. I could easily want to strangle her in one minute and then go out to dinner with her the next. She understood me like no one else and we'd always shared our deepest darkest secrets.

What she knew about me would easily fill a tell-all biography if I was famous or anything. Fortunately my lack of fame hadn't tempted Jonette to sell me out.

But now that my thoughts had started down that other road, I couldn't stop myself from connecting the dots. Jonette was lying about Dudley. I knew that as sure as I knew my name.

What I didn't know was how big a lie it was. Over the years, Jonette and I had been in the trenches many times, and she'd never had homicidal tendencies before. What would make her lie to her closest friend?

CHAPTER 5

I pulled up near Mama's whale of a car in the empty golf course parking lot. "I'll see you at home."

Mama didn't move a muscle. "Oh. I couldn't possibly drive. My heart, you know. We'll pick up my car tomorrow."

Jonette opened her door.

Her car was parked clear across the lot. "Wait, Jonette. I'll drive you over," I said.

"No thanks. I wouldn't want to put you out in your *hour of need.*"

It wasn't very sporting of her to go away mad. I wanted to grill her but of course I couldn't with Mama present, which was why I'd stopped at Mama's car first. Given Jonette's history with Dudley, I had to be sneaky if I wanted to pry her secrets out of her. "I'll call you," I said.

I watched her limp to her car, waiting until I knew for sure that her tin can cranked up and I didn't leave her stranded.

"You and Jonette settle your differences?" Mama asked.

I gripped the steering wheel tightly. Protecting Mama from Jonette's secrets involved walking a fine line. I loved them both dearly but everyone knew there were some things you didn't tell your Mama, no matter how old you were. Even though my Mama thought she knew everything, some of Jonette's secrets would make her hair stand on end. "Now why would you think that? You caught me about to strangle her there at the hot dog stand."

Mama tsked. "The way you girls go on. I've never understood how you two could be best friends one minute and mortal enemies the next. And then when the mud slinging stopped you'd be inseparable again. Is Dudley's death driving a wedge between you?"

I wondered how much Mama knew about Jonette and Dudley. Had Mama known that Jonette's mother had thrown her out like garbage because of Dudley? Mama had never questioned me about my wanting Jonette to come live with us.

But as a mother, I had a new perspective on that incident. If one of Charla or Lexy's friends asked to move in with us, I would worry about the legal ramifications. I'd also worry that the child's mother would be frantic until they learned of their child's whereabouts. Without a doubt, I would phone the child's mother. Is that what Mama had done?

"We didn't settle a darn thing," I said. "Jonette is holding out on me and it's irritating the daylights out of me. I'm worried that she's somehow mixed up in this mess with Dudley."

"Jonette's had a hard life," Mama said as I headed over the mountain to Hogan's Glen.

"I'm not in the mood for one of your lectures, Mama. If you recall, I'm the one who found the dead body today. I'm the one whose life is currently in the toilet, and I'll be damned if I'll let you lecture me about Jonette falling on hard times. This is supposed to be *my* hour of need."

Mama sniffed. "Don't get snippy with me, missy. Just because your father deeded the house over to you in his will doesn't mean I won't throw you out of my house."

I edged around the slow traffic in the right lane as we descended to the valley. It was a sore point with her that Daddy had entrusted the house to me.

I knew he'd done it because he'd trained me to think like him, but Mama was certain I had ulterior motives and that I'd made him change his will. "Look, neither of us is going to throw the other one out, so don't threaten me with that. Someone killed Dudley, and I'm afraid it might have been Jonette. Why else would she lie to me?"

Mama did a double take. "Bite your tongue. Our Jonette? A bloodthirsty murderer? Does she even own a gun?"

"Not unless she's taken to keeping multiple secrets from me. But in this day and age, you never know who'll be toting guns." I had three guns under my bed, but that was beside the point.

"You're right," Mama said. "I see stories on the news of kids shooting kids, of fathers killing their entire families. I tell you. The world's going to hell in a handbasket."

Personally, I didn't see how the entire world would fit in a handbasket, whatever that was. But I agreed with the sentiment.

There was too much craziness out there in the world. We didn't need it coming here to Hogan's Glen. "You don't mind if I invite Bitsy to stay, do you? We're just a few blocks from the funeral home and it would make everything so much easier for her."

Mama waved my comment off. "It's your house. Invite whomever you like."

It didn't take a genius to interpret that remark. She didn't want me to invite Bitsy to stay over, but she couldn't come out and say so because it would blow her self-proclaimed image as grand lady of the manor. She liked to appear as if she were the only sane person in a world flush with insanity.

Mama gripped the arm rest so tightly her knuckles gleamed. "Will she be bringing those hellion boys of hers? And that monster dog? The one that ate all my roses last summer?"

Bitsy had gotten her sons a second Saint Bernard after Dudley claimed the family dog in their divorce settlement. But the new dog had landed in a house of apathy and had grown up with very little supervision. Consequently, Mozart had no manners, but he was part of Bitsy's family.

"Definitely. The boys are old enough to go to a funeral. Artie's thirteen to Grant's twelve. They'll be fine."

Mama shuddered. "I'm calling my heart specialist as soon as I get home. With all this confusion, I'm going to need a tune-up."

I did my best not to roll my eyes. Mama's world revolved around her. What did it matter that a man was dead and a family was grieving? The only thing that mattered to Mama was herself.

I recognized Charlie's sleek BMW sedan in our driveway as I pulled in. My ex-husband lounged on the steps, waiting. In spite of my resolve to be firm, my heart lurched at his disheveled appearance. His thinning dark hair needed combing. His cotton dress shirt looked like he'd slept in it.

A short-haired Saint Bernard drooled on Charlie's shoulder. I recognized Dudley's dog at once and I ached for her loss. Madonna must be awfully confused. With Dudley not coming home last night, the dog had to think she'd been abandoned.

Dealing with Charlie in a civil manner took every bit of composure I possessed on a good day. This hadn't been a good day, and I didn't feel like being polite to anyone, much less my ex-husband. Life had handed me lemons and I didn't care for lemonade.

CHAPTER 6

"Shit," I muttered as I fumbled for my purse.

"Watch your language, Cleo," Mama advised. "It's not becoming for a lady to swear all the time."

"Mama, I don't have to be a lady around my ex-husband the adulterer."

"We could wait in the car until he goes, but that would inconvenience us. Rise above your feelings, dear." This from the woman who had forever barred Charlie from darkening the doorstep of our two-story Victorian house.

The fact that he'd had enough courage to wait on the steps for our return showed how desperate he was.

Charlie rose and walked toward my car. We were of equal height, he and I, and he'd never liked me to wear heels. The wonder of it all was that I'd let him tell me what to do for so long. Since the divorce, I'd binged on shoes with heels. Too bad I was still in my golf shoes.

When Charlie saw Mama in the passenger seat, he veered wide around her and ended up at my door. I saw the glassy tears in his baby-blue eyes and my wrath cooled a notch.

My instincts told me he was here for consolation. My brain reminded me he was married to another woman.

"I see you've heard the news," I said.

He reached for me, but I kept the car door between us. It was the best defense I could come up with on short notice. As a result, the clumsy embrace ended almost as soon as it began.

I swallowed my triumph with a dose of guilt. Charlie's color was off and his hands trembled. Even if he'd ruined my life, there was no reason for me to sink to his level. I was a bigger person than that.

"I'm sorry for your loss." I cleared my throat delicately. "I know you and Dudley were very close."

He pinched his nose to keep tears from flowing. "I can't believe he's dead."

If I turned my back on him and skirted around the car to Mama's side, he should get the message that I wasn't still his supportive wife. But in spite of all he'd put me through, I felt his pain.

I girded myself with facts. He was married to Denise. He'd betrayed my trust. He didn't deserve my sympathy. A little compassion was all he was getting from me.

I darted around the back of the car and assisted Mama from her seat, taking her arm as if she were a delicate hothouse flower. "It's real enough," I said. "I found the body."

Charlie trailed after us, the dog at his heels. "Why didn't you call me?"

I would not let him make me feel guilty. He wasn't my responsibility. "We're not married anymore, remember? You have a brand new wife. Go home and let her comfort you."

He kicked at the loose stones in the driveway. "Damn it, Cleo. I heard the news from Britt Radcliff and I detest that man. How do you think that made me feel?"

Mama answered for me. "Like the yellow-bellied snake you are?"

I patted her arm. The last thing I needed today was a trip to Intensive Care. Mama's hatred of Charlie ran deep. "Hush, Mama. Don't get all worked up. You have to think of your heart."

Charlie muttered something under his breath. "Will you just stop a minute, Clee? I need to talk to you."

I glared at him over my shoulder. Apparently he was used to my fierce stare, as he didn't quake like the old men at the discount store. Pity.

I could have used a bit more respect from Charlie, but his needs had always come first. Dismissing him would be great for my ego, but what if he wanted to discuss the children?

"I have to get Mama settled," I said. "If you have time to wait, I'll come out when I'm done."

Madonna politely pressed her head under my hand. I petted the very large dog and then slipped inside the house.

"How long you going to make him wait?" Mama asked when we were safely inside.

"Forever would serve him right, but the girls will be home from school soon. I'd just as soon be done with him before they get here. Maybe ten minutes?"

In that time, I went to the bathroom, fixed myself a glass of water, took off my golf shoes, and donned my faded pink slippers.

I called Bitsy but she didn't pick up the phone. At the tone on her answering machine, I invited her and the boys to stay here. When I ran out of things to do, I stepped out on the porch.

Charlie patted the seat next to him on the porch swing. I had too many memories of sitting beside him in that very swing, nestling my head on his broad muscular chest. Not going to happen today.

I sat in the nearby rocker. Madonna came over and placed her whole head in my lap. I scratched behind her ears. "What are you doing with Dudley's dog?"

Charlie's teary blue eyes peered out of his gaunt face. "When I heard about Dudley, I went and got her from his house. I wanted to keep the dog but Denise threw a fit. Says she's allergic."

Yeah right. Denise didn't want Charlie spending time with

anyone but her. She hated sharing him on the weekends with his daughters. Having a dog around would definitely cut into her Charlie time. "So?"

"So, I thought of you. The dog likes you, so it's all set."

Warning bells clanged in my head. Was Charlie telling me what to do? That was so not going to happen. "What's all set? I didn't agree to anything."

Charlie exhaled deeply. "You don't have to keep her for long. Bitsy and the boys will take her home after the funeral."

I had enough responsibility with Mama and the girls. Reasons why I couldn't keep the dog churned out of my mouth. "We live on a busy road, Charlie. This dog isn't used to traffic. What if she wanders out on the road? Kids are in and out of here all the time, and they won't always remember that the dog can't go out unsupervised. You should make other arrangements. Why don't you kennel the dog?"

"I can't put her in a cage." Charlie's voice broke. "She was Dudley's dog. Doesn't that mean anything to you? Where's your heart?"

My chin came up. Charlie didn't have the market cornered on grief. "He was my friend too. But he wasn't a very nice person. Why did you let him be so mean to folks down at the bank?"

Charlie scowled. "Dudley always looked after the bottom line. The Board didn't care about his methods as long as the balance sheet looked good. That's why he got the job of financing that new development."

"I can't believe you'd bring up White Rock at a time like this. That farm acreage won't pass the percolation test. People are still laughing at Dudley about that boondoggle. Old Man Wingate must have laughed all the way to the bank with his pot of gold."

"Dudley got the job done." Charlie's blue eyes filled with

heat. "He had a plan that both the buyer and the developer liked. Wait and see. The whole community will benefit from the larger tax base."

The only thing that farm had going for it was its proximity to the Hogan's Glen city limit. Nothing Charlie said to me would convince me Dudley had been thinking of the community's welfare when he brokered that deal. I'd stopped trusting Charlie's version of the truth after that little matter of adultery. "People didn't like the way Dudley did business."

"Losers always complain. Their time would be better spent looking after their own bottom line. It wasn't Dudley's fault bank customers had financial troubles."

"That's a stupid thing to say." I saw red. My hands clenched in tight fists. "I'll bet it was one of those irate customers that did him in, and I wouldn't blame them. Dudley had no right to play God with the bank's money."

His eyes narrowed. Snide comments about his bank had not been allowed when we were married. "Well now. That would put Jonette at the top of the suspect list, wouldn't it? Which underscores my previous point. She's a loser."

I didn't have to take his condescension anymore. My opinion was just as valid as his, especially when it came to my best friend.

I jumped up and yelled down at him. "You never understood Jonette. All you ever saw was that when I was with her, I wasn't there for you. Jonette didn't murder anyone. She's my friend and I believe she didn't do it."

Charlie went very still on the swing. "You're a hypocrite if you can stand there and lecture me about friendship. My best friend is dead and Jonette probably murdered him. Where's your compassion? Don't you feel anything for me?"

If he only knew the things I felt for him, he'd be taking cover behind his car. I was sick and tired of his attitude about Jonette.

I had more sympathy for the grieving dog than I did for my ex-husband.

It was past time Charlie got the message through his thick skull. "You threw my friendship and compassion back in my face when you committed adultery. You made promises of fidelity, and you broke them over and over again. I won't be your friend, and you want to know why? Because I don't trust you."

Charlie stood up and grabbed me by the shoulders. I thought he was about to shake the daylights out of me, but at that moment, the girls walked up the sidewalk from school. Madonna woofed in greeting and bounded over to intercept them.

Charla dropped her bookbag and hugged the Saint Bernard. The color of her wavy chestnut hair exactly mirrored the dark brown of the dog's tri-colored coat. "Did we get a dog?" she asked me. Then she noticed her father standing behind me on the porch. She abandoned the dog, which bounded over to Lexy.

Charla ran up the stairs and hurled herself at the two of us. Charlie had no choice to let me go and catch her. "Daddy! I knew you two would get back together," Charla exclaimed.

Before the girls appeared I'd been thinking of wrapping my fingers around Charlie's thick neck and choking the life out of him. I swore inwardly. Reining in my temper was my only option right now. "I'm afraid we have some bad news for you girls. Lexy, come on up here."

Lexy edged up to my side. She wasn't as naïve and impulsive as her sister. Charla, on the other hand, had thrown her arms around Charlie and was hanging on for dear life. The dog sat next to Lexy and wagged its tail hopefully.

I looked at Charlie, hoping he'd be the man here and do this hard thing for our broken family. His blue eyes filled with tears and he looked like a puff of wind would blow him over.

Another minor twinge of sympathy bubbled out of the

dangerous emotions circulating through me. Charlie had lost his best friend. I could afford to be magnanimous just this once. "It's about your Uncle Dudley. He's no longer with us."

Charla lifted her head from her father's chest. Her eyes looked watery. "Uncle Dudley? What's wrong? Is he in the hospital?"

All eyes were on me. I wanted to spare my girls this pain, but there was no way to soften the news. My heart swelled with grief. "Afraid not, sweetheart. There's just no easy way to say this. Your Uncle Dudley is dead. Murdered."

"Are you sure?" Lexy asked.

I nodded slowly. "Real sure. I saw him myself." The wind seemed to go out of Lexy. I reached for her and hugged her close.

My eyes met Charlie's over our girls and I knew that, no matter what, we were aligned in our feelings for our children. For the first time since the divorce, I didn't feel quite so alone.

My heart melted enough to realize that having a dog here for a few days might not be such a bad thing. It would give us something external to focus on as we dealt with our grief. "Your father wants us to keep Madonna until Aunt Bitsy and the boys get here. It's a big responsibility. We'd have to keep track of her so that she doesn't accidentally wander out onto the road."

Lexy scooted out of my arms and hugged the dog. She'd inherited Charlie's jet-black hair, which exactly matched the thick eyebrow markings on the dog. "I'll watch her, Mom. She must wonder what the heck's going on and I know what that's like. Can she sleep in my room?"

Charla disengaged herself from her dad and followed Lexy and the dog inside the house. "No way. She's staying with me. I'm the oldest. I get first pick. Mom!"

Charlie looked momentarily pained at their squabbling. "Thanks for taking the dog, Clee."

I marveled that we were in accord. Not that I was in danger of succumbing to his boyish charm, but it was the first time since the divorce that I hadn't felt like strangling the life out of him. And it meant a lot that he'd been here when I told the girls about Dudley, even if he didn't say much.

While we stood there, my next-door neighbor came home. Ed Monday waved, then unloaded four shopping bags from the office supply place and ambled into his house as fast as a three-hundred-pound man could move.

My neighbor was something of a weird duck. His blinds and curtains were never open. I imagined the inside of his house to be dark as a subterranean crypt. Maybe he was a nudist and liked privacy so that he could prance around in his birthday suit.

Beside me, Charlie shoved his hands in his pockets. What should I do with him? If I invited Charlie in, Mama would probably have a heart attack. The girls were so busy with the dog, they'd forgotten all about their father. Speaking of the dog, I wondered what kind of food she ate. "Does this dog come with accessories?"

"Huh?"

So much for being on the same wavelength. I rephrased my question. "Dishes, leashes, bowls, food, dog bed? You know, dog stuff."

"It's in my trunk. Just a minute."

Charlie lugged the doggie gear to the porch. "Keep the girls away from your neighbor, Clee," he warned.

I figured he wasn't talking about nice old Mrs. Waltz in the house to my right. I glanced over at Ed Monday's heavily curtained house. "Why? Do you know something about him?"

Charlie lowered his voice and leaned in close. "I've seen him down at the bank a lot these past few weeks. Several times I heard raised voices when he was in with Dudley, and the last time we had security escort him out of the building."

My eyes rounded and my throat constricted. "Ohmigod," I whispered. "You think Ed killed Dudley?"

Charlie's eyes narrowed. "I don't know, and I don't trust him, that's for sure. Be careful and don't let the girls go over there. I'm glad you'll have the dog here for a few days."

So was I. There was a murderer running loose in Hogan's Glen. A big dog like Madonna would help me feel safer late at night.

Charlie left then, and I was spared the embarrassment of reminding him that he wasn't welcome in Mama's house, even though technically I owned the house. As long as my mother lived here, this would always be her place, no matter what the deed said.

If what Charlie said was true about my neighbor, I had plenty to worry about. I'd never considered reclusive Ed Monday to be a threat in the year he'd lived next door.

A lawn service cut his spartan yard, and he didn't have any flower beds to weed. We'd collected his newspapers the few times he'd gone away for a weekend, but that was it for neighborly interaction.

Ed looked like someone's grandpa. Sixtyish with a receding hairline and a protruding stomach. He didn't throw wild parties. A perfect neighbor.

Ed hadn't been here long enough to be mad at Dudley on general principle so the most likely cause for his atypical behavior was a money problem. What kind of financial trouble did Ed have? Insufficient funds? Gambling debts? It worried at me like an infected splinter.

I didn't want to agree with Charlie, but my family's safety came first. Until I knew more about what was going on in this community, I was going to assume everyone was guilty of murder, Ed Monday included.

Why couldn't life be as simple as an accounting problem? In my everyday world, I plugged financial information into spreadsheets and the answers came out automatically. Only real life didn't fit into tidy columns of numbers. Life didn't follow formulas. Life was messy.

My family wouldn't be safe until Dudley's killer was behind bars. Until then I'd be wise to remember that a killer walked our streets. I had just begun to think I was finally on the road to recovery, but Dudley's murder scared me witless. No matter how much my life was messed up, I was still in better shape than Dudley.

CHAPTER 7

"I'm gonna walk the dog after dinner." Lexy shoveled the dinner I'd so lovingly balanced and cooked to perfection down her throat as if she were in an eating contest.

"No you're not." Charla turned to me with anguish written all over her big brown eyes. "Mom, tell her that's not fair."

"Madonna likes me more than you," Lexy quickly interjected. "Can she sleep in my room tonight, Mom? Please?"

At the mention of her name, Madonna thumped her tail on the kitchen floor.

"Mo—om," Charla said. "Tell her the dog is sleeping with me."

It didn't matter to me who took care of the dog, but I couldn't take much more of this bickering. My patience was shot. All I wanted was to go to bed and forget today ever happened. The dog would be gone in a few days. By then, hopefully, the world would be normal again.

I looked up from buttering my roll and dispensed justice. "Lexy, you already had a turn walking the dog. Charla can take her out after dinner. Madonna will sleep in the kitchen. Don't get too attached to this dog."

Lexy's eyes brightened. "Can we keep her, Mom? We've never had a dog before. I want Madonna to be our dog, Mom."

The dog's tail thumped again and she looked expectantly at the table. I willed her to stay in place. If she stood, her head was high enough to rest comfortably on my plate and she outweighed me.

Speaking of plates, Charla's was untouched. Why wasn't she eating? Meatloaf was one of her favorite foods, and tonight's dinner was cooked to perfection. Was she in the throes of an eating disorder?

Charla joined forces with her sister. "We need this dog, Mom. It's like fate, or something. Her coat matches all of our hair colors. How perfect is that? It's like she was made for our family. Can we keep her, please?"

I felt my resolve wavering under their combined onslaught. Madonna was a very nice dog. "This situation is temporary. Bitsy's boys just lost their father. We can't take this dog from them, too."

Both faces fell. I felt like an ogre for laying it out for them in black and white, but it didn't help to shield them from the truth. This way they wouldn't get too attached to the dog. "Brownies for dessert," I said with forced cheer.

"I'm not hungry." Charla pushed away from the table and headed outside with Madonna.

Lexy glared at me and stomped off to her room.

Wasn't it just like Mama to be off at bingo night when all the fireworks happened in our kitchen? Standing firm required lots of chocolate. Good thing I had an entire tray of turtle brownies.

Before I turned in for the night, I walked the dog. I didn't know if Madonna had to go out again, but I figured it wouldn't hurt to try. I tucked a plastic grocery bag in my jacket pocket just in case there was anything to pick up.

We walked on the sidewalk past Mrs. Waltz's house and down to the end of the block before we turned around. The street was empty and I was glad for the corner streetlights. Madonna padded slowly at my side, her head leaning against my leg, as if she would perish without that human contact.

She was in a strange place and her person was long gone. My heart ached for her. I'd love to make things right for her, but I didn't know how.

A passing car slowed, then crossed the street to our side. The driver's window rolled down.

I didn't recognize the car and felt uneasy. What if the person who killed Dudley was stalking our streets looking for potential victims? I tightened my grip on Madonna's leash. How fast could I sprint back to my front door?

"Hey, Mrs. Jones." The woman tapped on the side of her car. "Hey, Madonna."

Madonna's ears perked up at the familiar voice and she dragged me over to the car. Up until that point I'd been walking her. Now she was walking me.

I squinted into the boxy little sedan. Murderers didn't go around greeting folks and their dogs, did they? A familiar freckled face smiled at me as she leaned out to pet Madonna.

Katie Morales. She used to baby-sit for my kids when we lived in the old neighborhood. These days she cleaned people's teeth for a living. "Hey, Katie. What brings you downtown?"

"My boyfriend has a place out on Alternate Forty. I was on my way home when I saw you walking Madonna. I just had to stop and say hello. How you holding up, sweetie?"

In answer, Madonna licked Katie's entire face. Her tail wagged a few times before it dropped back between her legs.

"She didn't eat her dinner," I said.

"She won't eat if she's upset. When Mr. Davis had me watch her, I hand fed her for the first day or two. Once she got used to the change she was fine."

"You still living with your parents?" I asked. Katie's parents were Dudley's next-door neighbors.

"Yeah." Katie used both hands to massage Madonna's whole face. "I'm saving my money so that when I get married next year we'll have enough for a house down payment."

"You're engaged?"

Katie grinned. "Not exactly, but it won't be too much longer, I don't think."

"You should be careful being out this late. The police don't know what happened to Dudley. I wouldn't be out here myself if I didn't have to walk the dog."

"Madonna and I are used to being out this time of night. I usually saw her and Mr. Davis walking the neighborhood every night when I got in from Adam's."

I liked information to fit in neat little boxes. It seemed that Katie knew something about Dudley's final hours. "Did you see Dudley walking his dog last night?"

"Now that you mention it, I did see him, but he didn't have Madonna with him. He waved at me, though, just like he always does."

A chill snaked down my spine. Katie may have been the last person to see him alive. "Do you remember what time that was?"

"Sure do. Adam's mother always makes me clear out by eleven on weeknights. It takes me fifteen minutes to get home, so that would make it eleven fifteen."

Madonna suddenly arched her back and hunched her hindquarters in. A smelly, gooey mess piled up beneath her. My plastic grocery bag wasn't big enough to hold all that.

Katie held her nose. "Gross."

"She must not be feeling too good."

Katie recoiled into her car. "Gotta run. If you need anyone to pet-sit Madonna, keep me in mind. Madonna and I are buds."

Katie sped off. What I was going to do with the gloppy mess on Mrs. Waltz's sidewalk? Holding my breath, I scooped up as much as possible in my bag, then I ran and threw the bag in my trash can. Yuck.

I'd never missed this part of owning a pet. It was one thing to care for a sick kid. They were your own flesh and blood, after all. Doggie diarrhea was above and beyond the call of duty.

I thought about Dudley's neighborhood as I locked the door, started the dishwasher, and went to bed. Across the street from his house was a fallow farm field. That field backed up to the number six green on the golf course. Had Dudley planned to meet someone on the golf course? He could have walked there in less than ten minutes.

Madonna cried pitifully in my kitchen. She was in a new place, with strangers, and she couldn't possibly understand that Dudley wouldn't be coming back to get her. Tough love wasn't meant for situations like this. It wouldn't hurt anything if she slept in my room for a few days.

The dog seemed overjoyed by the change in plan and leaped into my bed. This wasn't what I had in mind, but I was too tired to argue with a dog that outweighed me. On the bright side, the dog generated heat and she really wanted to be with me.

Why did Madonna think sleeping in a bed was acceptable? The only reasonable explanation was that Dudley had trained the dog to sleep with him.

Dudley, the super stud, sleeping with his dog. Was he so hard up that only his dog would sleep with him? I'd never once suspected Dudley was lonely. He always seemed to have something going on. I yawned and snuggled into my side of the bed and dozed off.

I awakened with a big dog head lying on my chest, my sensible cotton nightgown sopping wet with doggie drool. The shock might have killed a lesser mortal, but I'd raised two kids and knew how to roll with the punches.

"Mom!" Charla burst into my bedroom, her red hair waving like a bright flag. "The dog's missing."

"I've got her," I said.

Charla's face fell and darts of jealousy shot out of her brown eyes. "No fair. She slept with you? In your bed? Don't you get detention for that?"

I edged out from under the dog's massive head. "Nobody said this household was a democracy."

Charla appeared to consider the import of the dog wearing me down. And in that second I knew trouble was brewing.

"Can I have a fringed leather motorcycle jacket? Can I? Can I?"

"As soon as I win the lottery." I shooed her out of my room.

I called Britt right after I sent the girls off to school. "Got some detective news for you," I said.

He yawned into the phone. "What kind of news?"

"I found out something last night. Dudley was in the habit of walking his dog every night about eleven-fifteen. The night he was killed, he went for a walk without his dog."

"And you know this because?"

I winced at his sharp tone. "I know what you're thinking. I'm not as nosy as Mama. I was out walking Dudley's dog, minding my own business, and Katie Morales stopped to see the dog. Katie comes home the same time each night and always sees Dudley out walking his dog. On the night he died, she says he went out alone."

"Did she see anyone else?"

"I didn't grill her. Figured you'd do that."

"Good. Keep your nose out of this investigation."

If I wanted to talk to people about Dudley's death, I would. I owed it to Dudley and his dog to make sure the police put his killer behind bars. "You sound tired."

Britt yawned again. "Stayed up all night working the case."

My ears pricked up. "What do you know?"

"We have a suspect in custody. Forensic samples and fingerprints went to the crime lab in Baltimore a few hours ago."

"Did you arrest someone?"

"Not yet."

"Why the heck not?"

"Circumstantial evidence. No murder weapon."

"Who is it?"

"This is police business, Cleo. You'll find out when the rest of the world does."

"You're holding out on me."

"It's my job to hold out on you. Keep that in mind."

As a kid I'd always hated it when adults said they did things for my benefit. Britt's statement rubbed me the same wrong way. I didn't like being kept out of the loop.

If he didn't have the gun, what were the odds he had the right person in custody? Telling me to stay out of the murder investigation was just like waving a red flag at a bull. Nothing suited me more than charging off to do a little investigating on my own.

I bet there were plenty of folks he hadn't considered before he'd zoomed in on his current suspect. There's no way he could have done a thorough investigation in less than twenty-four hours.

Because I did the taxes for most of the people in Hogan's Glen, I knew lots of dirt that he couldn't possibly know. The more I thought about it, the more I liked the idea of beating Britt at his own game.

The race was on. May the better woman win.

When I took Mama to get her car later that morning, the golf course parking lot was crowded. We had to weave through narrow rows of parked cars to get to her big clunker. I handed

Mama the grocery list after I installed her in Shamu.

"Just get the things on the list," I cautioned, narrowing my gaze to make sure she got my point. "No substitutions."

She gave me her patented look. The one where she slits her eyes, purses her lips—but not for long because she'd get wrinkles—and juts out her chin. The look that says Cleo, you've said something monumentally stupid.

"I was buying groceries before you were a gleam in your father's eye," Mama said.

Mama never shopped with a list. She bought what struck her fancy. I'd grown up with foods like tuna pot pie, Vienna sausage chow mein, and cheese doodle croutons. There were no limits to what Mama wouldn't mix or match when it came to food.

Self-preservation demanded I take charge of the cooking as soon as I moved back home. "Mama, don't get crazy on me today. You're to buy two pounds of ground turkey, two bags of salad, and lasagna makings. Bitsy and the boys wouldn't know what to do with your culinary creations."

Mama slapped her hands against her steering wheel. "Masterpieces. My dishes are masterpieces, and you're wrong. Boys will eat anything."

She was probably right, but why take the chance? "Well then, let me be wrong with normal lasagna. I expect very ordinary ingredients for my ordinary main dish tonight. Don't bring home a gallon of picante sauce just because it's on sale."

"You're so bossy these days, Cleo," Mama grumbled. "You're absolutely no fun at all. I know exactly what you need."

I groaned because I knew what was coming out of Mama's mouth next. She and Jonette were united on this front, and the last thing I needed was to be reminded of my nonexistent sex life. "I gotta run, Mama. Have fun at the grocery store."

Mama wasn't put off by my hasty retreat. Her clarion tones, though intended for my ears only, rang out like the Liberty

Bell. "You need to get laid, Cleopatra Jones. And if you don't do it soon, I'm going to move out. I can't stand your bitchiness much longer."

I ignored the elderly gentlemen puttering around their cars, hoping against hope they didn't have their hearing aids turned on. Heat steamed from my face.

Ever since my divorce, I've felt out of step with everyone else. Not that I'd ever marched to the same beat as the world, but at least I'd been on a parallel course. Lately I had come to realize that I was running blind through life without a map.

Fumbling in the dark wasn't my style. I needed some semblance of order to my world and the only way I could accomplish that was through organization.

I stood next to the Gray Beast, holding my car keys as I reviewed my plans for the day. I had a stack of Homeowners Association audits to complete which is why I couldn't be spared for routine chores like grocery shopping for our houseguests.

I mentally ticked off my list of things to do. I needed to phone Jonette this morning to finesse the info she'd been withholding. We'd both feel better afterwards. Besides, our being on the outs with each other would only get worse if Bitsy arrived before we resolved our differences.

After I finished with Jonette, I needed to write out instructions for Charla and Lexy to put fresh linens on the beds. Then, if my work day went smoothly, all I would have left to do this evening would be to throw dinner together.

"Cleo?"

That sexy rumble needed no introduction. My hormones danced a little jig and I struggled to maintain my composure. Mama might be right about sex deprivation. Now that I was aware of Rafe, I couldn't stop wondering how it would be between us. "Hello, Rafe. Big turnout today."

I couldn't help but notice the way his big brown eyes smiled at me. Had he heard Mama hollering across the parking lot about my lack of a sex life?

From the corner of my mind came a reminder of my resolve to trust no one, to assume that everyone I came in contact with could be Dudley's murderer. I had to view Rafe in the same light, even if I was physically attracted to him.

"Today's our Senior Invitational," Rafe said. "Mild temperatures always increase our turnout."

I fanned myself. My core temperature soared with long and lean Rafe standing next to me. His intent gaze made me feel as if I were the most compelling female in the universe.

Heady stuff indeed, now that I recognized my need for a male to pleasure me. A smile percolated up through my protective shield before I could stop it.

Rafe's bedroom eyes warmed perceptibly. "I wanted to encourage you and Jonette Moore to finish your round for the Ladies League anytime this week. Just let one of us in the pro shop know what time is convenient for you."

His eyes seemed to be singing a siren song. Something along the lines of "Come to me, you beautiful woman, and I will show you the secrets of the universe." My body recognized the tune.

I was primed for him to touch me again, greedy for his touch. I'd never felt quite like this before and it didn't seem to fit the guidelines I'd established for exercising caution. I craved the sensual release that only he could give. And all it would take was a mere touch.

My brain computed the various ways I could inadvertently touch him. It could be something as blatant as an "accidental" stumble or as innocent as pretending to shoo a bug away from his fair head. The possibilities were endless, especially for someone living in the rich fantasy land I currently inhabited.

Common sense was slow to return, but when it did it was

something of a shock to realize I didn't have a hibiscus flower in my hair or a grass skirt swishing around my private parts. Instead, I had on a very practical taupe jacket dress and boring sling-back pumps.

Definitely not sex goddess clothing. Definitely not someone a golf pro would be interested in. Most definitely not someone who was exercising caution. "Uh. Sure. I'll check with Jonette and we'll come out soon."

My keys felt very warm in my hand. I should get in the Gray Beast and leave, but I just stood there wishing for some way to prolong our conversation. What could I talk to a golf pro about? What?

A coherent thought intruded on my fantasies. Lessons. I needed golf lessons. Caution flew out of my head altogether. "I wanted to ask you about your lesson program."

"You'd like to take lessons from me?"

His incredulous tone caught me by surprise. Had I missed something about the quality of my game? Did he think I was already good enough to go on the Pro Tour?

Maybe the man needed glasses. I'd been halfway decent before my divorce. Now my game was in the category of exceptionally terrible. I swung too hard, but golfing was so therapeutic I didn't really care about my score.

What I cared about was spending time alone with Rafe Golden. I envisioned melting into his hands as he adjusted my grip, monitored my hip rotation, and measured my swing plane.

At this point in my sexless life, I didn't have the slightest problem with paying a man to be attentive to me, even if it was under the guise of golf instruction. "Unless you think I don't need lessons," I added demurely.

I could see him struggling not to smile. Then he gave up and laughed out loud. "Lady, I can shave ten strokes off your game in one lesson, guaranteed. I thought you'd never ask. I've had my eye on that flat swing of yours for months."

My hopes plummeted. He'd been eyeing my flat swing? Not my luscious supple body? I groaned aloud. "That bad, is it?"

He inclined his head towards the pro shop. "Let's go inside and check my schedule for an opening. I'd love to teach you what I know about the golf swing."

Hmmm.

I quickly weighed the possibilities. Spend a few minutes with Rafe or drive to work?

My hormones made the decision for me. "All right." I'd never been in the pro shop in a dress and heels but there was always a first time for everything.

A few moments later I was regretting my decision. Amidst the gray-headed seniors in their colorful golf attire I faded into the woodwork in my dull, taupe-colored suit. I couldn't have been more uncomfortable if I'd worn an evening gown to the swimsuit competition of a beauty pageant.

Just when I was ready to bolt out the door, Rafe put his hand on the small of my back and guided me towards the counter and his assistant, Jasper Kingsland. The sudden electrical stimulus radiating from his touch brought an abrupt cessation of brainwaves as a hundred and twenty volts of pleasure short-circuited my system.

Needless to say, I kept moving forward and thought I was being extremely discreet about not jumping up and down and screaming "Yes! Yes! Yes!" But the golf ball I stepped on pitched me off balance to the right and into a display of state-of-the-art titanium drivers. I'd been wanting to take some of these demos out and hit them.

I was hitting them all right. First with my head and then with my shoulder and then with my hip. Golf balls that had been resting atop the display flew across the room like freshly popped corn. Two seniors went down as one overhead fluorescent light shattered with a loud pop.

The entire Titleist floor display tipped and fell on top of me and the seniors. I envisioned the headline for tomorrow's newspaper: "Seniors Crushed, Sex Crazed Divorcee Trashes Golf Shop."

CHAPTER 8

Rafe knelt next to me. "Cleo, are you all right?"

I blinked back tears. What a disaster. I was too embarrassed to move, too humiliated to find out what parts of me still worked. Obviously my brain was fried.

Glancing around the pro shop, I saw that the two felled seniors were scoping out my undies. I shot them my death glare as I assumed a more modest position. Only, my legs weren't cooperating.

I just wanted to ooze into the tight weave of the bright green industrial grade carpet. I suppose someone had picked this cheery green color because it looked like grass, but frankly it wasn't doing a thing for me. It wouldn't suck me down for love or money.

"Cleo? Is anything broken?" Rafe asked.

Only my pride, my self-respect, and maybe the heel of my shoe. "I'm okay."

I abandoned all attempts to right myself and stared into the very concerned eyes of the hunk hovering over me. The dark brown of his eyes reminded me of thick chocolate melted over perfect vine-ripened strawberries.

I imagined myself feeding him those very strawberries as he lounged beside me in a secluded glade wearing only a smile. In my mind's eye, he sensuously licked the chocolate off of my fingers, one at a time.

Back in the real world, I tried my best "come hither" smile

and willed my arms to reach for this edible chunk of man candy. He must have been receiving me on the same level because he scooped me up in his arms.

"Jasper, check the seniors and see if they need medical attention," Rafe said. "I'm taking Mrs. Jones back to my office."

Hot damn. Privacy.

And a man that could turn me on with just a touch. He had one arm around my waist and another around my legs. My blood sang the Hallelujah Chorus and my heart pounded double time. Virtual fireworks exploded in my head as he threaded his way past rows of golf bags and large buckets of mustard-colored range balls.

I envisioned him kissing me senseless as he settled me on his lap, then we'd have sex on his desk or maybe the floor. Only that green carpet didn't extend back here.

In this less customer-friendly area of the shop, the floor was bare concrete with a drain in the center of the room. I shivered at the image of being naked on that cold, stained cement. Okay, so the floor was out.

Chair sex suited me just fine.

I rubbed my fingers in a light caress of that downy hair at the base of his neckline and he jumped, dropping me on his desk. Fortunately it was clear of staplers and cups of pens and lamps and things that would hurt to sit on.

As soon as contact between us was broken, my brain activity increased to the fifty percent level, just above survival functioning but still locked in terminal stupidity. "What'd you do that for?" I asked.

He barred his arms across his chest. "I didn't mean to drop you. Sorry."

I ignored the strong urgency I felt to leap off his desk and back into his arms again. A few more brain cells came back on-line and I realized I owed the man an apology for ruining his store.

To keep myself from reaching for him, I gripped my hands tightly together in my lap. "I'm sorry too. For destroying your display, for possibly endangering the lives of your senior customers, and for falling at your feet, twice."

He seemed to relax when I stayed put. "What's with that, anyway?" he asked.

I assumed he was talking about my clumsiness around him. "Don't know." No way was I going to try to explain the NASCAR-like spate of hormones even now corrupting my thought processes.

One of the life lessons I had learned about dealing with alpha males like Rafe was that their egos needed absolutely no artificial inflation. If I told him that his touch melted all my bones, he'd think he was hell on wheels. And then he'd run off and try his luck with another female.

Been there. Done that.

"Rafe? Rafe, honey? You back there?"

Case in point. That lilting voice belonged to Christine Strand, the head of our Ladies League. Over the years she'd irritated me by throwing herself at Charlie. And from the way Rafe flinched, I could tell she wasn't exactly his favorite person either.

"Wait here," he muttered. "This won't take but a minute."

I used the minute to compose myself. I realized my taupe dress was hiked up a little too high on my thighs to be respectable, so I jumped down to jiggle everything into place.

I'd forgotten about my shoe being on the injured reserve list and the heel promptly came off, causing me to clutch at the desk as my ankle twisted with the broken shoe. Pain arrowed up my leg and took my breath away. I cried out in agony.

Between waves of pain I was struck by the bittersweet realization that I had only myself to blame. If I'd been thinking, I would have kept to my busy schedule today. The smart thing to do was to stay away from Rafe until I knew who had murdered Dudley.

The murder had happened here on this golf course. Who had better opportunity to commit a crime here than someone who worked here? I shouldn't have let myself be swayed by marauding hormones.

The Assistant Pro, whipcord-thin Jasper Kingsland, heard my cry and fixed me up with a bag of ice on my left foot while Rafe took care of Christine and the next foursome of seniors. Jasper cleared off Rafe's chair and repositioned me to prop my foot on Rafe's desk.

Did Jasper ever take off that navy-blue Nike swoosh cap? I'd yet to see his hair, but from the fullness of his dark bushy eyebrows, I guessed his hair must be of a similar texture. I pictured a dark unruly mop on top of his acorn-shaped head. The resulting image didn't look much like a golf pro, more like a monk. No wonder he wore the cap all the time.

The ice brought blessed relief to my throbbing ankle. "I'm having the worst luck lately at this golf course," I said. "First I stumble over a dead body and then I almost destroy the Pro Shop."

"The Pro Shop will be fine," Jasper said, his face tightening into a scowl. "As for Dudley, he only got what he deserved."

"Oh? Did you have a grievance against Dudley?" My throbbing ankle quickly took second place to my curiosity.

"That man was a crook and I'll never forgive him for the rest of my life." Jasper's spine went steel shaft rigid.

Jasper didn't like Dudley. It sounded like his dislike ran deep. Was it deep enough to cause him to murder Dudley?

Jasper Kingsland had been the assistant pro here for a few years, moving here after his mother relocated to the area. Because I was an accountant, my thoughts turned to money.

His salary couldn't be much.

Was his beef with Dudley over money? Dudley had been a long-time member of Hogan's Glen Golf Club. Did he owe the club money? I couldn't imagine a few outstanding cart fees driving someone to commit murder.

Thing was, I could sit here and guess all day and never come close to the truth about Jasper's feelings. If I wanted to know Jasper's issue with Dudley, I had to ask. "Why do you say that?"

As soon as the words were out of my mouth, I realized my folly. If Jasper Kingsland had indeed murdered Dudley, and if he suspected I was onto him, I was endangering myself. For all I knew, Jasper had a gun tucked in one of these dusty gray file cabinets back here and he'd murder me on the spot.

I wasn't ready to die. I had girls to raise, a Mama to take care of, and a dog that had already been traumatized once this week.

Why wasn't I some feminine bombshell that could infatuate a man by merely blinking my lush eyelashes? If I had Marilyn Monroe's allure and Kathleen Turner's deeply sensual voice, Jasper would have trouble remembering his name in my presence. I definitely needed male befuddlement if Jasper was the killer. It wasn't like I could get up and hightail it out of here.

I was in no position to defend myself with anything other than the small ice bag on my ankle. My only other weapon would be turning him in to the Internal Revenue Service for a tax audit.

I'm sure something questionable could be found in his taxes if the IRS nosed around a bit. Silently I practiced my lines if he came after me. *Stop! Or I'll sic the IRS on you.*

Not exactly blood-tingling suspense but it was the best I could do on short notice. I sat very still and tried to look as nonthreatening as possible.

Jasper kicked the daylights out of the file cabinet in the corner, and it scared me so much I almost fell out of my chair.

The man had a very short fuse.

"Do you remember that news story about the teachers' pension fund that was drained?" Jasper asked and I nodded. "My mother had her life savings in that fund," he continued. "She worked her entire life and for what? So some crook could skim all the money out of her account."

I tried to make some sense out of what Jasper said, but in my mind I was already running out of this room. At the same time, I watched him to see if he would suddenly pull a gun from a hiding place, or decide to kick my chair out from under me. If he shot me at this close range, I'd be a goner. "But Dudley worked at the bank. He didn't have anything to do with the teachers' pension fund."

"You're wrong." Jasper's thick eyebrows drew together in one long unibrow. "He was the only one on the Teachers' Fund Advisory Board that had the insider knowledge to pull off a job like this. The rest of the folks were just ordinary Joes like me."

Jasper wasn't making any sense, but he'd finally quit pacing around the office. I thought about his accusation and couldn't reconcile Dudley the swindler with the Dudley who used to vacation with me. Jasper's story just didn't ring true. "I don't get it. If Dudley was involved, why wasn't his name mentioned in the paper?"

Jasper picked up a broken golf club shaft and whacked it against his dark brown slacks. I think I wet my undies. I definitely didn't like being stuck back here in Rafe's office, but my ankle throbbed too much to stand. Why weren't there any golf clubs within my reach?

"You're kidding, right?" Jasper asked. "Dudley had connections. He hushed this up so no one even knew he was involved. I'm thinking he poured all that stolen money into that White Rock boondoggle. Dudley Do-right was definitely Dudley Do-wrong in my book. Every time I saw the man I wanted to whack him with my five wood."

That was an odd choice. The driver was the largest club in a golfer's bag. If I was going after someone and wanted to do serious damage to them, I'd whack them with my driver. "Your five wood?" I repeated lamely.

Jasper snorted and tossed down the broken shaft. "Hell yes. He's not good enough to hit with my driver. I paid four hundred dollars for that club. But my five wood, it's solid enough, but best of all, I never use it, so I wouldn't miss it when I broke it on a low-life scumbag like Dudley."

In my estimation, Jasper didn't seem to be homicidal, just mad. He was talking about doing something to Dudley, but that was a typical male reaction, talking about violence. And he did appear to be the type to use a golf club instead of a gun, but I really wanted to know if he owned a gun. So I asked him.

He stopped pacing and stared at me. "You're joking?"

I wasn't joking and I felt very much like I'd asked the wrong question. Did I have some bizarre death wish? Taunting a potential murderer wasn't good for longevity.

The air temperature in here seemed to drop twenty degrees. I shivered. How fast could I throw my ice bag at him and limp out of here?

"Where is she? What have you done with her?" Jonette said.

Relief swept through me. I'd never been so glad to hear Jonette's familiar voice in my life.

"Calm down, Ms. Moore," I heard Rafe say. "Cleo's in my office with Jasper. I'll escort you back there as soon as I'm finished with this customer."

"Forget that," Jonette said. "I'm not waiting for anything. I've already wasted too much time waiting and I have no patience left. Get out of my way."

I could just imagine Jonette sailing around the counter and threading her way through the crowded storage area. But what if Rafe and Jasper were in this murdering thing together? Were they tag team murderers? Was Jonette putting herself in harm's way by joining me in the back office?

"Cleo!" Jonette bellowed. "Where the hell are you?"

"Back here." I tried not to look at Jasper's unibrow or his clenched fists. Something was very screwy with that young man. I didn't want to hang around here and find out exactly which screw was loose. "I had an accident."

"Me too, and the accident is named Detective Britt Radcliff." Jonette rounded the corner and saw me. "You're hurt," she said.

Jonette's face was deathly pale and she wore yesterday's golf clothes. Coffee stains dotted her white polo shirt, deep creases lined her red golf skirt. I cautiously stood up. "I'll be fine. I need to get to work." I would have been fine too, except my ankle gave out immediately.

While I demonstrated my proficiency with cuss words, Jonette steadied me and dragged me out of there. "Let's get you home."

I wasn't headed home, but any place was better than this pro shop. I felt like a nursery rhyme character as I limped out, one shoe on and one shoe God knows where. The carnage in the pro shop had been stacked to one side and Christine Strand was nowhere in sight.

As I passed Rafe and his cluster of aged customers, he emoted concern. He could emote all he wanted. I was getting the hell out of there.

Jonette propelled me forward and into the parking lot. I didn't even protest as she stuffed me in her tin can of a car. "Dammit, Cleo. What happened to you? It's not fair you're hurt when it's my hour of need."

My blood ran cold. "Your hour of need? What happened?"

"I spent the night at the police station. Britt thinks I murdered Dudley."

CHAPTER 9

Damn Sam. She had me there. An overnight in jail trumped a busted ankle any day of the week. "You can't be serious."

Jonette started her car up and sped out of the lot. "He held me overnight while they searched my house, my car, and my bank accounts. I got strip-searched by a female officer. As if I could hide a gun in my privates. What the hell is wrong with the cops these days? Why aren't they out there catching the real crooks?"

My head pounded at her angry sentences. I felt like the rug had been pulled out from under me, again. I couldn't quite take it all in. "Start at the beginning. What happened after I dropped you off at the golf course yesterday afternoon?"

"What happened? I'll tell you what happened. Detective Britt Radcliff happened. He ruined my life. That's what. I'll be lucky if I still have a job after not showing up last night."

I rubbed my temples. "I don't understand."

Jonette ran a yellow light. She held one hand on the steering wheel, the other waved feverishly in front of me. "How hard can it be to follow? If I don't show up for my shift at the Tavern, I get sacked. Dean has to have reliable help."

"Calm down," I said, thinking of our precarious safety in this tin can. "Dean's not gonna fire you. He's got the hots for you and you're the best worker he's ever had. We'll tell Dean what happened and everything with your job will be fine."

"Easy for you to say," Jonette grumbled. "You don't have a

gay man living in your house, taxes you can't pay, and a crummy car that will kill us both if I wreck it."

"Speaking of which, slow down. Where are we going?"

"We're going home," Jonette said. "I need some TLC and by damn I'm gonna get it. This is my hour of need, I tell you."

My work could wait. Jonette needed me. "I could use a cup of tea," I said as she rocketed into my driveway and slammed on the brakes.

Jonette must need TLC desperately if she was willing to let Mama see her distress. I hoped Mama took her time at the grocery store so that Jonette and I had time to talk this out.

Of all days for me to sustain an injury, this had to be the worst. I had house guests coming in tonight, a funeral to attend, a temporary dog that needed walking, and two daughters to watch over until the murderer was caught.

I hobbled determinedly towards the house thinking "ouch, ouch, ouch" with every step I took. When I was halfway there, Ed Monday emerged from his shuttered house, stooped down to get his newspaper, then waved his pudgy hand. I couldn't help staring at him.

Now that we had a murderer on the loose, Ed Monday's antisocial tendencies stood out like a flashing red light. I hurried inside.

"That man creeps me out." Jonette shuddered. "What is he doing in that dark bat cave? Isn't he over the weight limit for vampires?"

I couldn't quite get the image of Ed Monday flying through the night sky to come into focus. Some things were better left as a mystery. "I dunno and I don't want to think about Ed Monday right now. We've got enough to deal with as it is."

Jonette set me up on the sofa with an ice bag and a cup of tea. She sat down in the overstuffed chair and slipped off her shoes, sitting on her feet in the rose-covered chair. She was quiet and I respected her need to gather her thoughts.

Until Madonna woke up and came down the stairs to greet us, it felt like old times again, with me on the sofa and Jonette in Grandmother's chair. It made me wonder how many times life circled back in on itself. We'd sat here in this room and worked our way through our problems more times than I wanted to count.

Jonette cooed over the dog. Madonna wagged her tail vigorously and licked Jonette's face. "How'd you end up with Dudley's dog?" she asked.

"Long story," I said. I was glad to see her respond to the dog. She'd been quiet for a long time. "The short of it is that it's temporary. Bitsy and her boys will be here tonight so we're trying not to become too attached. Lexy and Charla had hissy fits last night. You know how they've always wanted a dog."

"I do." Jonette scratched under Madonna's chin. "I understand completely. Madonna is such a cutie."

Cute was definitely in the eye of the beholder. Mounds of runny dog poop were not cute. Slime trails of doggie drool were not cute. "She's not so cute at midnight when she is determined to sleep in my bed."

"Your bed?" Jonette stopped in mid-stroke. "What's wrong with her dog bed?"

I shrugged. "I'm guessing Dudley allowed her to sleep with him. I gave in because I didn't want to traumatize her further."

"You're a softie."

Since Jonette was talking again, I figured it was safe to get to the heart of this new problem. "Tell me about the police station. Why do they think you killed Dudley?"

"Because they've all got their heads up their butts," Jonette said. "It's no secret I didn't like Dudley. The man screwed me over, literally and figuratively, but I didn't kill him."

My instincts might be fouled up, but there was nothing wrong with my loyalty. Jonette was my best friend and she wouldn't lie to me about something like this. "I know you didn't," I said. "What I don't know is why the police think you did. What's the deal here?"

"I was the last person seen with Dudley." Jonette's hands fluttered in front of her face. "Don't yell at me. I was in his car and we were looking at properties that the bank was foreclosing on. We stopped for dinner at Bobo Burgers and the cashier remembers seeing us both there. When I drove home, I found out that my roommate was entertaining. I couldn't face *two* gay males, so I went out for another long drive. I just drove, and when it got dark, I headed home. My roommate was occupied, so he can't verify when I returned."

Jonette had always wanted a little farmette on the edge of nowhere with lots of furry animals romping around. Whenever she had spare time, she rode around looking for someone down on their luck that might want to give their place away. I'd ridden the back roads with her plenty of times, and I didn't doubt her story for a second.

Personally, I hoped she never scraped together enough money to pull it off because I figured the furry little animals would be cute for about ten minutes and then all hell would break loose and I'd get stuck with a dozen goats and llamas. "Surely someone saw you? Didn't you stop at any traffic lights? What about bathrooms? I know you had to pee if you were out for a long time."

"I stopped at the burger place near Sharpsburg, but I don't recall seeing anyone," Jonette said. "The parking lot was empty."

"Didn't you order anything? How could you walk in there and not get French fries?"

Jonette pointed to her hips. "I didn't get anything because I already ate with Dudley. Besides, I'm having trouble stuffing everything in my little tavern girl outfit. Big bellies and thunder thighs may be all right for the average thirty-something, but those of us in the public eye have to be aware of our appearance."

Jonette weighed a hundred pounds soaking wet. She'd never had a problem with her weight. "Shoot. You're no more in the public eye than I am."

"But you look nice," Jonette said. "That Rafe Golden is noticing how nice you look. And so are a lot of other men if you'd just lift your head out of the sand."

"I'm not a way station for hapless males." My growing desire to jump the golf pro wasn't something I wanted to hash over right now. It was too new, too dangerous.

I sipped my tea. The color seemed to be coming back to Jonette's face. She was sitting back in the chair instead of perched on the edge of it like she wanted to attack. "So, what are we going to do?" I asked.

We were good enough friends that I didn't have to explain. Jonette knew I was talking about Dudley's murder even though we'd talked around that subject.

"I'd like to string Britt Radcliff up by his heels," Jonette said. "I thought I was under arrest, but they were holding me while they searched everything I owned to see if I had any of Dudley's stuff. If Britt hadn't been our Sunday School teacher, I would have walked out of there last night."

"Did you ask for a lawyer?"

"Hell no." Jonette pounded on the upholstered chair arm. "I don't need one snake to fight another. I've had enough of lawyers to last me a lifetime."

This was no time for Jonette to indulge in her hatred of the legal profession. "But Jonette, you're not divorcing Britt. You should've asked for an attorney. They'd have gotten you out of there immediately."

Jonette sprung to her feet and paced my living room floor.

Madonna's tail thumped on the hardwood floor as she followed Jonette with her big brown eyes.

"Don't you think I know that now?" Jonette asked. "Britt kept being so nice, even though he locked me in an interrogation room. He brought me fried chicken when I complained of being hungry. It was only when they brought in another officer and made me tell the whole story again that I got worried."

I shivered and the ice bag fell off. Pain shot up my leg from my twisted ankle. I reached down and replaced the ice bag. "Why didn't you call me?"

Anger flashed in Jonette's eyes as she made another pass around the room. "I thought I could handle it. The thing was, just as I got used to the idea of one thing, the next thing came along and I said to myself, 'This isn't too bad. I can handle this,' and before you know it, I was ass deep in alligators. The mayor was down there."

"Darnell? What does he have to do with this?"

"When Britt brought me dinner, I heard the mayor yelling at him that having a murderer in town was bad for business. He told Britt to stick me in a cell and throw away the key."

"The only reason Darnell Reynolds got to be mayor is that no one else wanted the job," I said.

"How can you stand being around him?"

"You know how. I don't have to like all my accounting clients same as you don't have to like all your tavern patrons. Darnell Reynolds is a bug and we'll fix him."

Poor Jonette. She'd had men trouble all her life. She didn't need Darnell breathing down her neck. "Listen, Jonette. You have rights. Darnell and Britt can't take them from you, but you can give them away if you're not careful. If you get hauled down there again, don't just sit there and take it. Call me or Mama and we'll get you out of there."

"Thanks." Jonette's brown eyes glassed over. She blinked

furiously to keep the tears in. She wouldn't cry in front of me. She never had. Not even when her mom had kicked her out of the house. She paused in front of the window and took a few deep breaths.

I wanted to go to her and hold her like one of my daughters, but Jonette would knock me down if I offered her physical comfort. Emotional support was all she ever allowed.

"We grew up here and between the two of us, we know everyone in town," I said. "No way will the cops or the mayor know the kind of stuff we know. We'll figure out who really killed Dudley and show those stupid men up. All they have is circumstantial evidence. Speaking of which, what circumstantial evidence do they have?"

Jonette's shoulders slumped and she sat again. "Go ahead and fuss at me. I yelled at Dudley in his bank office. When the cops questioned folks down there, someone remembered me screaming that I was going to kill Dudley."

"See? You should have called me." I managed a thin smile. "I would have told the cops you've threatened to kill Dudley routinely ever since sixth grade when he called you a girl."

Jonette snorted and her eyes twinkled. This was just what she needed. "That's right. You make sure *Detective Dumb as Dirt* hears that. Dudley didn't think anything of my recent threat because I've been yelling at him for years."

No kidding. The cops were stupid if they thought Jonette's threat to kill Dudley meant anything. No way was I going to sit back and let them railroad my best friend. But it troubled me that she'd had dinner with him. I didn't know how to deal with that.

"What else do they have?"

Jonette rubbed her eyes. "They took my fingerprints. They are going to match up to the prints in his car and his house because I was in both places. They took the clothes I wore

Tuesday. There's nothing on them but dog hair."

Jonette held out her hand to me. "They trimmed my nails to see if I had fought with Dudley. I didn't, so that should help to clear me. Thank God I don't own a gun."

"Britt seems convinced you are guilty of murdering Dudley. You and I better figure this out and quick," I said. "What do you know of Jasper Kingsland and his mom? Jasper claims Dudley was responsible for the schoolteachers' pension fund theft. Jasper's mom had her life savings in that fund and now Jasper loathes Dudley. I thought he was going to blow a gasket when I asked Jasper if he had a gun."

Jonette leaped to her feet again. Did she put Mexican jumping beans in her tea? "Don't you know who Jasper's mom is?"

"No." I scowled up at her animated face. "But you seem to know. Tell me."

Jonette's face glowed. "Violet Cooper is Jasper's mom. Do you get it now?"

Violet Cooper. Now why did that name sound familiar? I thrummed my fingers on the back of the sofa. I remembered she moved here about ten years ago, but I couldn't come up with anything else. "I'm drawing a blank."

"Violet Cooper won every shooting award there is," Jonette crowed. "She's Hogan County's answer to Annie Oakley. I bet her house has more guns in it than a gun shop. I'm going over there right now to find out if she shot Dudley."

I couldn't let her charge off alone into such a dangerous situation. I stood up on one foot and grabbed her arm. "You'll do no such thing. If she's a murderer, you'll end up just like Dudley. We need a plan. How about this? Daddy did her taxes for a couple of years, but someone else did them this year. I'll pay her a visit under the guise of checking up on former Sampson Accounting clients."

"When?"

"Soon. Right after Dudley's funeral," I said. "I've got a million things to do before then. You still remember how to tape up an ankle?"

"Clee, I could tape your ankle with one hand tied behind my back." Jonette strode towards the kitchen cabinet where the first aid supplies were kept. She returned with a roll of athletic tape and a pair of scissors.

I sat back down and propped my foot on the coffee table. "Tape this bad boy up and then sack out in my room for a bit. I'd offer you your old room, but I haven't seen the floor in there since Charla took occupancy."

"No thanks," Jonette said. "I'll go to my place. I can't face doggie drool sheets just now." Jonette yawned. "I feel like I could sleep for the next hundred years."

"Don't do that," I said. "It's my turn to have an hour of need again. I'm sure to require your special attention."

That brought a faint smile to Jonette's bow-shaped lips. "Wouldn't have it any other way."

CHAPTER 10

After Jonette left, I realized my keys to the office were in my purse which was five miles away at the golf club. With this bum ankle, five miles was as unobtainable as the moon, even with Jonette's superb tape job.

I rooted through the kitchen junk drawer until I found a spare set of keys. Shoes were out of the question, so I wore my fuzzy pink slippers. I hobbled through the backyard to the detached garage which served as the offices of Sampson Accounting.

The décor of our three-room suite was early do-it-yourself. Daddy had framed and paneled the walls, hiring a plumber and an electrician to put in the utilities. Over the years, Mama had added indoor/outdoor carpet, plants, and curtains. File cabinets lined three entire walls. Computers and telephones topped the two desks.

The folders for the various Homeowners Association audits were stacked in the center of my desk. Mama might be a pain in the butt about some things, but she was a machine when it came to work. Everything had a place and you better get with the program or else. Daddy had been content with this arrangement, and so was I.

It had often occurred to me that if Mama understood accounting, I would be out of a job. There were times when I thought she understood tax law, balance sheets, and government forms just fine, but she avoided the intensive detail work of accounting, sticking to the glory jobs of answering telephones, filing claims, and billing clients.

I pulled up a chair, rested my ankle on it, then got to work. Within minutes I was deep into homeowner dues and association expenses. Numbers flowed in comfortable, satisfying sequences. Unlike the messiness of human relationships, accounting was a very straightforward process.

Mathematical computations required no interpretation of hidden subtext or reading between the lines. And, in the unlikely event of a numerical error, a mistake was easily corrected. Why couldn't emotions be as logical and orderly as numbers?

I'd finished up one of the smaller audits and started on the Shady Hills audit when Mama burst into the office like a cyclone. "Baby Girl, you're hurt?" she asked, hurrying to my side.

I appreciated her concern, but I was in the groove here in my safe world of numbers. "I twisted my ankle. No big deal. I'll be good as new in a few days."

Mama wasn't deterred. "What about ice? Aren't you supposed to ice an injury for the first twenty-four hours?"

"I already iced it." I handed her the completed audit report. "This is done and can be invoiced. I'm working on Shady Hill right now."

To my dismay, Mama tossed the report on her desk. Heck. I could've done that. I braced myself for Mama in her nurse-martyr role. I could already see the wheels of possibilities spinning in her head.

"Don't you worry. I'll take care of everything," Mama said. "Did you eat lunch?"

I brushed my hair back behind my ears. Couldn't she see I wanted to be left alone? "I'm not hungry, Mama. I have work to do."

"Don't leave me hanging. What happened to your ankle?"

Mama bustled about in the little mini-kitchen in the rear closet. I heard her crack ice out of the ice-cube tray.

The best way to get Mama out of my hair was to let her think she was helping, so I'd better cooperate with whatever she had in mind.

As I explained about the golf club display and twisting my ankle and Jonette's ordeal, Mama covered my ankle with a towel-wrapped bag of ice. "You've had a rough day," she said, her voice dripping with sympathy. "Let me pop over to the house and get you a bowl of chicken soup."

Mama wasn't Jewish, but she viewed homemade chicken soup as human duct tape. It was one thing she never modified the recipe for. She kept a supply of it in the freezer for emergencies.

"I'm fine, Mama," I said.

"Nonsense. Chicken soup can fix anything. I'll be right back." Mama departed in a flurry of footsteps.

I had to admit that the ice eased the throbbing in my ankle. It wasn't so bad having Mama fuss over me, and my plan had worked like a charm. Mama felt like she was helping and I was alone in my office. What could be better? I picked up the Shady Hills folder and oriented myself to the expense invoices and deposit slips.

I'd forgotten about the soup when Mama charged back in with the girls and the dog in tow. Mama's tray held a large bowl of soup with orange slices on the side, but more importantly, the cup of coffee that I needed to keep going. "Thanks," I said, shuffling papers to the side of my desk.

"Cleo, I've just had the most marvelous idea." Mama's face glowed like a light bulb. "Why don't you finish up out here while the girls and I prepare dinner?"

The rich aroma of chicken soup stirred the juices in my stomach. Okay, so I was hungry. I glanced at Charla and Lexy. They weren't protesting about helping Grandma which should have been a big clue something was up, but my brain was working out the details of the Shady Hills audit and I wanted to get back to it.

Turning Mama loose in the kitchen was risky. If she'd stuck to the grocery list, she couldn't have too many rogue ingredients to choose from for dinner. Her track record of being unconventional when it came to meal preparation shouldn't come into play.

"I guess that would be all right," I said slowly, inventing damage control on the fly. "The girls are supposed to change the bed linens this afternoon. Lexy, why don't you help Grandma in the kitchen? Charla, you set the table and make up the beds."

"Don't you worry about a thing." Mama adjusted the ice bag on my foot and patted my shoulder. She seemed giddy with excitement. "We'll have everything ready before you know it."

Mama's cheeriness put me on notice. Something was definitely up, and she didn't want me anywhere near the kitchen. Danger, danger, danger.

In case the girls didn't know the menu, I recited it as they left. "Lasagna, salad, rolls, iced tea, and a double batch of chocolate pudding."

My words were drowned out in squabbling as Lexy jostled the dog leash out of Charla's hand on the way out the door. I sipped the homemade soup and enjoyed the silence. There was nothing like working through a tangled accounting problem to sharpen one's wits. The pieces of Shady Hill fell rapidly into place.

While I formatted the audit report, I thought about the police investigation of Dudley's murder. Britt Radcliff and the mayor were wrong. Jonette wasn't a murderer. She had hated Dudley since forever, and she probably would still hate him on her deathbed.

If it weren't for Dudley, her life would have taken a much different path. But she wouldn't kill him because of that. She couldn't even kill her frog in tenth grade biology class, and she didn't have any reason to like it either.

If I was going to clear Jonette, I needed to question Violet Cooper, Jasper's mother. If Violet was as good a marksman as Jonette claimed, then she was a much more likely suspect than Jonette. And, if she had Jasper's quick temper, so much the better to paint her as the logical suspect. She'd never know that I was checking her out as I pried out of her who she was using for her accounting needs these days.

On my calendar, I scribbled a quick note to interview Violet Cooper on Monday. And if Violet wasn't the murderer, I'd keep looking until I found the real killer. Jonette wasn't going to jail for a crime she didn't commit.

Bitsy Davis, Dudley's ex-wife, wandered into my office about six with two scotches in her hands. Her blond hair hung lank about her pale face. The light in her sky-blue eyes appeared to have been snuffed out.

I closed the folder I was working on and hobbled around to sit with her in my guest chairs. "I've missed you, Bitsy. I'm sorry about all this."

"It isn't your fault." She embraced me then eased into her chair. "Trust Dudley to find new ways to screw up my life."

I knew exactly what she meant. Charlie's infidelity had cost me more than my marriage. I'd lost my self-confidence and opened myself up to the worst kind of pain. "How'd it go at the funeral home?"

"I wanted to put that SOB in the cheapest, tackiest coffin they had, but I couldn't do it." Bitsy drained her glass. "I bought the top of the line model because I couldn't bear for the boys to see me being hateful."

Children had a way of knowing things. I wouldn't be surprised if Bitsy's sons knew exactly what she thought of their father. My Lexy was plenty astute. She didn't need to be told that it was over between her parents.

I understood Bitsy's protective nature. Sometimes mothers did things for their kids that went against the grain. It was natural to want to shield your children from the hatefulness of the world. "I won't think any less of you for that." I covered her hand with mine and squeezed gently. "I understand."

"Damn him for getting himself killed." She closed her eyes for a moment as if she were summoning energy to continue. "Why did he do this to me? And why now? We were just getting to the point where we didn't argue over every little thing."

I'd never seen easygoing, mild-mannered Bitsy quite so shaken. Usually she took everything in stride, whether it was a tsunami or a broken nail. "I've been out of sorts since I found him," I said.

"I'm sorry you had such a shock, Cleo. This can't be easy for you, either." Bitsy gazed longingly at the drink I'd immediately put down. "I just don't know how I'm going to get through this."

Getting smashed had never solved anyone's problems, but who was I to judge? I handed her my drink. "Here. You need this more than I do."

She took my glass and knocked the contents back quickly. "How do you do it? How do you live in this small town where everyone knows everything about anything? How do you handle seeing Charlie with Denise?"

I grimaced. "It's hard, all right. But I was Cleo Sampson long before I was ever Cleo Jones and I'm not going to let him take away my hometown too."

"But the whispers and the covert glances." Bitsy's shoulders slumped. "Don't they bother you?"

I wasn't so good with this true confessions stuff, but Bitsy was my friend. It was eye-opening to see how raw her pain still was when she'd been divorced twice as long as I had. I had assumed the bitterness lessened with time.

"Sure," I said. "But I don't let that stop me. What's hard for me is realizing I've stored up bits and pieces of my day to tell Charlie and then I remember I don't do that anymore."

Bitsy nodded in agreement.

Maybe it was helping her to hear that I was so dysfunctional. I shared another slice of my soul. "When Charlie heard about Dudley, he came over here expecting me to comfort him as if I were still his wife. It was extremely awkward."

Bitsy nodded again, tears filling her eyes. She clutched her hands tightly together in her lap. "I know what you mean. Every time I heard a woman's name linked with Dudley's I wanted to yank the hair out of her head. Maybe if they had all been bald, Dudley wouldn't have looked at them."

I searched her gaunt face. Her color was off, greenish even. "Bitsy, is there something you're not telling me?"

Bitsy set down the glass so hard I thought it would shatter. She ran her fingers through her lank hair. "You're never going to believe this. I'm embarrassed to admit it, but it's not something I can keep hidden for much longer. I'm three months pregnant, Cleo. With Dudley's baby."

I blinked in astonishment.

She was pregnant?

With Dudley's baby? Never in a million years would I have guessed such a thing. Questions like how and when surfaced in my head and I torpedoed them immediately. Pregnant. I was stunned by the news.

I'd rather be run over by a herd of wild elephants than let Charlie sleep with me again. And Charlie had only slept with one other woman. Dudley had slept his way through the alphabet.

After disbelief rolled through, anger swept in. Given that Bitsy was pregnant, she should be taking better care of herself. She had no business drinking that scotch.

"Are you trying to give that baby brain damage? What's going on in that head of yours?" In spite of my good intentions the next question slipped out. "How could you be pregnant by your ex-husband?"

Bitsy bent her head forward and wept. I mentally kicked myself to the street and back for opening my big mouth. This wasn't an accounting problem I could shift around until everything fit in the right blanks. I wished I could take back my words, but I kept my mouth shut to keep from digging the hole deeper.

When her tears subsided, Bitsy said, "I got pregnant in the usual manner. Do you remember that Dudley refused to have a vasectomy like Charlie did after Lexy's birth? Once I divorced him, I discontinued using birth control. And in a moment of weakness three months ago, I allowed him to charm his way back into my bed. Everything felt so good and right between us. I believed he wanted us to be a family again. But when I came to town to see him afterwards, he was entertaining a woman for lunch. After waiting in his office for two hours, I knew I'd been had."

Poor Bitsy. She'd given Dudley her heart time and again and he'd never cherished her love for the precious gift it was. Dudley had been a fool and it had cost him everything.

Lord, Lord. Pregnant. How was she going to deal with that? In this day and age there were other options when it came to pregnancy. Would she choose to keep the baby? "What are you going to do?"

Tears brimmed in her eyes. She inhaled shakily. "I'm having

the baby. It's all I have left of Dudley."

I exhaled slowly. Bringing a baby into the world when there were two people sharing the parenting load was a lot of work. Doing it alone was gutsy.

"Did Dudley know about the baby?" I wanted to recall my uncensored question immediately, but the damage was done.

Bitsy stood and walked over to look out the gingham-framed windows, her hand curved protectively over her womb. Now that I knew about her pregnancy I saw that she was already rounding. "He knew. And he seemed relieved because in his mind, we *had* to get married again, only I wouldn't have it. Not when he hadn't mended his ways. He swore he'd changed and that he deserved a second chance, but I foolishly believed him."

Bitsy turned to face me. "Oh, Cleo, what am I going to do? I loved that man beyond all reason, and now he's gone and gotten himself killed. How am I going to raise this child on my own? I can't bring myself to tell Mother or the boys about the baby."

I could just imagine Mama's hysterics if I was three months pregnant with a dead man's baby. And my Mama had adored the ground Charlie walked on until he'd cheated on me. Bitsy's mother had hated Dudley from day one and she constantly found ways to let Bitsy know she'd married beneath herself. I didn't know how Bitsy lived with that harpy.

My heart went out to my friend. "I'll help you any way I can. Are you going to stay in Virginia?"

Bitsy strolled back across the office and stopped near my chair. "I don't know. I want to move out, but Mother was so good to take us in after the divorce. I hate to uproot the boys again, but what choice do I have? Mother has every right to throw me out on the street. I'm an unwed mother at thirty seven. My father is probably spinning in his grave at the disgrace."

All Bitsy had ever wanted was Dudley, and he hadn't lived up to her trust and love. The least I could do was to offer her shelter. "Bitsy, you and the boys are welcome to stay here for as long as you like. It won't be good for the baby if you and your mother are arguing a lot."

Dudley had paid Bitsy child support. With his death, all of that would stop. A cold chill snaked down my spine all the way to my throbbing ankle. How would Bitsy make ends meet? Was she financially unable to leave her mother?

What if she actually took me up on my offer and came to live with us? At that thought I turned slightly green. How could I afford to feed three and soon to be four more people? Would I need a second job?

Bitsy's lower lip trembled. She reached over and squeezed my shoulder. "You'll never know what your offer means to me. You've always been my friend, Cleo. Thank you for standing by me. Thanks but no thanks."

She took a deep breath and stood tall. "We should be okay financially. I was worried at first because his investment accounts were cleaned out, but Dudley always lived larger than life. He always had one deal or another on the horizon where he was going to make it big. Fortunately for me and the boys, Dudley never changed the life insurance policy he bought early on in our marriage. I'm the sole beneficiary of that policy."

Dudley had bragged incessantly to Charlie of how well off he would leave his family in the event of his untimely demise. If memory served me correctly, Bitsy stood to receive ten million dollars from that policy. She'd never have to worry about money again.

Because my mind is always thinking of ways things fit together, another thought occurred to me that I couldn't make go away. Even though Bitsy lived in another town, she'd been wronged by Dudley. Could she have shot him knowing that insurance money would free her from him and her mother for the rest of her life?

How could I ask her if she had an alibi for the night of his death? She was my friend and this was definitely her hour of need. Later when things were calmed down I could, in a nonthreatening way, ask her about her alibi. Right now Bitsy needed my support, not my suspicion. "I'd forgotten about the insurance policy. How do you go about getting that money?"

Bitsy's face turned an interesting shade of green. I recognized that shade from my pregnancy days. Bilious green. Moving quickly, I opened the bathroom door and flipped on the light and the fan.

"I already contacted them." Bitsy brushed past me into the bathroom, closing the door.

I heard the sound of retching. The fan kept the sour odor of vomit contained. With any luck, all that scotch would come back out too.

Just then, Bitsy's youngest son, Grant, dashed into the office. The door crashed against the wall with a loud bang. "Mom! Aunt Cleo! Come quick. The dogs are fighting."

CHAPTER 11

"Hey, Grant." I crushed him in an embarrassing hug. Dudley's slate-gray eyes stared back at me from the boyishly angular face of his youngest son. At thirteen, Grant was all elbows and knees with manly feet he had yet to grow into.

I glanced at the closed bathroom door. Grant didn't need to find out about his mother's pregnancy this way. Who knew how long Bitsy would need to pull herself together? The least I could do was handle her dog problem.

"I'll take care of this, Bitsy," I said to the door. "Take your time and join us in the house when you're done."

"Okay," she said.

I followed Grant outside. The two Saint Bernards were behaving in less than a saintly manner. There was a lot of teeth snapping, rolling on the ground, and general racing around. But there was a distinct masculine gleam I recognized in Mozart's eye when he chased Madonna that gave me the biggest clue to what was going on. I was certain canine mating behavior was unsuitable for an impressionable teen.

I was about to suggest to Grant that we leave them alone when Grant observed in a squeaky voice, "Great gravy. Mo's humping her."

Good thing my teeth were still original or they would have fallen out for sure. Regardless of the level of Grant's sexual education, I wasn't prepared to discuss doggie sex with him. It had been traumatic enough talking to my own kids about the facts of life. That settled it for me.

I wasn't going to come between consensual sex between two jumbo dogs, and even if Grant was familiar with procreation, he didn't need to watch. "Grant, why don't you go inside and help set the table for dinner?"

Grant remained intently focused on the dogs. "Look at him go. He's never done my leg as many times as that. Do you think they'll have puppies?"

The awe on Grant's boyish face made me groan. Men and boys. Leave it to them to be amazed by another male's prowess.

What would Bitsy do if these super-sized dogs reproduced? Having never had dogs, I didn't know how long the gestation period was, but quite possibly Bitsy could be having puppies about the same time as she was having her baby. Thank God I wasn't in her shoes.

I latched the wooden gate and shooed Grant into the house. I didn't need to see the dogs go at it either. It was a sad state of affairs when your pet had a sex life and you didn't. I might as well have a big "L" for loser tattooed on my forehead.

As I passed through the kitchen, I sniffed lasagna in the air and a faint tang I couldn't quite place. A sense of foreboding flitted through me. "Mama? How long until dinner?"

"It's all ready, dear," Mama said. "We're in the dining room." I followed her voice to discover that Grant had spread the word. Everyone had their noses pressed up against the glass to see the doggie antics.

This was not good. Would I be arrested for showing doggie pornography to minors? What would my oddball neighbor Ed Monday think of all the yipping and racing about? Would he murder us for disturbing his peace? I hoped not. At least not until after dinner. I was starved.

I hugged Dudley's older son. Artie blushed furiously. Mostly because he was fourteen but also because he seemed embarrassed to be caught watching the dogs go at it. "When are you going to talk your mom into moving back to Hogan's Glen so that we can see more of you?" I asked as I ruffled his wavy hair.

Artie had gotten the best combination of his parents' physical features. From his father, serious gray eyes and dark poetic hair; from his mother, a cherubic face and lush eyelashes. He was as handsome as sin and looked as innocent as a lamb.

Artie's voice was as deep as Dudley's had been. "Mom said we might be moving back."

Charla squealed with glee. "Really? That would be so cool. Mama, Artie plays football. He's the starting quarterback on his JV team. If they moved back, that'd be awesome."

Artie seemed fairly enthralled by Charla's exuberance. Charla was four months older than Artie, but because of their birthdates, they'd been in different grades throughout their education. I'd be worried about his potential attraction to my daughter if I didn't know Artie.

He'd sooner cut off the nose on his face as do anything with a girl. But maybe that was the old Artie. Now that his voice had changed and peach fuzz adorned his chin, maybe hormones ruled his mind, in which case, Charla should watch her step around him.

How much of Dudley's philandering ways had his son inherited? I shuddered to think of a second generation of Dudleys let loose on the general populace.

Were my daughters in danger from these potential womanizers? Would there be a repeat demonstration of what was going on out in the backyard in a bedroom upstairs with Artie and Charla as the participants?

Not if I had anything to do with it. "Why don't we all sit down to supper? I'm sure you boys must be starved."

"Yes ma'am, I'm right hungry," Grant answered as he slid into a seat.

I started for the kitchen to help bring the food out but Mama stopped me with a curt look. "Cleo, sit down and rest that foot of yours. We'll get the food out here. Where's Bitsy?"

Bitsy was becoming intimately acquainted with my office toilet, but I wasn't going to mention that. "She'll be along in a minute."

I glanced over at the table. The bases of all the silverware were perfectly aligned, the floral patterns on the gold-rimmed china plates were precisely oriented in the same direction. The linen napkins and the tablecloth looked like they'd been freshly pressed. And the centerpiece of massed candles was absolutely stunning. Charla had outdone herself.

Her usual idea of setting the table was to throw things down as she dashed around the table. She deserved praise for making the effort to achieve such a wonderful presentation. "Nice job on the table, Charla."

"Lexy did it," Charla said as she placed a basket of rolls on the table while Lexy filled the crystal glasses with iced tea. Charla gave me her best two-hundred-watt smile.

"We switched jobs because I wanted to cook with Grandma."

I noticed Artie reeled under the force of that smile, and I made a mental note to keep close track of that boy. Charla didn't need to experience the joy of motherhood at fifteen.

Another jolt of anxiety shot through me as I complimented Lexy on her elegant table setting. I'd counted on Lexy keeping Mama on track with the cooking. Surely Charla wouldn't have helped Mama prepare something inedible for company?

Bitsy came in and sat down next to me. She took a roll and pinched a bit off the edge to eat. She still looked a bit pale. I felt sorry for her, but I couldn't quite forget that insurance money. Bitsy had ten million dollars worth of reasons to murder her ex-husband.

How was I going to get through this dinner if I kept thinking about that insurance money? The list of things I didn't want to think about at dinner just kept getting longer and longer. There was doggie sex outside, Bitsy's love child, and the teenagers sizing each other up at my dinner table.

All my troubles were related to sex. And there was a murderer on the loose. I couldn't forget that. Keeping my family safe was my top priority. Safe sex for my daughters came in a close second when survival was an issue. A mother's job was never done.

Charla lay hot pads on the table, then disappeared as Mama brought out the casserole dish full of bubbling lasagna. I heaved a sigh of relief. So far, so good. Charla returned with the salad, and that's when I knew trouble was afoot. The salad was a colorful composition worthy of artistic greats like Picasso and Rembrandt.

The dark green spinach leaves ringed the lighter iceberg lettuce. Another concentric ring consisted of purple cabbage, followed by an orange ring of grated carrots and cheddar cheese, a red ring of cubed tomatoes, and an unidentifiable blue lump in the center. All of the rings were perfectly concentric. "What? How?" I sputtered.

Mama beamed. "This is Charla's creation. She calls it Rainbow Salad. Didn't she do a nice job?"

"How'd you make it look like a bull's-eye?" Grant asked.

"Nested mixing bowls," Charla said. "I put in the spinach, then the upside down bowls. As I completed a layer, I removed a bowl."

Clever. But what was the blue stuff? "And the center?"

"Ricotta cheese," Charla said, in a tone that suggested we were annoying her with our remedial questions. "It was the wrong color for my rainbow, so I fixed it with food coloring."

Okay, no reason to panic. Ricotta cheese was edible, even if it was royal blue. Only, the ricotta cheese should have been in the lasagna. Not good.

Fear hammered through my veins. If Charla had been in charge of the salad, then Mama prepared the lasagna. Unsupervised.

I eyed the cheesy, bubbling mass with growing suspicion. There was a distinct fishy odor in the midst of all the regular lasagna smells. What had she done? Mama cut into the mass and carved out a jumbo slice for Artie. He stared at the lump on his plate. "It's green."

Mama nodded. "I played with the recipe a little to personalize it. This is my new signature dish."

I held my breath, afraid to ask what else was in the lasagna besides spinach. Why hadn't she put the ricotta cheese in the lasagna? I wanted to snatch her up and shake some sense into her. "Mama," I started.

She raised her hand. "Just give it a try. I'm sure you're going to love Spickle Fish Lasagna."

Bitsy turned green and pressed her napkin to her lips. "Excuse me," she muttered, fleeing from the room.

Artie took a big bite. We watched him chew in morbid fascination. His eyes grew very moist as he pondered the taste sensation of Mama's main dish. After a few moments, he swallowed. "Interesting. You have to try it."

Mama beamed as she dished out generous servings to everyone. I noticed that Artie hadn't taken another bite of his "interesting" lasagna and some sixth sense kept me from digging into mine. However, when Charla, Lexy, and Grant all took big bites of their lasagna, Artie couldn't keep the laughter inside. I watched the teens eating lasagna turn green.

Lexy spit hers out on her plate. Charla and Grant followed suit. "What is this stuff?" Lexy asked. "It tastes vile."

"There's tuna fish in here," Grant said.

"The pickle relish is crunchy. Grandma, you didn't say it

would be crunchy," Charla admonished.

I picked apart my vile-smelling helping. Spinach, pickle relish, and tuna fish. In lasagna. For grieving houseguests.

It was just too much. I wanted to howl with frustration. I should have known better than to trust Mama to follow a recipe.

"Don't eat this," I cautioned as I gathered up the plates. I had visions of summoning paramedics to come save us from food poisoning. "I'll order pizza and we'll eat in about thirty minutes. Meanwhile, have some rolls."

"What about my salad?" Charla asked. "Can we eat that?"

"Your salad should be fine. I'll call the pizza delivery place from the kitchen." I glared heatedly at my mother. "Mama, I'd like a word with you."

Charla sniffed at my sharp tone, but I couldn't worry about her delicate feelings right now. I lifted the huge pan of lasagna and limped into the kitchen. I heard Mama say something to Charla as I ordered the pizza, then I waited for Mama to come to me.

I was spooning the awful casserole into the trash when she marched in. It was all I could do not to retch at the fishy odor emanating from the pan.

My frustration boiled out of me. "How could you do this, Mama? Bitsy's going to think we're out to murder her entire family."

Mama's spine was so stiff you could iron on it. Her amber-flecked brown eyes glittered with fury. "It's not my fault her ex-husband got killed. If he'd kept his thingy where it belonged none of this would have happened."

"This isn't about Dudley's womanizing. How could you embarrass me this way?"

The slack muscles in Mama's forearm arm flailed as she shook her finger at me. "You've made my life a living hell by keeping me out of my kitchen. What fun is plain lasagna? Spickle

Fish Lasagna is an original."

She had me there, but the reason Spickle Fish Lasagna wasn't on anyone's menu was because it tasted terrible and smelled worse. But what about her other statement? Had I made her life a living hell?

I had curtailed her creativity in the kitchen because her meals weren't edible. It was a simple economic decision. "I'm sorry that I limited your creativity, but I had reasons for doing so."

Mama pounded her fist on the kitchen counter. "Your trouble is that you're wound too tight all the time. If you don't release all that stress, you're going to end up just like me."

Seeing as how Mama could run me into the ground any day of the week, I didn't see that as much of a problem. But she was right about me being wound tightly. Between my divorce, living with Mama, running my business, dealing with Charlie and the girls, and finding a murdered friend, I was over my limit for stress.

I sighed deeply. A stress-free woman would be generous with her own flesh and blood. I wanted to reinvent myself and here was a good place to start. "Why don't we compromise? I'll agree to let you cook again, say dinner two nights a week. You can try out your creativity on us. How does that sound?"

Mama grinned big. "Sounds mighty fine to me."

For a split second, I wondered if I'd been had. Mama had been wanting to cook again, and the kids had wanted pizza for dinner. Both were getting exactly what they wanted, and it seemed entirely too coincidental to me.

At the sound of a car in the driveway, I turned toward the door. "There's the delivery guy. Grab a stack of clean plates and I'll bring in the pizzas in just a sec."

I glanced at the nook where I normally kept my purse. It wasn't there. Nor was it anywhere else in the kitchen.

All right, I could be flexible. I'd let the pizza guy in, then find my purse. I opened the door. Much to my surprise, my purse hung in mid-air right under my nose.

"Looking for this?" a deep sexy voice asked.

Here was another stress I didn't need. I could see Rafe's dark brown eyes smoldering sensually through the loop of my purse strap. A snap of recognition jolted through my system as I went on full golf pro alert.

"Thanks, I was just looking for my purse."

I had to be careful here. Rafe could be using his sex appeal to find out if I suspected him of being a ruthless killer. Was I up to the challenge of playing it cool? If this were a poker game, I'd be holding my cards close to my chest.

"You left it at my shop this morning." Rafe reached behind him as if he were going to retrieve his billfold from his back pocket.

Surely this long, lean man with gilded hair wasn't a cold-blooded killer. My female instincts were shouting at me to kiss him before he got away, but my head said to keep my distance. These were dangerous times for Hogan's Glen.

"Along with this."

My broken shoe. He'd had it stuck in his pocket. That was rather intimate for our casual acquaintance. But. A storybook handsome man with a shoe standing at my door. Wasn't this every woman's fairy tale?

Who was I kidding? Fairy tales didn't come true for thirty-five-year-old divorcees. I snatched my shoe without making direct contact with any part of his delectable body. "Thanks. Sorry I left my stuff behind."

"Mom!" Charla bellowed as she walked in the kitchen. "Are you hogging all the pizza?"

A look of irritation flashed across Rafe's face. Was he annoyed at the interruption? Did he plan to seduce my suspicions out of me? My pulse leapt wildly at the thought.

I accidentally put all my weight on my taped ankle as I turned to face Charla. Pain lanced through me lightning fast, and I clutched the counter to steady myself. "False alarm. It isn't the pizza guy."

Charla stopped at my side, her arms barred across her developing chest. She was cute and young and perky. All the things I left behind after her birth. "Charla, have you met Rafe Golden? Mr. Golden is the golf pro down at the course. Rafe, this is my oldest daughter, Charla Jones."

"Hello." Charla scowled at Rafe.

I didn't understand her instant dislike, but maybe she wasn't mad at Rafe. Maybe she was mad at me. I made an effort to soothe her pride. "Your salad looked lovely, Charla. I plan to have some as soon as the pizza gets here."

Charla's scowl stayed in place. "It's all gone. I wish we'd taken a picture of it."

I deposited my broken shoe on the counter and squeezed her shoulder. "You can always make it again when it's just us."

Processing what she'd said, I realized that Bitsy's boys must be starving if all the salad was gone. "Take the chocolate pudding out and we'll have the pizza for dessert."

"Yes!" Charla pumped her fist in the air. She skipped away with the pudding.

I turned my attention back to Rafe. It was impossible to miss how completely his broad shoulders filled the doorframe. Against my will, liquid heat pooled in my lower abdomen.

I couldn't believe he was here, at my house. Rafe Golden was standing here in my kitchen, looking at me like I was dinner. What was I going to do with him?

Even if there wasn't a murderer on the loose, I had good reason to be careful. My female instincts had malfunctioned with Charlie and I had no reason to believe they were working now. For a moment I allowed myself to believe that Rafe's interest in me was on the up and up.

What did Rafe expect from the women he pursued? Sultry voices and steamy nights under satin sheets? If so, he'd missed the boat with me. My sheets were clearance sale percale and the only time I'd ever had a sultry voice was when I had laryngitis. "Would you like to come in?"

He shook his head to indicate no. "I wanted to schedule your golf lesson."

My golf lesson. Time with Rafe all by myself. Through the mixed brain messages of "be careful there's a murderer on the loose" and the "hot dog what are you waiting for," I managed to sound coherent. "When did you have in mind?"

With those words, a whole new world of terror opened up for me. Committing to a lesson meant that I would spend time alone with a man that seemed very interested in me.

What clothes would I wear? How would I style my hair? I had the distinct impression Rafe had a steady diet of buffed and polished women. Looking down, I saw my taped ankle and my ratty pink slippers. Buffed and polished wasn't my natural state.

Rafe whipped a day planner from his pocket. "I wasn't sure about your ankle," he said, studying the entries in his planner. "I have an opening tomorrow afternoon or we could schedule something next week."

The new and improved me wanted that golf lesson. I wanted to believe he wasn't a murderer. "Tomorrow won't work for me. I've got houseguests through the weekend and Dudley's funeral on Saturday. What about next week?"

He flipped the page to Monday. Christine Strand had his one o'clock slot. Two o'clock was open. "Two o'clock works for me."

While he penciled me in, I had a moment where my thoughts were my own. If I trusted my hormones that Rafe wasn't a murderer, that still left his assistant with plenty of means and opportunity to kill Dudley.

What did Rafe know about Jasper and Dudley? Information could be right under my nose if I only had courage enough to ask him. I wanted to clear Jonette, so I needed to start asking questions about the murder.

I could be subtle. Rafe would never know I suspected a golf course employee of killing Dudley. "The other day I spoke with Jasper about Dudley. What's your take on their relationship?"

His gaze narrowed shrewdly and I wondered if I had been subtle enough. "Seeing that Dudley is dead, they don't have a relationship. Prior to that, Dudley was treated just the same as any other golf club member. It's not our policy to discriminate against our members."

His response didn't net me any new information. I'd never clear Jonette at this rate. To heck with being subtle. I might as well state what I thought and see how Rafe reacted. "Jasper told me he didn't like Dudley very much."

Rafe shrugged. "Who did?"

CHAPTER 12

Lexy and I wore black to Dudley's funeral. Charla had insisted her Uncle Dudley wouldn't want her to be so inhibited. She opted for a confection of dark indigo swirled with lavender and plum. Mama wore one of her conservative church suits and her triple-stranded pearls.

To fit my foot in my black high heels, I'd foregone taping my ankle. A decision I had been regretting as I stood by Bitsy in the church foyer while the townspeople filed past. I prayed for a short-winded eulogy and the fastest liturgy on record.

Dudley's parents were long dead and his estranged brother wasn't coming up from Florida for the ceremony. Bitsy had insisted that we sit in the family pew with her, so we all proceeded together to the front row. In a church packed with perfumed mourners, I was exceedingly glad to have a reserved seat.

Why were all these people here if no one liked Dudley? I wanted to berate them for their ghoulish curiosity. Did they expect to see his unhappy banking customers egging his closed casket? Did they hope for a pew of his discarded mistresses to ogle? If so, they were wasting their time.

I had read somewhere that killers had a fascination with attending the funerals of their victims. Was the killer here? Was it someone I knew personally? I shuddered at the thought, but my brain locked onto that idea. I did a quick inventory of people I knew that might be suspects.

Jonette had purposefully stayed away. She topped the list of police suspects because she'd had run-ins with Dudley her entire life. I didn't think much of their detecting ability if they thought Jonette did Dudley in.

Jasper was here, sitting next to Rafe. Both of them had unrestricted access to the golf course where Dudley was killed. Because of Dudley being involved in the teachers' pension scandal, Jasper also had a motive to kill Dudley. There were no women sitting with Jasper and Rafe so I assumed Jasper's mother wasn't here. I needed to go question her on Monday.

Bitsy was here. She'd inherited a pile of money upon the death of her ex. She had ten million reasons for wanting Dudley dead.

Ed Monday was conspicuously absent. If Charlie was right about Ed being the killer, I was wasting my time checking out the assembled mourners.

Many of my accounting clients were present and they nodded back at me. Our mayor, Darnell Reynolds, looked especially florid. Perhaps the skinny man in the bad suit sitting next to him had something to do with that. Of all the people I had observed in the church, the mayor looked the most upset. I'd see if I could corner Darnell at the reception and find out what was wrong.

Detective Britt Radcliff stood in the back of the church. His gaze met mine, then moved on, as he scanned the packed church. Was he looking for potential suspects too?

The words of the funeral service rolled over me. Dudley had been a royal prick most of the time. In that I agreed with Jonette. But just because someone behaved badly was no reason to kill him. If that were true, spouses would kill each other when things went haywire and no one would need divorce lawyers.

This was the first time I'd been in church since my marriage ended. I mouthed the words of the service and hoped the roof didn't fall in on me. Sitting in these old fashioned wooden pews and seeing the familiar scenes on the stained glass windows took me back to a time when I believed in God and my husband.

Now I mostly believed in myself.

It was impossible to miss the stage whisper and rustlings of papers of a very restless person in the pew directly behind me. My hearing automatically tuned in to the beacon of noise. I recognized that syrupy voice immediately. Denise. I strained to hear what she was saying to Charlie, but I couldn't quite make out her words.

Ordinarily I wouldn't care what she said to Charlie. She'd fought for him and taken him from me. Their discussions were none of my business, but still I wanted to know what had her so irritated. I know it was petty of me, but nothing would make me happier than to have their newfound bliss turn to sewage.

I fumbled with my program and glanced over my shoulder. Grim lines etched Charlie's pale face. Either Dudley's death had hit him very hard, or something else was going on, something very unpleasant between him and Denise.

A spark of triumph flashed through me and I glanced fearfully toward the arched ceiling. It wasn't charitable of me to want his marriage to fail. But how fair was it for him to ruin my life and then ride off into the sunset with a younger, perkier woman?

I'd naively thought everything was great in my marriage and look what had happened. We'd been getting along fine, we'd had a synergistic partnership both in and out of bed, or so I thought. His infidelity had hurt all the more because I didn't have a clue.

Denise knew he'd cheated on me. Wouldn't she wonder every time he was late that he was out screwing someone else?

I would. Jonette had been right about that. I wasn't the type to forgive and forget adultery. Charlie had burnt his bridges with me. It was up to me to rebuild my life.

My hormones were telling me to take a long look at the golf pro, but I wasn't sure I could trust my hormones either. How stupid would I be if I trusted Rafe not to hurt me? Heck, he might even be a cold-blooded murderer. With my instincts so out of kilter I couldn't be sure about anything.

I glanced at Rafe out of the corner of my eye and found him staring at me. Our gazes met and held. I felt myself growing warm. What was he thinking? Did he want to murder me or sleep with me? Was my overactive imagination seeing things where there was nothing to see? It was possible that the man flirted with women to build his golf lesson business.

I wished for a different reality. I wanted to believe that he found me as exciting as I found him. I wanted to believe that I wasn't washed up at thirty-five.

I managed a little half smile, and his eyes warmed. I couldn't bring myself to look away. How could I when looking at him made me feel so alive and desirable? And no harm had ever come from looking. My hormones did a little happy dance and I smiled the knowing smiles of women in the TV commercials for male potency.

"Mama!" Lexy scolded, sounding more like the parent than the child. "Pay attention."

I broke eye contact with Rafe and faced the masses of flowers next to Dudley's coffin. Lexy was understandably concerned about my interest in the golf pro. In her mind, her physical education teacher, Mark Hayes, and I were a match made in heaven. A match that would ensure she passed PE with flying colors.

After Rafe delivered my purse three days ago, Lexy grilled me about his intentions in a way that reminded me of Daddy way back when. With blazing green eyes, Lexy made it clear that she didn't think a golf pro was the man for me. She was entitled to her opinion, but frankly Mark Hayes didn't make my blood sing or my knees melt the way Rafe did.

We stood for the final hymn. Dudley lay before us, shrouded in lilies, in the best casket money could buy. Money could buy lots of things, but it hadn't bought Dudley happiness.

Bitsy dabbed at her tear-filled eyes. Her sons stood like stoic soldiers in their dark suits. Did they remember coming to this church when they were boys? They'd moved away five years ago, practically a lifetime to a kid.

We filed out of the church and into the reception hall. I stood at Bitsy's shoulder and helped her with people's names. I continued with my silent detecting, but I came no closer to figuring out who killed Dudley.

When I had a chance, I crossed over to greet Darnell. He introduced me to Robert Joy, the skinny man that was still glued to Darnell's side. I knew that name from somewhere.

It took me a few minutes of idle conversation to access the information in my brain. Robert Joy was the developer from Dudley's White Rock housing development. The farm that wouldn't perk. After a few more pleasantries about the large turnout and the tasty food, I decided I wasn't good at subtle. My style was going directly at something.

"May I have a word with you privately, Darnell?" I asked.

Robert Joy left us alone.

Darnell mopped his brow with his handkerchief. "Thanks. I was beginning to think I couldn't shake him."

"What's wrong, Darnell? I've never seen you so agitated."

"It's that damn White Rock. Robert Joy won't leave me alone. I wish I'd never run for mayor."

Darnell was my mother's age, and he'd gotten into mayoring because he couldn't stand being retired. He was also my wealthiest client and the dirt wad who wanted to put Jonette in jail. "It can't be that bad."

"It can. Robert expects me to annex White Rock into the city."

"Why?"

"So that he can build more houses on the property. Having city services changes the size of the lots."

"And that's bad because?"

"I can't talk about it." Darnell mopped his brow again. "I can't believe Dudley stuck me with such a mess."

"Dudley had a reputation for looking after the bottom line. You should know that by now."

"Yeah, but he could talk the skin off a mule. I bought into his stories of a bigger and better Hogan's Glen and now he's not here to keep Robert Joy in line. I'm between a rock and a hard place here, Cleo."

"Dudley had that effect on people."

"He was also my friend. We pushed many projects through the town council over the five years we worked together. I owe it to his family to find out who killed him."

My eyebrows shot up. "How are you going to do that?"

"I've told the police force to leave no stone unturned. We're moving decisively on this. I expect there to be an arrest in the next few days."

"Sounds like you already know who did it."

"We're very close to making the arrest."

I couldn't take his smug attitude any longer. I wanted to squash Darnell for being such an insect. Instead, I stood up for my friend. "Jonette didn't do it."

"You are too close to her to be objective. I'm sure this was a personal situation that got out of hand."

"You're making a big mistake to focus on Jonette. I'm telling you she didn't do it."

"Cleo, I don't tell you how to do my taxes. I'd appreciate it if you'd butt out and let me do my job."

"Every time you come in my office, you tell me how to do your taxes. Take off your rose-colored glasses and face the facts. There's a murderer loose in our town."

"Not for long," Darnell said.

Robert Joy returned with a plate of chicken wings and I moved on. There nothing else I wanted to say to our pigheaded mayor.

An hour into the reception, I realized Bitsy's color was way off. She was pale as a sheet. I sat her down in a quiet corner. "What's wrong, Bitsy?" Other than being pregnant and burying your ex-husband, that is.

Pain clouded her sky-blue eyes and her shoulders sagged. "I don't feel good. I'm worried something might be wrong with the baby."

I held her hand and tried to be calm. I didn't want her to lose the baby. Bitsy needed someone to take care of her.

I caught Lexy's eye and waved her over. Now I just needed to remember if there were any health professionals here. Britt Radcliff was the closest thing we had to a doctor or paramedic in the room. "Bitsy's not feeling good. Go get Detective Radcliff," I instructed Lexy.

Moments later, Britt assisted Bitsy to a pew in the empty chapel in the church undercroft. "Lie back and put your feet up," he said. "Bend your knees."

Bitsy followed his suggestions and the tightness in her face subsided. Some color came back in her face.

Artie appeared in the doorway, concern adding years to his cherubic face. "What's wrong with Mom?"

I motioned him forward. "Come on in, Artie. Your Mom needed to take a break."

Britt inclined his head toward the door, indicating that he wished to speak with me privately. I touched Artie's shoulder as he stood watch over his mother. "I'll be right back, Artie."

Outside in the hallway, I said, "Thanks, Britt. Bitsy is in a bit of a mess."

Britt leveled his very direct, police officer, lie-detecting gaze at me. "She's pregnant?"

I squirmed uneasily beneath the weight of his truth serum gaze and I had nothing to hide. Maybe this man was good at his job. Maybe he wouldn't let the mayor railroad him into arresting Jonette.

Then I remembered something else. A few days ago he'd asked me if I was pregnant. "Is that all you think about? Pregnant women?"

The corners of his lips flexed briefly in a mock smile. "I'm not as stupid as I look. During the funeral, I noticed her scratching her stomach the way my wife used to when she was carrying. That plus the green undertones in her face clued me in that something was amiss. Am I right?"

I hesitated. Bitsy expected me to keep her secret, but the situation warranted an explanation of her behavior. I hoped she'd forgive me for breaking her confidence. "She's pregnant, but she doesn't want it getting out. Her boys don't know."

Britt's piercing gaze never wavered from my face. "Who is the father of the baby?"

I swallowed thickly. "Dudley."

"Ah."

I could almost see wheels spinning in his head. What connection had he made? "Ah?"

He steepled his fingers under his chin. "She's already put in for the life insurance money."

My eyes opened wide. "You know about that?"

"It's my business to know these things."

I rushed to follow his logic. Bitsy had profited from Dudley's death. Was Bitsy the person the mayor expected to be arrested in the next few days? "Is Bitsy a suspect?"

"Yes."

My loyalty to Bitsy took offense at his conclusion, even though I'd drawn a similar one myself. Did he know about Dudley's recent betrayal of Bitsy? "Bitsy doesn't even live here anymore. I'm sure she has an alibi."

Britt leaned close and lowered his voice. "An eye witness placed Bitsy at the bank earlier this week. Just because Bitsy doesn't live here, doesn't mean she couldn't have done it. I'll be checking her story, same as I will my other suspect, but with the pregnancy and the insurance settlement she had plenty of motive to do the man in."

It was up to me to remind Britt that he'd known Jonette and Bitsy for years and that they were good people. "Don't railroad my friends. You're completely off base in your investigation. Bitsy would never kill the father of her unborn child for an insurance settlement. Bitsy would have much rather had Dudley, believe me. And, Jonette has been threatening to kill Dudley on a daily basis since they met in elementary school. If Jonette was going to kill him, she wouldn't have waited this long to do it."

"Stay out of this. A man was murdered."

"You let Jonette go because of what I found out about Dudley Thursday night. I can't stand by and do nothing."

"Jonette's not in the clear. Her prints are in his house and in his car."

I'd been expecting this bad news. "I'm sure there's a very good reason for that. Did you ask her?"

Britt started to reply but stopped when he saw we were no longer alone.

"Aunt Cleo?" Artie tugged on my sleeve. He had loosened his tie and taken off his jacket.

"Yes?"

"Mom wants to go back to your place. Can you get someone to drive us? I'm not old enough to drive."

Poor Bitsy. My heart swelled with compassion. She was overwhelmed by events. Having to deal with the start and end of life all at the same time was too much to bear. To top that off, she'd just lost the man she loved.

My thoughts veered into crisis management mode. If I took Bitsy home, who would stay here to represent Dudley's family? Only one name came to mind. Charlie. He was Dudley's best friend. He'd have to do.

I placed my hand on Artie's shoulder. He was trying so hard to be grown up, but I could feel him shaking under my hand. "I'll take Bitsy home. Give me a minute to bring my car around."

Artie nodded and went back to wait in the chapel with his Mom. Britt walked me back upstairs to the reception hall. "You don't have to do this," Britt said. "I can drive Mrs. Davis to your place."

He'd probably grill her all the way there, and she'd end up more upset than when she left here. No way would I put Bitsy through that today. Good thing I had a ready-made excuse. I pointed to my fat, throbbing ankle. "I don't mind. My ankle is bothering me with all this standing. I twisted it the other day and it's not right yet."

As luck would have it, Grant and Lexy stood with Charlie by the dessert table in the reception hall. It was a bittersweet triumph to see that I stood a good three inches taller than my ex. I explained the situation to him. "Bitsy is worn out and needs to rest. I'm taking her home. You're going to have to stay and represent the family, Charlie."

Charlie nodded in tight-lipped silence.

I exhaled slowly. I'd been bracing for resistance, but he didn't seem to mind being told what to do by a towering Amazon. What would have happened in our marriage if I had changed tactics with him years ago and done as I pleased?

I turned to Lexy. "Would you and Charla stay and help Mama with the cleanup? The church ladies are here, but I'd feel better if Mama had someone with her that wouldn't let her get too riled up."

Lexy nodded. Last week's fight with Erica Hodges over how the coffeepot was supposed to be cleaned out was still fresh in our minds. Mama had very strong ideas about cleanliness in the kitchen. "No problem."

"Grant, do you want to stay here with your Uncle Charlie or to come with me?"

"Mom's all right?" Grant asked.

I managed a thin smile. Now that I had acknowledged my twisted ankle, it had begun to throb. "She'll be fine with a little rest." Please, God, don't strike me down for that white lie. Bitsy wouldn't be okay for about another six or so months, but it wasn't my call to tell her children about her pregnancy.

I started towards the exit. An electric charge jolted through me as someone touched my shoulder. Recognition flashed in the aftermath of that stimulus. Only one man had the power to turn my bones to mush with a mere touch. I turned toward him. "Yes?"

Concern ringed Rafe's eyes. "All this walking around isn't good for that ankle of yours."

No kidding. My ankle was now twice the size it had been when I dressed this morning, and it throbbed incessantly. Rafe's concern was admirable, but completely unnecessary. "I'll be fine. I'm on my way home now."

"Let me help you." He slipped an arm around my waist and walked us towards the door.

I should have said no, but he moved too fast for me. Besides, his added support took weight off of my ankle. My arm slipped around his waist to further secure the connection and my hormones soared like Roman candles.

We moved as a three-legged creature, only I felt as if I were floating on air. I could definitely get used to this. Would my attraction to this man place me in danger? I hoped not.

After locating my car in the parking lot, I fumbled in my purse for the keys. Between the throbbing of my ankle and the dancing hormones flooding my bloodstream, it was difficult to think clearly.

"May I?" he asked.

He could. In fact, he could do just about anything and I wouldn't protest too much. I handed him my keys and allowed him to drive the Gray Beast up to the side door of the rectory. I went to unbuckle my seat belt. "Thanks. I'll take it from here."

He caught my hand before it reached the buckle. "Stay put. I'll get Mrs. Davis and drive you both home."

I tried to pull my hand free, but he held fast. "You don't have to do that," I said. "We can manage."

"I want to help. Don't move, I'll be right back."

Didn't men think women could do anything? What did they think we did all the time when they weren't around? My protest was halfhearted and I knew it. Rafe was being helpful. And he must be interested in me because he kept seeking me out.

My spirits perked up a bit. It was flattering having a handsome man pursuing me. Darn flattering.

As long as he wasn't the murderer, that is. It wouldn't do me any good to slide further down the food chain of Mr. Wrongs.

Rafe carried Bitsy out, and my hands clenched in fists. My hormones screamed foul. If this was a football game and I was the referee, I would have thrown a yellow flag on the ground and stomped on it.

Darn it.

I couldn't have it both ways. Either I was attracted to the man or I thought he was a murderer. If I didn't make up my mind, I would go crazy.

I wanted my life to have zing in it again. Even if I tabled the suspicion stuff, there was still the matter of his flirting with other women.

Was he even a good catch? He always seemed to have a woman in his arms. Didn't the man have any self-control?

CHAPTER 13

I limped to my front door and unlocked it. My plan was to stand there like the grand lady of the manor while Rafe did his Masters of the Universe impression and carried Bitsy to her room, but one look at the utter destruction in my living room and I felt like I'd been sucker punched.

Spots swam before my eyes. Not now. I didn't need to feel lightheaded now. I clutched the hutch with both hands until my vision cleared. I willed air back in my lungs and glanced fearfully around my house.

Lamps were on the floor. Pillows were shredded. Grandmother's wingback chair upended. Magazines strewn across the floor. Mama's special cobalt-blue vase smashed, the bright yellow daffodils mangled.

My knees trembled from the exertion of standing here and not collapsing into a puddle on the floor. I felt violated. And scared. Was there a burglar in the house? I heard a crunching of paper and rustling of fine fabrics. Adrenaline surged and I tensed to flee.

First one drooling dog head appeared over the back of the sofa and then the other.

No burglars. Hellion dogs.

The grinning dogs eased off the splattered sofa and padded over to greet me. As if I'd let them live after they'd trashed my house. I yelled at them, but no sound came past my lips.

If my kids had done something like this, I would not have

any trouble screaming my head off. I'd make the kids clean up the mess and I'd yell some more. Maybe even stomp around a bit. All that irate body language would be lost on these sexually replete dogs.

I sank down on the wooden bench in the foyer. This bench was usually a last stop on the way out of the house, a place where I put things I didn't want to forget to take with me. I'd never once used the bench as a way station to get into the house.

I just couldn't go any farther. I reminded myself this dog situation was temporary. Bitsy would take the hellion dogs and go home tomorrow. Then I'd have my life and my house back.

Rafe carried Bitsy in. I heard Artie's sharp intake of breath. Catching his eye, I shook my head in warning. I didn't want Bitsy to know. She had enough on her mind right now with the funeral and her pregnancy.

Luck wasn't with me. Bitsy's eyes were fully operational. "Oh my God!" she exclaimed. "Put me down. Right this minute."

I staggered to my feet and issued a terse command to Rafe. "Take her upstairs. I'll clean this up." If there was any mercy in this world, he would listen to me and get Bitsy upstairs.

"You'll do no such thing, Cleopatra Jones. This mess will take you all night to clean up." Bitsy squirmed out of Rafe's arms like a cat stuck in a large pickle jar and landed on her feet. "Damn these dogs. This is all Dudley's fault. If he hadn't insisted on the biggest dogs in the world, we wouldn't be living with such giant berserkers."

I hitched an arm around Bitsy's shoulders. "You have enough to worry about right now. I'll deal with this. Maybe you should think about some sort of dog-proof interior gates when you get them both home."

"What?" Bitsy stared up at me, white-faced.

I prayed she didn't throw up in here, although it wouldn't make that much difference. What was one more pile of goo in the aftermath of a dog orgy?

I pushed that thought from my mind. "Gates. You know, like when the kids were little and we wanted them to stay out of the living room so we'd have at least one room in the house that wasn't littered with toys."

Bitsy ignored my comment about gates. "I'm not taking either dog home. I hoped to leave Mo here with you."

My heart stopped. I heard a rushing of wind and saw a very bright light. The carnage of my living room swirled through my head. I couldn't face this level of disaster on a routine basis. "I thought you knew I was dog-sitting Madonna until you took her home with you."

"My mother hates dogs," Bitsy said. "If I even take Mo back with me, she's going to have a fit."

Mothers are supposed to drive us crazy. That's their permanent job description. It amazed me that Bitsy hadn't grasped that elementary concept. "Move out."

Bitsy cast another quick glance at Artie. "I've been thinking about that."

With the baby on the way, she would need more space, a place where both dogs could run and be happy. And with her insurance windfall she could afford to live anywhere.

Surely if Bitsy had time to think things over, she'd keep the dogs. I'd just have to let Bitsy get accustomed to the idea. "You need your own space."

Bitsy swayed against me. Tears pooled in her eyes. "It doesn't matter. I can't handle the dogs, not with everything else."

I felt like crying myself. Bitsy wasn't the only one facing major life changes. Damn Charlie for sticking me with Dudley's dog. Damn Dudley for dying and leaving behind a huge mess.

There definitely wasn't room in my bed for two of these huge dogs. Mozart would have to find another home. That was all there was to it. "We'll think of something."

When Bitsy had started crying, Rafe and Artie herded the dogs outside. Their return spurred me into action. I leaned over and picked up a broken lamp off the floor. Aunt Ida's lamp. Wet spots that I earnestly hoped were doggie drool dotted my sofa.

Bits and pieces of something unidentifiable lay among the wreckage. I hoped it wasn't something one of the girls had treasured. They'd bitch and moan for years.

It wasn't until I found a larger piece that I recognized what it had been. "My slippers! They ate my slippers. That's it. I'm taking both dogs to the pound right now."

Bitsy slumped into Grandmother's chair, relieved that a decision had been made. All I needed were my purse and my car keys and both dogs were history.

Rafe caught my arm as I tried to stomp out of the room on one foot. "What?" I shouted in his face.

His wonderfully sculpted lips quirked. "You do fireworks real nice, hon. But it's Saturday afternoon. The pound is closed. Why not keep the dogs separated tonight and regroup in the morning?"

I wasn't ready to be placated, especially not by someone that might be a murderer. And I damned sure couldn't handle the sexual tension thing that happened every time this man touched me. I tried to put on a pleasant face but from the way Rafe leaped back, the Antichrist look was back. "Go away."

He caught my head in his hand, tipping my chin up until I met his gaze. "Cleo, don't be angry with me. I want to help."

Banked embers smoldered behind his expression and a heat wave swept through my body again. How could someone show such concern for another person's welfare and be a murderer? I was so confused. My brain wanted to trust this man. My hormones already did.

"Why don't I take Mozart home with me for the night?" Rafe asked. "I'll bring him back tomorrow when things are calmer."

Getting Mozart out of the house would be a big help. Stepping away from Rafe, I glanced over at Bitsy for approval. She nodded her agreement. "Do you need to check with the boys?" I asked.

"Not for this. But I should talk to them soon. About a lot of things."

No kidding. The issue of what to do with the dogs would be the perfect lead into the topic of the baby. "They should know, Bitsy. The sooner, the better."

Rafe and Artie packed up Mozart's dish and dog food for his sleepover. Rafe slipped his arms through the handles of the book bag holding all the dog gear. Mozart pranced at the end of his leash. "I'll bring Mozart back tomorrow," Rafe said. "That should give you ladies plenty of time to figure out what to do."

Now that he was standing across the room from me, my brain finally started working again. He'd driven my car here from church. How would he get back there? "Do you want my keys?" I offered, thinking I wasn't going anywhere until he brought the dog back.

"No thanks." He shook his head in denial. "Mo and I are up for a long walk."

Rafe was leaving. He had been a big help. Was I just going to stand here like a bump on a log? I should thank him. "Wait." Operating on instinct, I limped across the room to kiss him on the cheek.

Only, he tricked me by turning his head and catching my kiss full on the lips. The piece of gummed up slipper sole I'd been holding dropped out of my hands. His lips touched me hesitantly at first, as if asking for permission.

A whisper soft sigh escaped my mouth. My brain tried to reason with my hormones without success. This elation I was feeling wasn't supposed to be happening.

My body responded to him as if it had all the answers it

needed. My hands fisted in his shirt and I instinctively nestled into his heat. If the house had been on fire, I'd have burned to a crisp because all I could think about was kissing Rafe. Hunger seared my every thought as I yielded to him.

His hand stroked the back of my neck and all I could think of was how much I wanted this. I'd been dreaming of this kiss for days. Maybe years.

I heard a soft cooing sound and was horrified to realize that it welled up out of my throat. Rafe pulled away. All my senses screamed, "Don't stop," but it was too late. I'd awakened us from the sensual spell.

His hand moved from my neck to my face and he caressed my cheek with his thumb, all the while smiling at me with those big brown lady-killer eyes of his. I struggled to pull air in my lungs.

I wanted to say something profound, but I was speechless. After a moment, I found my voice. "Damn."

His wonderful smile reached all the way to his twinkling eyes. "I don't often get that response. What does it mean?"

I took half a step back and breathed in air that wasn't laden with male pheromones. My response had been the most honest I could give. Damn pretty much summed up how I felt.

As in damn he stopped, damn he kissed me, damn he was a great kisser, and damn what was I going to do if he was the murderer. "Damn pretty much says it all."

Rafe's warm chuckle resonated through every pore of my body. Masculine pride and delight gleamed in his eyes. The man was thrilled that I'd been reduced to swear words. I took another step back. It was either that or kiss the smug grin off his face, and I didn't think either of us was ready for that. Especially not before an audience.

An audience?

Heat seared my cheeks as Rafe walked out the door with

Mozart. I turned to see both Bitsy and Artie watching me with rapt fascination.

"Well." This from Bitsy.

"It-it-it's not what you think," I offered in my best Elmer Fudd imitation, realizing my hair was tumbling down about my face and neck. Where was my hair clip? I scoured the floor until I found it.

"Does Charlie know about Rafe?" Bitsy asked.

Ruthlessly, I shoved my hair back into the clip. "Charlie doesn't need to know. He's married to another woman, remember?"

"Only because you divorced him," Bitsy reminded me.

The door flew open and Grant, Charla, and Lexy blew in, with Mama close on their heels. Everyone talked at once and I couldn't understand a blasted thing they were saying. In my hyperaware emotional state, I couldn't take it. I screamed, which silenced everyone.

Mama clutched her heart and staggered to the dog drool sofa. At the last minute, she noticed that the sofa didn't look right and changed course for the wooden rocker. "My heart. My heart," she cried.

My own heart raced. How could I have forgotten for a moment that Mama had a delicate constitution? "I'm sorry, Mama. I shouldn't have startled you like that. Are you all right?"

Mama gripped the arms of the rocker and heaved in a shuddering breath. "What in the blazes is wrong with you people? First you ruin a perfectly good funeral by walking out early, then you scream at a woman with a heart condition. What's this world coming to?"

Mama looked suspiciously okay to me. Her color was good. Her mind was sharp. And all of her limbs seemed to be working fine, judging by the rapid pace at which she was rocking.

I exhaled slowly. Okay. I hadn't jeopardized Mama's health.

Time to figure out what else was wrong. "What made all of you come in here talking a mile a minute?"

"Some man stole my dog," Grant shouted in my ear.

"Oh, that." I waved off his comment. "We can explain." I glanced at Bitsy, who'd decided to sit on the doggie drool sofa.

"I sent the dog home with Cleo's boyfriend," Bitsy said. "The dogs tore things up here while we were at the funeral and I couldn't deal with Mozart's antics along with everything else today."

"What?" Grant said, his face a junior version of male befuddlement.

"Oh, for Pete's sake, Grant," Artie said. "Think about it. Mozart humped Madonna the whole time we were gone."

"Oh," Grant said, the chaos of the room finally registering. "Is Mo coming back? Mo is going home with us tomorrow, right?"

"We need to talk about some changes now that your father is gone," Bitsy said.

We exchanged a look and I knew that she was ready to have that talk with her sons. I shepherded Mama and my girls into the kitchen. I prayed Bitsy would tell her boys everything.

Charla stomped into the kitchen in front of me, stopping next to the butcher-block array of knives. Molten amber shot out of her eyes.

"Since when is the golf pro your boyfriend?" Charla demanded. In the next breath, she asked, "Does Daddy know?"

CHAPTER 14

I'd changed my clothes three times before I found the perfect outfit for my two o'clock golf lesson. With my thick ponytail fed through the back opening of my Callaway cap and my conservative navy shorts and off-white golf Polo, I looked every bit as professional as a scratch golfer.

No way did I look seductive or flirty like Jonette did in her two piece hot pink ensemble with matching pink anklets. My shortie socks were white, and came up just high enough to cover the precautionary tape on my mostly mended ankle. This upcoming golf lesson could be considered my first date with Rafe, and I didn't want anything to mess it up.

I could control how I looked but not how I thought. I couldn't get the questions out of my mind that I'd fielded about my ex. I didn't care if Charlie knew about Rafe. Charlie gave up his right to have any say in my behavior long ago. So what if I'd kissed Rafe? He wasn't *really* my boyfriend.

Which wasn't to say I hadn't been thinking about dating him. Ever since that magical kiss, I had been thinking of what it would be like to be with Rafe. To find out if we had anything in common besides a case of mutual attraction.

Who was I kidding? I wanted to kiss him again in the worst way, but I didn't have any experience with men other than Charlie. I needed to take this slow so that I didn't get in too fast or too deep.

Caution had me put a room full of furniture between us

yesterday morning when Rafe brought Bitsy's dog back. I had hoped distance would minimize the magnetic pull he exerted, but increasing our linear distance didn't do a bit of good.

My entire body seemed aware of each breath Rafe took. I might as well have stood next to him for all the good distance did me. I could no more escape this magnetic attraction between us than the moon could suddenly veer out of the earth's orbit.

Before he left, Rafe sent me a searing glance, a veritable laser beam of desire that revved up my insides. I stood there in my kitchen and warred with my impulse to drag him upstairs and have my way with him. I congratulated myself on my self-control as he left unmolested.

I wasn't disappointed that he didn't kiss me again. No, siree, I was taking it slow. That's the way the new Cleo operated.

Before my lesson, Jonette and I played our interrupted round of golf from last week. I whacked my drive off the number six tee. Jonette's tee shot already lay in the center of the lush green fairway. I felt strong today, charged with energy and anticipation.

My ball trickled to a stop a few yards short of hers. I smiled in triumph. Things were going my way for a change. "What did you do over the weekend?" I climbed into the cart and Jonette drove us down the paved cart path.

"Nothing much. Went to the funeral. Worked. Dodged Britt Radcliff. Thought about Violet Cooper."

Dang. In the flurry of getting Bitsy, her boys, and Mozart off and dressing for my lesson I forgot about interviewing Violet Cooper today. No problem. The new Cleo was flexible. "I'm headed over to see Violet after my lesson. You wanna come?"

"Wild horses couldn't keep me away," Jonette said. "When are you going to tell me about kissing Rafe?"

My mouth dropped open. "How did you know?"

"Your Mama called me," Jonette said with a toss of her head.

"Spill it, Clee. Was it as good as you thought?"

"Mama knows?"

Jonette grinned. "You kissed the man in front of two witnesses. Did you expect them to keep the big kiss a secret?"

Of course. My audience. No wonder so many people had populated my kitchen when Artie announced that Rafe had returned the dog.

I whacked my ball again. It landed in the rough bordering the fairway. Jonette hit her second shot and it landed short of my ball, but still in the freshly mowed grass of the fairway.

How could I distract Jonette from the big kiss? I thought of remaining mute the rest of my life, but I had too many things to say, too much unwanted advice to pass onto my children. When we got up to the green to putt, I couldn't help gazing over the hill down at the crime scene. "What was he doing out here, Jonette?"

She wasn't deterred one bit. Her expertly plucked eyebrows rose in challenge. "Don't think you can fob me off with Dudley's murder. I want to know about you and Rafe. It was hot, right?"

Hot was putting it mildly and Jonette was a bloodhound when it came to these kinds of details. If I didn't give her something, she'd dog me until I did. "You were right, Jonette. Rafe isn't a training wheels kind of guy. I forgot everything when he kissed me, and I probably would have jumped him right then and there in the foyer if he hadn't broken off the kiss."

"So, there is life after Charlie?"

I couldn't help but grin at that remark. No longer did I want to burrow into a hole to escape my troubles. There was a big world out there and I wanted to sample more of it. Especially Rafe Golden. "Definitely." Two putts later I holed out and headed for number seven.

"What's next with Rafe?" Jonette asked.

Next would be ripping his clothes off and letting our imaginations run wild. After stewing in my own lust for twenty-four hours, I was ready to abandon my taking it slow plan. This was a new day, a new me. I wasn't going to let the world pass me by. "I have a golf lesson with him after we finish up here."

Jonette whistled appreciatively. "Man, I'd pay good money to watch that lesson. You wouldn't even know I was there."

I would just as soon my lesson with Rafe be private, but the location of the lesson area was highly visible. Maybe it wouldn't be such a bad idea to have Jonette nearby.

If I did something mortifying, Jonette would step in and rescue me. "I don't mind if you watch. I hope I'm not indulging in a foolish fantasy with Rafe."

Jonette's assessing gaze flickered over me. "You're no fool, Cleo. If Rafe Golden doesn't realize what a gem you are, then you're better off without him."

"Thanks."

Jonette was right. If Rafe didn't appreciate me, he certainly wasn't any great catch, and I would be better off learning that before things went any farther.

When we finished our round, Jonette took our completed scorecard into the pro shop. I drove the cart over to the driving range where the pro held all of his lessons.

Since my chip shots were inconsistent, I hoped Rafe would work with me on my short game. Not that other areas weren't in dire straits also, but chipping was a good place to start.

As I rounded the seven-foot-high ligustrum hedge, the first thing I saw was Christine Strand glued to Rafe. Steam shot out of my ears as I realized they were kissing. Hot tears seared my eyes.

Damn. Damn. Damn.

I saw red and smashed the accelerator to the floor. I wanted to hurt Rafe for hurting me.

Running him over with a golf cart seemed a just punishment in my book. Only, my jingling clubs warned of my not so stealthy approach, and Rafe's head shot up. His wounded gaze caught mine. How dare he look so hurt? I was the one who ached inside.

I should never have gone with my hormones in making the decision to believe Rafe's interest in me was sincere. I'd had it right when I thought he might be the killer. He'd certainly killed my hopes of trusting a man again.

How could he kiss us both in the same week? He *deserved* to be run over. Multiple times.

I bore down on Rafe, knowing that the time to stop was passing. Rafe shoved Christine out of the way.

He wasn't going to move. He *wanted* me to hit him? This man was crazy. If I killed him, I would go to jail and never see my girls again. No man was worth that.

I slammed on brakes and just barely nudged him with the cart. Good thing I had my dark glasses on. He couldn't see how close to tears I was. With my self-control shot, all that remained was my cloak of threadbare dignity. "Forget the golf lesson. I won't be rescheduling."

"I can explain," Rafe growled, his hands on his hips.

"I don't want to hear it," I said, but that was a lie. I wanted to know why he'd kissed me. I wanted to know why it mattered so much that I'd seen him kissing Christine. I ground my teeth together in frustration.

Rafe grabbed the cart steering wheel and slid in the driver's seat like he was going to drive my cart. My choices were to get squashed or to move out of his way. Ever the pragmatist, I moved over, making certain there was a wide gulf of space between us on the seat.

"Don't be mad," he said.

I wouldn't look at him. "Being mad would imply I cared."

"You do. And you and I both know it. Dammit, Cleo, *she* kissed me."

"I don't care," I said. "That kiss was a mistake."

"It certainly was."

I gasped. I was, of course, referring to the wonderful, earth-shaking kiss we'd shared on Saturday.

Rafe swore again under his breath. "The kiss today was a mistake. I didn't participate at all. She threw herself at me."

I didn't have to listen to this. "Stop the cart and let me out. You've got your lesson with Christine to finish."

He ignored my request. "I promise I won't ever have another lesson with her if that will make you happy."

I exhaled sharply. "Happy? Do you know what would make me happy? I would be happy if I ran you over with this damn cart. That would make me happy."

His brown eyes blazed. "But you didn't. Run me over."

He had me there. He had been in my sights, but I lost my nerve. Truth was, I couldn't bear to hurt a fly. Not even a two-timing fly. As thrilling as kissing Rafe had been, I wasn't about to waste one day of my life on a worthless cheat.

Life was just too short. "Let's forget these last few days ever happened, okay? Chalk it up to temporary insanity."

"Insanity? That's what you're calling this thing between us?"

His voice was dangerously soft. I shivered in spite of the eighty-degree temperature. I didn't want to get in a discussion of "us" when there was no us. I nodded. "Insanity. That's my story and I'm sticking with it."

Rafe threw back his head and laughed. "I like you, Cleopatra Jones. You're a breath of fresh air."

How did you deal with a crazy person? Other than my family, I hadn't run into too many of them. Should I try to placate him or get as far away from him as possible? I decided on the haul ass strategy. "My car's over there."

His lips quirked. "I know where your car is. I know how many miles are on it. I know your air conditioner is shot. I know the transmission sticks as you accelerate. I drove your car, remember?"

"You can't hold that against me." I waved off his comments. "You volunteered to drive the Gray Beast."

"Your car has a name?"

"That car is my nemesis," I said. "It'll run long after all the other cars in the world stop. It's like that annoying bunny on TV. Daddy bought that car for me to learn to drive on because it was so safe. It's been a member of our family ever since, even if it is butt ugly."

"I like that you drive a safe car."

Dang. He was sounding nice again. I liked him better when he was acting crazy. How could I put him in a box and deal with him if he kept changing personalities on me?

He stopped next to my car, took the car keys from my hand, and deposited my clubs in the trunk. Jonette walked over to claim her clubs. "What happened to the hot golf lesson?"

My face turned beet red. Jonette colored in return as her words filtered into her brain. "It's awful hot out here today, isn't it?" she said to cover the telling silence.

Rafe handed me my keys, but he didn't let go of them. A startling electric current flashed between us. He waited until he saw the spark of acknowledgement in my eyes before he said a word. "Since it's my fault we have to reschedule, your make-up lesson will be complimentary."

I wasn't planning on rescheduling, ever. He'd just have to give that complimentary lesson to another woman. That's what I thought, but I wisely kept my mouth shut. I did not want to get into a heated discussion with him in front of Jonette.

Rafe held on to the keys for a moment longer, then he gave

my hand a warm squeeze and drove off in the cart.

Jonette fanned herself. "We're lucky your gas cap is on tight. There were enough sparks out here to blow up this entire parking lot."

I gestured towards the passenger door. "Get in."

Jonette groaned. "What now? I swear your life is a soap opera, Cleo. Why can't you have a private affair like everyone else? Why do you have to conduct a torrid romance in the golf club parking lot?"

I glared at her over the top of my sunglasses. "Hush, Jonette. I'm invoking the hour of need clause in our relationship. Get in."

"Oh, all right," Jonette grumbled, tossing her clubs in my backseat. "But only if you tell me what happened."

"After we get out of here." I headed west on the highway towards the mountain road.

"You want to know what happened?" I said when I felt capable of speaking without swearing. "I'll tell you. Christine happened. She was all over Rafe like melted butter and he wasn't resisting until he saw me. I lost my cool and tried to run him over with the golf cart."

"Good for you." Jonette clapped her hands in delight. "Did you hit him?"

Remembering my cowardice, I grimaced. "Barely. I lost my nerve at the last minute. Jonette, why do I attract losers? Why can't I find someone who's faithful? Rafe saw me coming, pushed Christine out of the way and just stood there. He dared me to hit him. The man's a lunatic."

Jonette laughed and laughed. "He's perfect," she said when she could speak again.

I signaled a right turn. "Of course he's perfect. He's also a cheater. And we haven't even had a real date. All we've had so far is some chemistry and a kiss."

"Hey, don't knock it." Jonette wiped the tears of laughter from her cheeks. "Most women would kill for that much."

"Yeah, but I'm not most women. I want a man who'll do as he's told, who'll come when he's called, and who only sleeps in my bed."

Jonette started laughing again. "Sounds like you want a dog."

"Nothing wrong with a well trained dog."

I laughed at the image of Rafe on a leash. My instincts told me it would be exceedingly dangerous to tie that man close to me. He'd have me in bed in two seconds flat, but, on the bright side, I'd finally have some relief from the sexual tension that sparked between us.

I'd never been one for causal affairs, but this man tempted me to do things I'd never done before. How far would the new me go? Would I give him another chance?

If only Charlie hadn't destroyed my faith in my instincts. Never before had I felt like I was drifting through life without a rudder. Without that built-in self-check of my tried and true instincts, how could I be sure that I didn't do something exceedingly foolish?

I assumed Rafe didn't kill Dudley. How big of an imagination stretch was it to think that his interest in me was more than superficial?

My heart wanted to believe in the power of love. My head knew it wasn't worth the risk.

Who was I deluding with all this self-analysis? Even after catching him with Christine I still wanted him. The new Cleo Jones was an animal.

CHAPTER 15

The house where Jasper and his mother lived had an uncared-for look, like the owners had moved to Florida a few years ago and neglected to sell the place. High grass filled the yard in front of the tired two-story clapboard house. Trees encroached on the house from the sides and rear, as if the forest was reclaiming the acreage and the forest was winning.

Two beagles reclining on the junk-filled porch bayed at our approach. I stopped in the rutted, weed-choked lane. My golf cleats might come in handy if I had to make a rapid getaway through this thick growth.

There were no cars in the drive, no sign of recent civilization if one didn't count the satellite dish on the sagging roof. In my mind I could hear banjos twanging like they did in that movie about isolated inbred country folk.

Didn't Rafe pay Jasper anything down at the golf club? From the looks of this place Jasper desperately needed a raise. And a bush hog to find his yard again. At the golf course Jasper had access to all kinds of mowing machines. Why didn't he bring one home and clean up this mess?

Or, did he like hiding out in the woods? This level of overgrowth would certainly discourage visitors.

Jonette reached up and locked her door. "I'm not getting out. This place is too spooky."

"You are too getting out." I hit the master lock button and unlocked all the doors. "I'm trying to keep your butt out of jail.

If I'm risking my neck for you, the least you can do is provide moral support."

Jonette eyed the high grass and frowned. "I'm going to get ticks and God knows what else if I step foot out there."

So was I, but what was the point in whining about it? I opened my door. "What's a few ticks among friends?"

The beagles bayed louder as we approached the porch. The eerie noise reminded me of the sound hunting dogs made when they found something that smelled like dinner. I sure hoped these dogs didn't have food on the brain.

I stopped short of the badly warped, unpainted porch steps. If I had to defend myself against the killer dogs, I had my keys, my pocketbook, and Jonette. Not an arsenal by any means. If I was going to take investigating seriously, I would have to be better prepared for danger in the future. It might be time to dig Daddy's pistol out from under my bed.

I hollered above the din of barking dogs, "Mrs. Cooper? You in there?"

"Okay. We did this." Jonette tugged on my arm. "No one's here. Let's go."

I stood firm. A thump inside alerted me that someone was in the house. "Wait."

When no one greeted us, I tried again. "Mrs. Cooper, are you in there?"

The interior door creaked open. I heard an unmistakable sound of a gun being cocked. A metallic cylinder thrust through a hole in the screen door. "Who wants to know?" a gravelly voice called out.

The object in the door was a rifle barrel, and it was pointing right at me. I moved a few paces to the side and the gun didn't follow. The dogs continued barking for all they were worth.

"Let's get out of here." Jonette stood directly behind me and tugged on my belt loop. "This woman is crazy."

"I'm Cleo Jones and this is my friend Jonette Moore, Mrs. Cooper." Something was not quite right here and I wasn't ready to go until I figured out what it was that was bothering me. "We're here to talk to you about your pension fund. I believe you know my mother, Delilah Sampson."

As I spoke, the gun barrel angled towards my new location. Interesting. Did Mrs. Cooper have poor eyesight?

The gun wobbled. "Hush, dogs," she said and the dogs hushed. "You say you're Dee's daughter?"

"Yes ma'am," I answered. "I was a Sampson until I married Charlie Jones down at the bank."

"Those goddamn cheaters at the bank," Mrs. Cooper grumbled. "You're married to one of them?" She stepped closer to the door. More gun barrel slid out, but I could make out her rounded petite frame. Short white hair frizzled around a well-lined face. A faded floral shift spanned her plus-sized figure.

The gun lined up on me again. I scooted sideways out of self-preservation. Who knew when she would pull the trigger? "Not anymore. Please, Mrs. Cooper, I need to talk to you."

"How do I know this isn't some trick?" Mrs. Cooper asked. "Are you going to take my house away from me next? You'll have to drag me out of here. I won't come willingly."

"Mrs. Cooper, I don't want your house," I said. "I want to know about your pension fund. How long ago did the money disappear?"

The rifle barrel followed the sound of my voice to my new location. Violet Cooper may have called off the dogs, but she wasn't taking any chances. I whispered to Jonette to stay put when I moved next time. I wanted to see what Mrs. Cooper would do if we split up.

"Two years ago." Bitterness ate through her voice like battery acid. "Those GD crooks at the bank took all my money. Do you think I want to live like this? It's all their fault. I got to have an eye operation. Every dime Jasper makes goes toward that surgery. I won't have the procedure done until I can pay for it."

"Don't you have medical insurance?" I asked.

She snorted. "Hell no. I don't need insurance. I had the pension fund instead. Fat lot of good that did me. You were right to get shed of that banker fella. They're crooks, every last one of 'em."

The gun followed me to my new location. Poor Mrs. Cooper. She was stuck in a falling-down house while Jasper worked for peanuts at the golf course. It would probably take him fifty years to come up with enough cash to pay for her eye operation on his minimum-wage salary. I'd speak with Mama to see if her cronies in the hospital auxiliary couldn't do something to help Mrs. Cooper. "What kind of operation do you need? Is it that new laser surgery?"

"Cataracts. Got 'em in both eyes. Can't see worth a damn unless I look out of the side of my eyes, but the surgery is supposed to be a miracle cure. That's the trouble with getting old. Your body wears out just when you finally get good sense. Then it's a steady diet of doctors."

"What do you think happened to the pension fund?" I asked. All the while I was thinking, could investigation really be this easy? It seemed surreal that I could be this calm when someone was pointing a gun at me, but there it was. I was investigating Dudley's murder, and I was going to beat the cops to solving the case.

"Someone took it, that's what. The po-lice couldn't figure out who done it, so I didn't get a dime of my money back. My life savings. Everyone on the advisory board came out squeaky clean, but it was those bank crooks that took my money. I think that Donnie Davis did it. You know him? I believe he goes by the name of Dudley."

Here was another trail back to Dudley. Was this a coincidence?

"I know him, but I'm sorry to say that he's dead. He died last week."

Mrs. Cooper visibly started. "Serves him right. Well, Daddy always said you can't take it with you. What did that Dudley do with my money? If he turns up with an extra two hundred and fifty thousand dollars, it's mine and I want it back."

"I hear you, Mrs. Cooper. I'll look into it. I promise."

"What did you say you do?" she asked.

I caught Jonette's eye and edged backwards down the rutted lane. "I'm an accountant, Mrs. Cooper. My Daddy used to do your taxes for you, and I'd be happy to have you as a client again. Thanks for taking the time to talk to me this afternoon. Bye now."

Jonette and I hopped back in my car and I backed rapidly through the knee-high weeds. "Hell. Violet Cooper couldn't see to kill Dudley if she tried."

No matter how much I wanted Jasper's mom to be the killer, it just wasn't happening. Unless she had someone drive her to the golf course and back, and then lead her out on the dark fairway, Violet Cooper just wasn't a plausible suspect.

I continued my thinking aloud. "She's practically blind because of those cataracts. She tracked our location by the sound of my voice. She had motive, all right, and the skill to shoot a man, but she doesn't have the wherewithal to pull a murder off. And she'd rather have her money back than Dudley killed. I don't see her as a murderer."

"You're such a softie," Jonette retorted crisply. "I bet Violet Cooper could kill if she had to. I'll bet she wouldn't have any trouble pulling the trigger on someone, especially if it was Dudley."

I breathed a sigh of relief when I reached the main road and mowed grass. There was something to be said for civilization. "But she would've needed an accomplice and Jasper's too hotheaded to pull it off. She's not the one, Jonette. The murderer has to be someone else."

"I wanted it to be her."

I patted Jonette's hand. "So did I."

"Now what?" Jonette asked.

"Now we keep asking around to find out who else had trouble with Dudley or the bank."

"Great. That narrows it down to just about anyone who ever had a mistake on their bank statement. It's a wonder Detective Brain Dead didn't accuse Bitsy of killing her ex."

My hands twitched in response and I ran off the road. I jerked the steering wheel, but the Gray Beast bounced along the shoulder until it was good and ready to come back on the road again.

"Damn Sam," Jonette said. "You trying to kill me?"

"No. You startled me. I keep forgetting you don't know."

"Don't know what?"

"Bitsy is already on Britt's suspect list."

"And you harbored a criminal in your house?" Jonette asked in amazement. "I always knew Bitsy was nuts. No woman could love Dudley unless something was wrong with her."

"Bite your tongue, Jonette. You don't know what you're talking about. Bitsy's got it tough. You wouldn't want to be in her shoes, either."

"Well now you got my curious up. What's wrong with her shoes?"

"Bitsy and Dudley were on the verge of reconciling their marriage but something went very wrong. Bitsy was about to say yes, but Dudley stood her up at the bank. Something about a two-hour lunch with another woman. Now Bitsy's in line for a large life insurance settlement, and that's not all."

"What are you talking about?"

I took a deep breath. I wasn't exactly betraying a confidence.

Bitsy had told her boys, and Britt knew. Jonette might as well hear it from me instead of down at the tavern. "She's pregnant with Dudley's baby."

"Ohmigod." Jonette whistled under her breath. "It's a wonder Britt doesn't have her sitting in a jail cell right now. If a man two-timed me while I was pregnant with his kid, I'd kill him for sure."

"Yeah, but you wouldn't have settled for one shot between the eyes, and neither would Bitsy." I turned off the mountain road back onto the highway. "Something just doesn't feel right about this whole thing. I believe Dudley's death has to do with his banking clients. Too bad I don't have an in there anymore."

"Don't." A panicked look crossed Jonette's eyes. "Do not for one moment even consider having anything to do with Charlie Jones on my account. That man is not good for you. I want you to stay as far away from him as possible."

The sun came out from behind a cloud and I could suddenly see every speck of dust floating around inside my car. "There's one thing I know for sure about Charlie Jones. He'll be coming around to see me soon. Charla will tell him about the big kiss. Charlie has been fine with me not having a life while he's playing house with his silicone bride, but he won't like this news."

"He doesn't have any say in it." Jonette poked me with her finger. "If you let him boss you around again, I'll kill you myself. Stay away from Charlie, Cleo."

"Don't worry about me," I said. "I have a plan."

Yeah. I had a plan all right. I just wish I had more confidence in it. My plan was like Mama's beef stew recipe. Throw a lot of ingredients in the pot and see what happens.

The trouble was, sometimes her stews came out great, sometimes they were disasters.

CHAPTER 16

When I walked out to get the mail the next day, I saw my neighbor Ed Monday doing the exact same thing. His round face was as red as Mama's gets when she's having one of her spells. Had he received some bad news? I could see the papers trembling in his hand from my front porch.

According to Charlie, my neighbor had been removed from the bank for yelling at Dudley. Escorted out by the security guard had been Charlie's exact words.

Charlie wasn't the most trustworthy of sources, but he'd succeeded in planting a seed of suspicion in my mind about my neighbor. Other than spend a lot of time in his dark house, Ed Monday had never done anything else out of the ordinary.

Something was bothering him now. Ed was my neighbor. What if he was having a heart attack?

Would he be offended if I invaded his personal space to check on him? Would he think I was being nosy? Probably.

Did that matter if he really needed help? I hated indecision, but the truth was, Ed wasn't a social creature. Oh, we waved faithfully in greeting back and forth in the yard, but he'd never accepted my dinner invitations. He'd never invited us over to his place.

I'd respected that, but now I was stuck. I couldn't walk away from a neighbor in need. What if the circumstances were reversed and one of my girls needed help? I would want my neighbors to help them, so it was good to be proactive about this kind of thing.

If it wasn't something I could help with, at least I would have made the effort. I walked over to the edge of my yard. "Ed?" No response. I tried again, louder. "Ed, you okay?"

"What?" He looked up from his letter and seemed genuinely surprised to see me standing nearby. His thick glasses glinted in the afternoon sunlight. His tired clothing and ratty black sneakers should have gone in the Goodwill bag long ago.

Did he resent my intrusion? If so, he'd just have to deal with it. I was on a mission of mercy. "I was getting my mail and I noticed you seemed very upset. Did you get some bad news?"

"Bad news?" he repeated.

The poor man was in shock. Time for me to be more forceful. I crossed the invisible line delineating our properties and sat us both down on the steps. I recognized the preprinted return address on the open envelope in his hand. It was from the Hogan's Glen Bank where Charlie and Dudley worked.

"Do you have a problem with the bank?"

"Those incompetent buffoons," Ed railed. "Every month they send me an erroneous statement. The numbers never match up with the ending balance from the last one. They keep notifying me that I'm overdue on loan payments, and I never obtained a loan from them."

I'd never seen Ed so distraught. "I'm sure it can all be straightened out with a phone call to the bank."

"Ha. That's what you think." His sweating, florid face tightened with anger. "I've been down to that bank a bunch of times. That Donnie Davis said he'd take care of this two weeks ago. He lied to my face. He's a liar and a crook and now, he's dead. What am I going to do?"

My puzzle-solving radar went on full alert. Dudley had looked into Ed's problem at the bank and now Dudley was dead. I could connect the pieces with the best of them, but I couldn't envision Dudley outright stealing from Ed Monday.

"I know someone down at the bank," I said. "I could have them look into it for you." Charlie owed me big time and I'd hurt him if he didn't answer my questions about Ed's account. Not that I expected him to share Ed's financial information with me, but he could discreetly check Ed's claim about his erroneous bank statements.

"What could it hurt?" Ed's shoulders slumped in defeat. "I'm tired of wasting my breath talking to those crooks. As soon as I get this resolved, I'm moving my account to another bank, even if the Hogan's Glen Bank is the only one in town."

I heard my porch door open. Glancing over, I saw Mama waving at me from our doorway. "Cleo, phone for you in the office," she called.

I nodded, torn between telling her to take a message and wanting to hoof it back over there to answer the phone. Maybe it was another Homeowners Association who'd heard of my wonderful accounting services. I turned back to Ed. "Do you want me to come back when I'm done?"

"I'm fine." With effort, Ed hoisted all three hundred pounds upright.

I searched his face quickly again. My neighborly sentiment was about used up, but he did seem less red-faced and his hands weren't visibly trembling anymore. I didn't feel too bad about abandoning him. "I'll let you know if my questions turn up anything down at the bank."

The quickest way back to the office was through my house. I hoped whoever had called hadn't hung up by now. Mama snagged my arm as I charged through the foyer. "Whoa there," she said.

I disengaged her fingers. "I need to get this call, Mama. I'll be right back."

"There is no call." Mama propped her hands on her hips. "I

made it up when I saw you over there with that man."

I rolled my eyes. Trust Mama to rescue me when I was trying to help someone else. "*That man* is our neighbor and he has a serious problem."

Mama gestured in the direction of Ed's house. "That man spends days at a time inside that tomb. I don't like the way his eyes look."

I blinked. Mama's line of warped reasoning was a good example of what happened when someone smashed the wrong puzzle pieces together. The assembled picture wasn't recognizable. "For heaven's sakes, what's wrong with his eyes?"

Mama fingered her triple-stranded pearl necklace. "They're shifty. That's what. I've been judging people all my life, and I know that man has a deep, dark secret. I wouldn't be surprised if he's an underworld crime boss or something."

I blinked again. "Ed Monday? If he were a crime boss in Hogan County, don't you think we would have noticed folks coming and going at all hours of the night? For your information, there's a recurring clerical error in Ed's bank account."

I took a deep breath. "I thought Ed was having a heart attack right there on his porch. Why don't we install bars on our windows and doors if you're afraid of him?"

Mama's small-minded accusation rankled my nerves. Was she just shooting her mouth off again? "If you're so worried about our shifty-eyed neighbor, why haven't you said anything before now?" I asked.

Mama pursed her lips momentarily. "That's not necessary and you know it. But you could exercise some common sense and not sit on the man's porch. He wants privacy, so leave him alone."

There was no point arguing with Mama when her mind was made up. "I'm giving him privacy."

"Mark my words. He's a bad egg. I tell you it's not natural

for a body to want to be by themselves that much. Something is very wrong over there."

Was Mama extremely paranoid or was she right? Either way I didn't want her to lecture me for another half hour. Time to change the subject. "What's the news from the beauty shop?"

Mama touched her freshly coiffed hair and beamed. "The word is out that the financing got pulled from that White Rock development. Margie Albright says that Robert Joy is spitting mad and is threatening a lawsuit and a big tell-all exposé to the newspaper."

That acreage had a colorful past. Sixty years ago, a house of ill repute had been located in those cornfields. It seemed poetic justice that people were still getting screwed on that parcel of land. "Who put up the money for that place?"

"All the ladies were speculating about it. Valley Land Company. Does that ring any bells?"

"Sounds familiar." I knew exactly who Valley Land Company was. I had filed tax forms for his corporation, but he'd meant to keep his name out of his business affairs. My lips pressed firmly together so that his name wouldn't leak out.

I was bound by confidentiality to protect my client's privacy. Not exactly lawyer-client privilege, but the same principle applied to conversations with my clients. If I spoke his name to Mama, she'd be on the phone before I could close my mouth.

Valley Land Company was the brain child of my biggest client. Blabbing would be very bad for my bottom line.

Time to change the subject again. "What's for dinner?"

Ever since the funeral, Mama and the girls had been cooking together. Both Charla and Lexy knew enough of the basics that Mama shouldn't ruin their cooking common sense at this stage of their lives. And, it gave the girls quality time with their grandmother.

I wish I'd had my parents over for dinner more when Daddy

was alive. In those days I'd been busy juggling so many balls in the air that when I left the office after spending the day with Daddy, going home to Charlie and the girls was all I could think about.

Mama squared her blazer padded shoulders. "Tonight's going to be turkey surprise."

My mouth went dry. Food surprises were not good things. "Oh? What's the surprise?"

"I don't know," Mama cackled happily. "I've left that part to the girls."

Water. I needed water. After filling a glass with tap water, I said, "Just make sure we can eat it. I can't afford to send out for pizza two or three times a week when dinner bombs. We don't want a repeat of Spickle Fish Lasagna."

Mama's expression grew solemn. I guess she didn't like being reminded of her big mistake. "How's the big romance coming along?" she asked.

My love life was not open to discussion with Mama. "Nothing to tell."

"I bet he'll be over here again soon and I'll ask him myself," Mama declared. "What are you doing to keep Jonette out of jail?"

What was with all the questions? Did Mama think she was a reporter for the five o'clock news? "I assume you're talking about Dudley's murder?"

Mama nodded, wiping dry the spot of water I'd inadvertently sloshed on the counter next to the sink.

Murder was much easier to talk about than my sex life. "I thought Violet Cooper had a good motive to kill Dudley because of her embezzled pension fund, but she can't see worth a damn, so that is a dead end. Now Ed's got this problem down at the bank and I'm thinking that might be something. Good thing I know someone down at the bank."

"Bad idea," Mama warned.

Mama's worst fear was that I would forgive Charlie and take back up with him again. "Charlie owes me," I insisted. "I may as well start collecting now because life is short."

"I don't want him in this house." Mama barred her arms across her chest.

"I didn't either, in the beginning, so I went along with you. But now that I realize he can't help being a jerk, it seems petty to make him wait outside when he comes over to pick up the girls."

Mama went all slitty-eyed on me. "Does that mean you're over him?"

The truth was, I did feel like I was over Charlie. Getting over someone was like one of those stock market tickers, where the net result was a one-way trend, but on a daily basis there were lots of little peaks and valleys.

At this very minute, I felt one hundred percent over him. Getting kissed by another man had a tendency to do that. "Yeah, I'm over him."

Mama narrowed her amber eyes as if she were going to protest, then she relaxed. "It's okay with me if he comes inside."

I hugged her. "Thanks. It should make things easier on the girls if we all act like adults."

Mama brushed me off. "No chance of that."

Someone pounded on my front door at ten o'clock that night. I wasn't expecting company, and I didn't feel comfortable about answering the door this late. Madonna woofed and padded to the door, her tail wagging.

I took that as a good sign, checked the peephole, and opened the door partway for my ex. Charlie wore the dark-green fishing vest I'd bought him three Christmases ago. His lure-adorned fishing hat sat squarely on his head. Dark shadows underscored his eyes. Charlie had aged twenty years since Dudley's funeral.

"Yes?" I asked.

Charlie petted the dog. "I know I don't have the right to ask this, but may I come in?"

It was much easier to be over Charlie if he wasn't standing right in front of me. "Why?"

His bloodshot eyes met and held my gaze. "Because, even though I messed up our marriage, you and I were always friends. I could really use a friend just now."

I usually joked about Jonette's bullshit detector being broken, but right now I wasn't sure mine was connected. It went against my grain to be nice to him, but I couldn't slam the door in his face either. He was the father of my children. "Come on in."

Charlie didn't budge. He glanced fearfully over my shoulder. "Your Mama isn't going to swoop in here and kick me out, is she?"

CHAPTER 17

"Mama's gone to bed for the night," I said. "You're safe."

He stepped inside as if the floor were made of ice. I steeled myself against his very familiar scent. What would I do with him now that he was in the house?

I cleared my throat softly. "Are you hungry?"

"I could eat," he said.

I fixed him a cup of decaf coffee while I warmed up the leftover turkey surprise. Keeping my hands busy helped to steady my nerves. "What's on your mind, Charlie?"

He sat down heavily at the table. "I wanted to see you and the girls. I miss our times together."

Just thinking of his betrayal made my blood pressure skyrocket. My days of being the stoic martyr were over. "You should have thought of that before you jumped in bed with Denise."

His lips tightened into a thin disapproving line. "We could have worked things out if you hadn't gone off half-cocked, Clee."

He had a lot of nerve assuming I was to blame for our divorce. The old me might not have argued with him, but the new me didn't cave to his displeasure. "Hold on. You can't blame our divorce on me."

"Why not? You're the one who filed for divorce."

"What did you expect? That I would welcome you with open arms when you'd been screwing another woman's brains out? Not in this lifetime."

Charlie shrugged. "Men mess up. It's part of the Y chromosome thing. I made a mistake. *You* turned your back on me."

I wouldn't let him paint me in this corner. "Damn you. It wasn't just one mistake. I will not stand here and listen to this. If you're unhappy with your lot in life, don't blame me. What's this really about, Charlie?"

He stared at his clasped hands resting on the heavy oak table. "I told you. I miss you."

I was not softening. I repeated that phrase silently until I believed it. "Have you forgotten that you're married to another woman? Are you trying to cheat on your new wife with me?"

"No." He glanced at me. "Maybe. Would you?"

I couldn't believe he'd even think such a thing. "Hell no. If you're having problems with Denise, work them out with her. I don't want to hear about them."

"If only it were that easy." He laughed mirthlessly. "She had an affair. When I called her on it, she bragged that she was sleeping with my best friend."

I didn't want to hear this, but I couldn't help but think that justice was being served. Charlie was going through exactly what he'd put me through, and it couldn't have happened to a more deserving person.

But. Denise and Dudley? "Do you believe her?"

The microwave chimed. Neither of us moved to silence it.

Charlie rubbed his entire face with his hands. "Because of her, the last words I said to my best friend were that I never wanted to speak to him again. I'm all torn up inside."

My brain processed this new information. Charlie had a strong motive for killing his best friend. He certainly knew how to handle a weapon. We'd shot skeet in the early years of our marriage. Light-years ago, but shooting was a skill a person didn't forget.

"What were you doing the night Dudley was killed?" I asked.

He visibly sagged. "I was home alone. Denise spent the night with her mother."

So he could have done it. He could have killed Dudley. He knew about guns, he was driven by jealousy, and he didn't have an alibi. "Does anyone else know about the affair?"

Charlie's shoulders slumped. "I don't know. I just have to get away for a little while."

This sounded familiar, like the Charlie I remembered. During our marriage, Charlie had often gone fishing when he didn't want to deal with his problems. His predictable behavior reassured me, and I relaxed my guard.

The microwave dinged again. This time I responded to it and removed Charlie's food. I discarded the wax paper covering the food and placed the plate in front of him.

"What the hell is this?" He pointed to the ring of dark romaine lettuce, the circular bed of smoked turkey, and the honey mustard smiley face on the purple fried egg. We'd had a whole one left over from dinner. I wasn't sure how the lettuce would hold up after heating, but hey, seeing as how I could be feeding a murderer, the crispness of his food really didn't matter to me.

"It's turkey surprise and if you don't eat every last bite, Charla's going to be brokenhearted. Mama's teaching her to cook."

"God help us all." He took a bite. His expression grew thoughtful as he swallowed. "Not bad."

"I'll tell Charla you liked it," I murmured as I refilled both of our coffee cups. "So, are you headed up to the lake for some fishing?"

"That's my plan, but it's so late, that what I'd really like to do is crash here, if that's okay."

It wasn't okay with me, not by a long shot. "You have a perfectly good bed across town, if you recall. One that has your wife in it."

Charlie forked in another bite, talking between swallows.

"Denise and I had a big fight tonight. I can't go back there and give her the satisfaction of winning. I told her I was going up to the cabin at the lake for a few days because I couldn't stand the sight of her. Could I stay here, please? I still have keys to Dudley's place, but I can't bring myself to go over there. I'd spend the night wondering where they'd done it."

Justice had indeed been served. "Welcome to my world," I said wryly.

Charlie grimaced. "I'm sorry, Clee. I had no idea what I put you through. I'd take it all back if I could. I don't know what I was thinking getting mixed up with Denise. I asked her for a divorce tonight and she told me to go to hell. She said she didn't plan on moving out, and if I wanted a divorce, I'd have to move out and leave her the house."

The idea of Denise getting my house in Hogan's Heights free and clear really bugged me. Technically it wasn't my house anymore, but still. What right did she have to it?

"I left tonight because I couldn't stand being under the same roof as she was," he said. "I'm exhausted. I don't feel up to a two-hour drive."

"You could stay in a motel," I suggested, sipping my coffee.

Charlie scraped his plate clean. "You know how I hate motels. I like sleeping in my own bed."

"You don't have a bed here. *If* I allowed you to stay here, you'd be staying on the couch."

He sighed deeply. "I couldn't sleep with you? I promise it wouldn't be sexual at all. I'd just like to sleep in a familiar bed."

I shook my head so fast my hair flew out of the clip and into my face. I shoved the loose strands behind my ear. Charlie was not weaseling his way into my life or my bed. "Absolutely not. As it turns out, my bed is a little full these days." I was referring to the Saint Bernard he'd foisted off on me.

Charlie scowled. "Is he here now?"

I felt my lips round into an "O" shape. He'd misunderstood what I said, and not for the first time. "You are my only guest tonight, unless you count the dog you stuck me with."

In typical Charlie fashion, he ignored the part about the dog. "I don't like you dating Rafe Golden. What do you know about him? Is he a child molester? We have to think about the safety and well-being of the girls."

It was a little late for him to wonder about the safety and security of the girls. If Rafe had been here, then at least there would have been a man in the house and they would be better protected than they were right now.

My relationship with Rafe was none of Charlie's business. I barred my arms across my chest. "Back off, Charlie. You don't have any rights when it comes to my social life. I'll make sure the girls' safety isn't jeopardized, but that's as much as I'm willing to concede."

"I heard he kissed you."

"That kiss appears to be common knowledge," I admitted.

"It upsets Charla that you're dating someone."

The guilt card wouldn't work on me either. "Give me a break. Charla has held on to the hope from day one that we'd get back together. Anything that impinges on her hopes upsets her. For instance, your marriage to Denise upsets Charla, but that didn't stop you from getting married."

Charla would be tickled pink that her Dad's marriage was on the rocks, but it would be a cold day in hell before I took Charlie back. Jonette was right. I'd always be wondering if he was cheating on me. I was *so* over him. "I'll get some clean linens and make up the couch."

Charlie followed me into the living room. "God, I can't believe you're putting me on the couch. My back is going to kill me tomorrow."

"You're welcome to leave and get a motel room. If you

weren't the father of my children, I'd turn you away for the night. Be grateful that I'm even allowing you to stay here at all. And don't go getting any ideas. This is just for *one* night."

He held up his hands in surrender. "Okay. You've made your point. I am grateful. I didn't know where else to turn."

That's what happened when your world turned to shit. I'd lived that life. Family was all you could trust when that happened. I guess that's why Charlie came here. We were the closest thing to family that he had. Friends and acquaintances just didn't cut it at times like these.

Thinking of acquaintances reminded me of Ed Monday and his banking problem. I tossed the embroidered throw pillows in the rocking chair. "Charlie, I need a favor. My neighbor is having trouble down at the bank. Could you look into it for me?"

"Mrs. Harris?"

"No, Ed Monday. He claims his bank statements are inaccurate. The bank insists that he has a loan that he didn't repay. He swears he never took out a loan. Could you see what's happening with his account?"

"Your weird neighbor? Why would I want to help him out?"

"Because I'm asking you to."

Ever the opportunist, Charlie asked. "What'll I get for it?"

I tossed a blanket at him. "You get to sleep on a lumpy couch. Don't push your luck."

CHAPTER 18

"Daddy!" Charla's voice rang joyously through the house. "I'm so glad to see you."

I heard Charla clear up in my room as I tied my shoes. My heart ached for the family she wanted us to be. In her greeting I heard yearning and aching and worst of all, hope. My oldest daughter truly believed her parents would get back together.

Supposing Charlie did divorce Denise, what would happen? Last night he'd sounded like he wanted us to try again. If I could trust what he'd said, he wanted me back in his life and in his bed.

Too bad. I couldn't get past all that he'd put me through. I couldn't pretend that his adultery and our divorce had never occurred.

I put on a determined face and went downstairs to fix breakfast. Time folded in on itself as the four of us sat down to eat at the kitchen table. Charla talked nonstop while Lexy sulked because she couldn't get a word in edgewise. Charlie's warm gaze rested as frequently on me as it did on the girls.

I could almost see the wheels turning in his brain as he tried his old life on for size. In the old days I would've gone along with his wishes so that I didn't make waves. I wasn't that person anymore. My purpose in life no longer revolved around making Charlie happy. The sooner he came to terms with that, the better for all of us.

Charlie offered to drop the girls off at school, and they left in a clatter of noise. Even my normally quiet Lexy seemed animated by her father's presence.

But, after they left, I sat down with a cup of coffee and wondered just what I'd done. I'd fixed Charlie his eggs just the way he liked them, the way I'd made them a hundred bazillion times before. I'd added that dollop of milk to his coffee before I sat the cup on the table in front of him.

Good heavens. I'd been acting like I was his wife. That wasn't going to happen. I wouldn't let it. Only, there was a lot of comfort in a familiar routine. And after sixteen years of marriage, I was very familiar with Charlie Jones.

He'd given me that unshaven boyish grin as he left, the one that had always melted me down to my toes. A part of me was whispering seductively in one ear, "You could have him again." But the other part of me was shouting, "You don't want him."

Mama walked into the kitchen dressed in her triple-stranded pearls, mauve suit, and burgundy pumps. "I heard a man's voice. Who was here?"

Mama's bedroom overlooked the driveway. She'd have to be blind to have missed Charlie's BMW.

I drew in a deep breath, bracing myself for the explosion sure to come. "Charlie spent the night."

Mama's penetrating stare would have broken another, lesser woman. "I thought we agreed that you were over him," Mama said.

"We did, and I am. He slept on the couch, Mama. He needed a place to stay."

"Hasn't the man ever heard of motels?" Mama poured a cup of coffee, then joined me at the kitchen table.

I'd already had this conversation with Charlie. "He's the father of my children. Even if he is a puke, I couldn't turn him out in the street."

"I don't see why the hell not."

Lord, you had to love my mother. She was unswervingly loyal in her convictions. "It was my choice. I don't see why we can't be civil about this."

Madonna must have sensed my distress. She came over and thrust her big Saint Bernard head in my lap. Her brown eyes radiated sympathy. I rubbed her head and she licked my hand.

"You always were softhearted, Cleo. Make sure that man doesn't take advantage of you again."

"Hey. I resent that remark. There's a difference in being softhearted and being stupid. I learned my lesson about Charlie already."

"Keep that in mind." After she felt her warning had time to sink in, Mama added, "What time are you going over to the office today?"

"Soon as I finish up here. I'd like to start with the Bluemont Hills audit." I also planned to make a phone call about Valley Land Company.

It had occurred to me during the night that Valley Land Company, the White Rock housing development, and Dudley's death might be connected, but I wanted to move cautiously. A lot of money was tied up in this stalled development. A misstep here could cost me my pride, my biggest client, or even my life.

Mama left and I did the dishes. This was good thinking time for me as I mindlessly loaded the dishwasher. Before Dudley's murder, I seemed to be caught in an out of-the-way eddy of life. Now it seemed as if my life was shooting through rapids, zipping from one exciting hydraulic to the next.

No longer was each day an ordeal to endure. I wasn't looking backward anymore. My future seemed as bright as the gleaming white azaleas and sunshine-yellow forsythia blooming in my yard. The new Cleo was getting on with her life.

My immediate goal was to find out who killed Dudley. I wouldn't let Britt send Jonette or Bitsy to jail for a murder they didn't commit. I had one or maybe two men, if you counted Charlie, who were interested in me, although I wasn't sure that either man was a good catch. But, hey, I had a future. Life was good.

I took a break from work and walked Madonna down to the bank to deposit the checks that arrived in today's mail. Since it was such a nice spring day, I chose the long way to the bank. Madonna and I went out the back door and cut through Old Man Putnam's driveway and over into the park. After that, we followed Schoolhouse Road west to Burkittsville Road and came up on the bank from the side street.

The first thing I noticed as I approached was that Main Street was a parking lot. Vacant cars pointed in the direction of the yellow crime scene tape surrounding the bank.

Had something else happened in Hogan's Glen? What danger lurked in our sleepy little town?

Questions churned in my head as I made my way towards the throng of people gathered at the barrier of crime scene tape. I recognized the massive bulk of my neighbor Ed Monday and stopped next to him, reining Madonna in close. Ed's bald head gleamed in the sunlight. I leaned around his portly figure to catch his eye. "What's going on, Ed?" I asked.

Ed glanced over at me and then back at the bank. "The bank guard was killed last night," Ed said, shoving his fists in the pockets of his worn jeans. "Shot. Right between the eyes."

I felt icy talons gripping my stomach. I believed something suspicious was going on at the bank, and now the guard was dead? Did the police see the same connections that I did? "The guard?"

Ed nodded glumly, his attention fixed on the scene before us. My mind started churning around the new pieces to this puzzle. How did this all fit together?

Why would the guard be shot, unless the bank was being robbed or unless the guard saw something he shouldn't have? Was this about White Rock or Valley Land Company? I glanced around the crowd, noting faces of friends and acquaintances. Our illustrious mayor was nowhere in sight.

I shivered in spite of the warm day. Hogan's Glen was not a good place to live these days. Two murders in less than a week was two more than we'd ever had. Two murders meant it wasn't a fluke circumstance. This was terribly serious. We had a serial killer in our midst.

What else connected Dudley's murder to this one? Anyone with half a brain could make the connection to the bank. Lots of money flowed through that bank, and who better to know the transaction details than a bank officer like Charlie or Dudley?

Charlie hadn't had an alibi for Dudley's murder. Suppose he'd gone to the bank first and murdered the guard before he came over last night? Had he used me to establish an alibi for the guard's murder?

Had I slept with a serial killer under my roof?

How well did I really know Charlie Jones? Just because I'd been married to him for sixteen years didn't mean that I knew him. I'd had no knowledge of his adultery until it smacked me square in the face. Maybe I'd missed the real Charlie Jones all these years. Maybe I'd only known the man he wanted me to see.

I exhaled shakily. There was no reason to jump to conclusions. Just because Charlie worked at the bank, that didn't automatically make him a mass murderer. Lots of people worked at the bank. But still.

I felt very uneasy. A killer was running wild in our town. How could I keep my family safe if the police couldn't catch this person?

Uniformed policemen stood on the sidewalk next to a cluster of bank employees. I watched in morbid fascination as Detective Britt Radcliff scribbled on his notepad, then moved on to question the next bank employee. The group shifted and I found myself looking right at Denise. She was dressed in one of her sickeningly flattering suits, her blond curls cascading about her face just so.

She caught my eye and smiled smugly. I didn't smile back. We were not friends.

Her smile was the same sort of smile she'd given me in the old days when she'd been sleeping with my husband behind my back. It was the kind of smile that said I've got hidden secrets.

Well, I had a secret too. Her husband spent the night at my house. He wanted to divorce her. I hoped the cops grilled Denise about this murder every bit as thoroughly as they'd grilled Jonette over Dudley's death.

I wasn't exactly friends with my neighbor Ed Monday, but at least I didn't want to spit on him every time I saw him. Ed appeared to be transfixed by the scene. He nearly jumped out of his shoes when I tapped his shoulder to get his attention.

Oops, I had forgotten about his need for personal space. "Sorry," I said hastily. "Didn't mean to startle you, but I wanted to let you know I have someone looking into the problems with your account."

"I hope it wasn't the bank guard." Sunlight flashed off of Ed's thick glasses.

I narrowed my eyes. Was that a joke? Did Ed Monday have a sense of humor? "It was someone else."

"Good," he said glumly. "Doesn't look like the bank guard would help me now anyway."

What was that old saying? Dead men tell no tales? The bank guard was dead. Dudley was dead. And if this continued, someone else would be dead soon. Everyone knew bad news happened in threes.

Would it be another bank employee? What underlying cause connected the murders? I didn't know.

"Hey, Clee. What's all the excitement?" Jonette joined us at the taped barrier, her leopard-print spandex short skirt and top leaving nothing to the imagination.

I motioned towards the bank. "The guard was killed last night."

"Damn Sam." Jonette whistled appreciatively. "This has the makings of a regular crime wave. What the hell is going on around here?"

I shrugged. "I don't know, but I have this vision of Denise sleeping her way through the bank hierarchy, killing them for sport."

Ed Monday shocked me by laughing. "That's rich," he said.

"That's jealousy talking," Jonette's amber-flecked eyes scowled at me in consternation. "Denise would be pained if she so much as broke a nail. I can't see her murdering anyone, and believe me, I've got her number. We've got something much bigger going on. I can feel it."

Jonette was about as psychic as I was, but in her current occupation as barmaid she came across all sorts of people. Perhaps she had some insight into Denise that I was missing. Or at least some objectivity. I couldn't be objective about the woman who had ruined my life.

It was very unsettling that we were having a major crime spree in Hogan's Glen. I had Mama and the girls to consider. "The bank guard was Bennett Glazier. Did you know him?"

"What do you want to know about Bennett?" Jonette asked.

My eyebrows quirked up. "You know him?"

Jonette nodded. "He's a regular down at the tavern. My guess is that last night he had his usual three whiskey sours, then he walked home. He lives in one of those duplexes over by the park. Bennett never hit on me, but he couldn't take his eyes off of my boss."

The bank was between the tavern and the park. Bennett must have seen something unusual at the bank on his way home and stopped to check it out. Or had his sexual orientation triggered a murderer's rage? "Dean and Bennett are gay?"

"Dean is not gay. I can attest to that one hundred percent," Jonette said. "As for Bennett, I'm not sure he was out of the closet, if you know what I mean. He was more like a wannabe, in love with Dean, but Dean wasn't interested. That unrequited love thing."

Ed Monday's ears turned pink. I guess this conversation was too racy for him. He ambled away, leaving me to wonder why he'd been standing here. Behind that shambling gentility, did a raging fire burn out of control? My instincts told me that he had a secret. I had two problems with that information.

First, my intuition was shot all to hell. How could I put much stock in my insights when I knew that I'd missed big on perceiving a major problem in my marriage? Second, not all secrets were large enough to kill for. What if Ed Monday had some minor secret that he didn't want getting out? Was that why he kept to himself? To keep from being recognized?

I couldn't pigeonhole Ed Monday any more than I could solve Dudley's murder right now. I didn't have enough information, but I couldn't help feeling that I knew more than I thought. What I needed was a block of time that I could sit down and think this out.

For instance, Jonette was the police's top suspect in Dudley's murder. How did she rank in their standings for the latest murder? She knew both victims. Some assumptions could be made from that.

Assumptions that would be dead wrong if you didn't know Jonette.

Voicing my suspicions to a murder suspect wasn't particularly brilliant, but I wasn't one to stick just my big toe in the shallow end of a pool. It was more my style to dive in headfirst in the deep end and worry about the outcome later.

"Don't shoot me for asking, but do you have an alibi for last night?" At her pained expression, I qualified my remark. "I know you didn't kill Bennett, but can someone verify your whereabouts last night?"

Jonette planted her hands on her hips. "Are you asking me if I shacked up with anyone last night?"

I groaned. Why was everyone obsessed with sex? I hadn't noticed this preoccupation until I didn't have a sex life, but now it seemed that sexual innuendoes were everywhere. "Jonette, who you sleep with is your business. In fact, I'd rather not know the details. All I want to know is, do you have an alibi for the time of the murder?"

"Seeing as how I don't know what time the murder was, that makes having an alibi a little challenging. Fortunately, I have someone who can corroborate my story. Britt's had a deputy tailing me for days now. I spent last night home alone with the police watching my house."

I exhaled sharply. "Well, that's a relief."

"No kidding," Jonette said. "I was worried about spending the rest of my life in an orange jumpsuit."

I nodded towards the thick knot of bank employees. "Do you think it's one of them?"

Jonette shrugged. "How the hell should I know?"

"I thought you knew everything."

"Don't confuse me with your mother."

I arched an eyebrow at her. "Fat chance of that."

CHAPTER 19

Denise knocked on my door several hours later. Just the sight of her in that wrinkle-free, cleavage-displaying business suit stirred the hair on the back of my neck. I wanted to take this opportunity to kick the crap out of her for ruining my life, but I was bigger than that.

Maybe.

"Cleo?"

"Yes?" I stood just inside the screen door. Not inviting her in, but not doing anything bad either. Mama had gone down to the church office to help fold the monthly newsletter and I was home alone, unless you counted Madonna who was snoozing on my bed.

Denise had been inside my house exactly one time and I'd vowed she would never enter it again. On that singular occasion two months ago, Denise had come to pick up the girls instead of Charlie. Since Lexy was still in the shower, Charla had invited her new stepmother up to see her room.

Denise had felt faint. I couldn't much blame her for that as Charla's room looked like it had been hit by a tornado. Anyway, I'd come home to find Denise in my bed. I'd gagged, evicted Denise, and then burnt my bed linens in the backyard.

I wanted to snap and growl at her on general principle. Instead I schooled my features into those of a woman who had moved on.

"Charlie won't be picking the girls up this weekend," Denise said. "He's off on a fishing trip and I'm just too frazzled to deal with the children after what happened at the bank this morning."

As if I wanted her alone with my girls. I'd just as soon send both girls to lion tamer school as to send them off to spend the weekend with Denise. "No problem. When do you expect Charlie back?"

Her thick lips drew down into a face wrinkling frown. "Don't know for sure. He left yesterday afternoon and I haven't heard from him."

And she wouldn't if I knew her husband. He'd come home when he was good and ready. It could be a few days, it could be a week or more.

That man didn't believe in calendars or clocks once he started fishing. He spent time up there clearing his head. And from what I'd seen, he needed to have his head cleared.

"I told the police I hadn't heard from him since early yesterday afternoon," Denise said. "They're up at the lake looking for him. They want to talk to him about Bennett Glazier's death."

That got my attention. First because Charlie would be pissed that anyone bothered him while he was fishing, and second because she was lying about the time he left. Was there more she wasn't telling me? "Oh?"

She wiggled and her boobs waggled and I remembered how those boobs had mesmerized my former husband. Was Denise using this opportunity to punish Charlie for threatening to divorce her? She didn't know him very well if she thought she could manipulate him that way.

"It appears Charlie stopped off at the bank on his way out of town last night," Denise said. "The police took Charlie's computer and they won't let the rest of us go back to work until they check out all the computers. Can you imagine how long that will take?"

I could imagine it all right. This was a small town and folks would be greatly inconvenienced. No telling how many would move their accounts to a Frederick bank after this. Our independent bank didn't stand much of a chance of survival if it remained closed for any length of time. "Oh dear."

It was possible that Charlie went to the bank and worked for a bit after he left her yesterday. But not probable. Charlie was a fairly linear guy.

If he was upset and wanted to go fishing, there wasn't any way in hell he would stop at the bank and work for a few hours. It was fairly miraculous that he'd veered off his course to spend the night here.

Denise pouted. "I don't even know if we'll be paid for the time we're closed. It's such a mess. I can't wait until the police clear out of there so that I can get back to work."

Was she nuts? If my workplace closed for a few days I'd be dancing in the streets. Denise sounded a little too good to be true right now. Was she practicing her speech for her boss?

Oh, wait. Charlie was her boss. She could practice on him anytime of the day or night. I ground my teeth together in frustration and a sharp pain shot up my jaw.

I would have to watch it or my teeth would soon be ground down to nubs. The whole Charlie and Denise thing was one source of major teeth gnashing. Dudley's murder was another.

Charlie had mentioned that he didn't have an alibi for Dudley's murder because Denise wasn't home. I was Charlie's alibi for the second killing. I couldn't ask Denise about her alibi for the second killing without sounding like I was interrogating her, but I knew something about her alibi for the first murder if I could just remember what it was. I strained through the bits of information stored in my feeble brain.

It came to me a moment later. She was supposed to be off

doing something with her mother that night. "It's nice to have family in times like these. I rely on Mama to help me out in a lot of ways. Do you have a close relationship with your mother?"

"My mom is terrific," Denise said with another annoying wiggle.

I don't know why she was posturing and jiggling her fake boobs under my nose, unless it was because she could. I certainly was not impressed, but I was getting closer to finding out where her mother lived. "Is she located near enough that you get to see her frequently?"

"She's in a retirement community about thirty minutes away. I go see her at least once a month."

Thirty minutes. That wasn't so far that Denise had to spend the night there before driving home. Why did she stay overnight? If it were me, I'd have wanted to be home in my comfy bed instead of sleeping on a borrowed cot.

How tacky would it be to ask the name of the place? Jonette routinely assured me that tacky was in the eye of the beholder, so I boldly kept the questions coming. "Does she like the retirement place? Mama has been making noises about one. I understand they have all sorts of activities and trips at these types of places."

Denise nodded energetically and everything wiggled. "Mom's made so many friends there she barely has time to fit my visits in her busy schedule. Montclair is the greatest. They even have Mom on an aquatic volleyball team."

Montclair. I had the name of the place. Now all I needed was to learn if Denise's presence there the night Dudley was killed could be verified.

Mama pulled up in the driveway and Denise suddenly seemed very anxious to leave. When I get to be Mama's age, I'm going to cultivate a reputation like Mama's so that people get the hell out of my way.

Denise tossed her head and her blonde curls shimmered. She waved goodbye in a Miss America–style minimal wrist rotation. "Once Charlie gets back in town, I'll have him call and reschedule his visit with the girls. Ta ta."

My fingers clenched into tight fists. I'd like to squeeze her ta tas until they popped.

Mama growled at Denise as she passed her on the steps. "What did that hussy want?" Mama asked.

I opened the screen door and stepped aside for her to pass by. "She canceled the girls' weekend visitation with Charlie. It seems he's gone fishing and she doesn't know when he'll return."

Mama snorted. "Fancy that."

"But she didn't just come here to tell me that. Did you hear about the bank guard?"

"Sure did. It's all Muriel and Francine could talk about down at the church."

"Denise implied that the police like Charlie for this murder."

Mama tugged at her ear as if she couldn't believe what she'd heard. "What?"

"I kid you not. Denise claims he worked on his computer at the bank after he left to go fishing. With the bank guard turning up dead today, it's no wonder they think Charlie might be involved."

"What time did all of this happen? Didn't Charlie spend the night here?"

"I don't know when the guard was killed," I said. "I was watching that TV show about cops and lawyers so it must have been after ten when Charlie arrived. Denise claims he left home in the afternoon."

Mama frowned. "Do you suppose he whacked the bank guard and then came here to give himself an alibi?"

I blinked at her choice of words. "Whacked the guard? When did *whacked* become part of your conversational vocabulary?"

Mama slipped her taupe pumps off and rested her stockinged feet on the coffee table. "We have weed whackers. I'm sure there's such a thing as people whackers too."

"Yeah, right. If this were a mob-run town. This is Hogan's Glen. Nothing ever happens here."

Could I have been wrong about the town too? I had always assumed Hogan's Glen reveled in its close-knit small town atmosphere. But then, I had also assumed Charlie was content in our marriage and I'd missed the mark there.

"Not anymore," Mama said. "With two murders, I guarantee you we're on the map now."

"What if Charlie committed the murders?" I asked. "Could I have been married to a murderer all those years and never suspected a thing?"

"People change. People do bad things. You never thought he'd cheat on you either."

My teeth clenched automatically and I braced for the shooting jaw pain. "Cheating and killing aren't exactly in the same league."

"That's why children should never do drugs."

"What? What are you talking about now, Mama?"

"Drugs. They're bad for you."

I didn't get the connection. In all the years I had known him, Charlie had never shown any interest in drugs. He liked being in control too much to ever let his guard down. "Are you saying Charlie is doing drugs? I can't believe he'd do that."

"I'm saying that it's possible to go a little ways down one road and find yourself in a whole new place with different rules. Once that happens, people don't know how to act and bad things happen. That's why they have gangs in the big cities. So that folks know how to behave. Granted it's bad behavior, but gangs have stepped into the vacuum of kids with no home training."

I didn't care that much about faraway inner-city kids and neither did Mama. She just liked to shoot her mouth off. "This is a little too bizarre for me. I don't know how we got from the bank guard's murder to inner-city gangs, but I can't save the world. As far as I'm concerned, if Charlie's gone off-road with bad behavior, he's got only himself to blame. He had a great life and he threw it away."

Mama's gaze narrowed. "Just make sure he doesn't drag you into this cesspool. I don't want my granddaughters having to go to prison to visit both of their parents."

My chest froze in mid-breath. "Prison?"

Mama waved her arm in a wide circle. "That's where they put murderers, remember?"

My head snapped back as if I'd been gut punched. "There's no way they could put me in prison. The closest they could put me to either crime scene is that I know how to play golf, I have a bank account, and I know my way around a computer. And if they use those criteria, they'd have to arrest half the county."

"Be careful, sweetheart." Mama patted my shoulder. "There's a rotten apple in this town and I don't want you getting too close."

Too late. I was already too close. The only way to get rid of a rotten apple was to throw it out of the apple barrel. I didn't want my family members to be the next victims of a deranged killer. Finding the killer was the only way I knew to protect them. Rooting out the rotten apple was my top priority.

I had three other reasons for finding the killer. Jonette and Bitsy and Charlie topped the police suspect list. Jonette had an alibi for the second murder. What about Bitsy?

I phoned Bitsy and her mother answered the phone.

"Bitsy's at a doctor's appointment," Mrs. Noblit said.

"I'm sorry I missed her. How is she doing?"

"As well as can be expected now that her life is ruined."

171

I guess Mrs. Noblit wasn't excited at the prospect of having a third grandchild. "Please tell her I called and asked after her. One more thing. Do you happen to know where she was last night?"

"Bitsy was right here serving tea to my bridge club. Why do you ask?"

I crossed my fingers and told a small fib. "I thought I saw her dining at the Boar's Head last night."

"You were mistaken. My daughter was right here."

I hung up. It seemed Bitsy had a solid alibi for the second murder. Of the three top suspects, that left the brunt of the suspicion on Charlie.

If Charlie was Britt's new top suspect, I had to get him cleared too. I'd been willing to find the real killer to clear Jonette and Bitsy, so how could I let the father of my children go to jail? Even though he had treated me badly in the past, I couldn't stand by and do nothing.

Like Mama, I couldn't envision a future where I'd be driving my daughters to prison to visit their father.

No way around it. I had to find the killer, now more than ever. Over the years, I'd found that it paid to take problems to the top of an organization. Right now I had plenty of questions for our mayor.

"Thank you for seeing me on such short notice, Mr. Mayor." I sat down in the paneled office. Darnell Reynolds had the American flag on one side of his desk and the Maryland state flag on the other. With his dark suit, white shirt, and narrow red tie, Darnell was the picture of patriotism.

"You said there was a problem with my taxes?"

I hadn't exactly said that. I'd hinted that was the case when I told his secretary that the mayor might have a visit by the IRS unless I got something straightened out immediately.

"I've been reviewing the new tax laws and believe we should rethink our strategy on the tax forms I filled out for Valley Land Company." I pulled out a large folder from my briefcase. I hoped it didn't come down to me opening the folder because I had nothing new to show him.

I was here on a fact-finding mission, hoping that I wouldn't piss off my largest client or get killed. "If it's not too much trouble, I'd like to review the assets of the corporation."

The mayor pounded his fist on his desk. "Dammit."

I flinched and gritted my teeth. I'd never known Darnell Reynolds to punch anything. Bugs like him usually scurried for cover when detected. There might be more depth to Darnell than I thought. "If this isn't a good time I could come back later."

Darnell circled behind me to close the door. I heard him click the lock. Every hair on my neck snapped to attention.

This was it.

I'd triggered the rage of a homicidal maniac and I was next on his hit list. I should have told my daughters I loved them this morning before I dropped them off at school.

I stood up, not wanting to have him lurking behind me. If he was going to shoot me, I wanted to see it coming. Daddy had always said that the best strategy for any situation was to have a good offense. I couldn't exactly dodge a bullet, but I could talk my way out of almost anything.

When I turned, it was to see Darnell resting his florid face in his hands. The bright color ran from the peak of his balding head down into his white shirt collar. Was he going to murder me with his tears? I hadn't expected this reaction.

A twinge of sympathy tugged at my heart. "Darnell? You okay?"

"No. I'm not okay. I was stupid enough to go into business with Dudley and it's going to ruin me."

"I don't understand," I said, hoping to draw him out. Folks told their accountants the oddest things. This past tax season, a woman had insisted that her vacation to Saint Thomas in the Virgin Islands was a religious pilgrimage. Another man tried to write off his wife's car as a company vehicle and she didn't even work for his company. I couldn't wait to hear Darnell's story.

"My life is unraveling and I can't do a thing about it. I won't be needing an accountant in prison, Cleo."

I wished I had thought of bringing along a tape player. If the mayor confessed to the murders, I'd like to have it on tape so that Britt Radcliff wouldn't think I had made up this story. "It can't be that bad."

Darnell clutched his heart the way Mama did when she had heart palpitations. I knew what to do. I steered him to his desk chair and handed him a glass of water.

"You're going to think I'm a foolish old man."

"I don't know what to think, but I'm going to call nine one one if you keep grabbing your heart."

"Don't call anyone."

I'd known Darnell Reynolds for years. Daddy and I had golfed with him on occasion. Darnell thought nothing of improving his lie when no one was looking and he always gave himself putts.

I didn't have any trouble imagining him planting a bullet in Dudley's head. "Tell me what's wrong. Maybe I can help."

Darnell sipped his water and gradually his flush subsided. "What's wrong is that Dudley made promises that I can't keep. When this comes out I'm going to be ruined."

"Promises?"

Darnell groaned. "He told Robert Joy the land developer that everything was greased for White Rock. That the mayor was in his pocket. That all the approvals he needed for annexation were a sure thing."

Dudley and his high financing. I wondered how much money Dudley made on this deal and where that money went. "Ouch."

"More than ouch. Once this becomes common knowledge, I won't have a job."

"I heard that you wanted out of the White Rock deal."

"I don't have any choice. I never promised Dudley or Robert Joy a single thing. I wanted my name kept out of this. That's why I formed the land corporation."

In Hogan's Glen, the procedure was for the town council to vote on matters that affected the community and the mayor had the deciding vote on the council. "How were you going to handle voting on the annexation?"

"I planned to abstain from the process. Other council members have done that in the past when there was a conflict of interest. There's never been any problem with that before, but Robert Joy is threatening to ruin me if I don't cooperate. I'm damned if I do and damned if I don't."

It all clicked for me at that moment. Darnell wanted to make money on the land deal but he wanted to be mayor more. With Dudley's assurances about the annexation being a sure thing, Robert Joy had already invested in land grading, surveying, and promotional materials.

Without the annexation, it was doubtful that more than a dozen or so homes could be built on that thirty-acre spread. Worse, the cushy profit margin for the developer disappeared. Those colorful advertisements hadn't come cheap. Robert Joy needed to recoup his investment on this project.

At last, I was in my element. I had a nose like a bloodhound when it came to following the money.

My heart wanted Darnell to be guilty of murder, but he was my client. It was to my advantage that he stay out of jail. "Have you spoken to Scott Michaels?"

"Hell no. I didn't want the city attorney involved."

"It's time to get him involved. Once you go on record with documentation about your intent to recuse yourself from the annexation vote, then you don't have to worry about Robert Joy."

Darnell's eyes flooded with relief. "It can't be that simple."

"Sometimes the simplest answers are the best."

"What about White Rock?"

"Annexation or not, you own the property. Worst case, you now own a farm, Mr. Mayor."

"What about my tax problem?"

His tax problem was a figment of my imagination. "Let's leave things as they are for now and revisit the new tax laws when everything else calms down."

I collected my briefcase and let myself out the door. Darnell had gotten caught up in one of Dudley's shell games. Darnell was upset about his reputation being ruined and losing his job, but was he upset enough to murder someone? I believed he was capable of killing and he certainly had a motive to kill Dudley.

If I believed the murders were about money, then I needed to follow the trail of the money. In the case of the White Rock development, the trail wasn't clear.

The mayor had plenty of money. The developer wanted money. The dead banker used to have money. Who had the money now?

I didn't have any new ideas, so I went back to the beginning and looked at everything with fresh eyes. Of all the suspects on my list, there was one I wanted to be guilty. I'd start with her alibi for Dudley's murder.

CHAPTER 20

With a killer on the loose and a town full of suspects, I didn't feel I could spare time for my Ladies Golf League this week. The police were no nearer an arrest than they had been last week. I had people to investigate, and best of all, Mama was busy organizing a church social this morning.

Montclair Retirement Center was a veritable town unto itself, a cluster of graciously designed three story buildings. Sweeping archways dominated the covered walks linking the complex. Rigidly pruned evergreens formed the backdrop for a riot of purple and yellow pansies lining the concrete sidewalks.

I signed a logbook, registering myself as an Official Visitor, while the youthful receptionist called the business office to see if someone was available to talk to me. Baby blue dominated the richly patterned carpet, the walls, and the upholstered furniture. Very soothing, even for someone as nervous as I was today.

I had so many possible murder suspects now that it would be a relief to remove someone from my personal suspect list. I was fairly certain this was a wild-goose chase, but my nagging conscience wouldn't let me overlook Denise Wonder Boobs.

The only person I'd completely ruled out as a killer was Violet Cooper, Jasper's mom, and that was because she couldn't see. Darnell and Robert Joy and Ed Monday were on my suspect list. Jasper could have done it, and if I was really being honest, Rafe could have done it too.

Charlie and Jonette and Bitsy were on the police department's suspect list. I didn't think Jonette or Bitsy did it, and I didn't want to visit Charlie in prison. So I had to find someone else to take the heat off these official suspects.

"Your mother is interested in Montclair?" Dr. Brinkley asked when I was seated in his pale-blue office. Montclair's head administrator had a gentle, jovial demeanor that put me in mind of Santa Claus.

Mama was now, whether she knew it or not. I needed a cover story so that I could verify Denise's presence here the night of Dudley's murder. I crossed my fingers and hoped God wouldn't fry me on the spot. "Mama is increasingly isolated as she ages. A place like Montclair with an activities program would put that spark back in her eyes."

Dr. Brinkley nodded enthusiastically and handed me a glossy folder. "Our dynamic program director gets everyone involved in activities."

The thought of living in a place where I didn't have to cook, with on-site facilities for haircuts and church, with a heated indoor pool and exercise room, along with a craft room and a quilting room seemed to be Paradise on earth.

"One of the things that led me to make a visit without Mama is that I'm concerned about security. How do you protect the elderly against outside threats?"

Dr. Brinkley puffed up with pride. "Our check-in procedure restricts entry into the residential area. Visitors sign our log-book. Then the receptionist cross-checks the name with our residents' approved lists before letting them through the locked exterior door. Each resident has a locked suite with no exterior entrances."

The logbook was the key. If I could look through the sign-in log I should see Denise's signature for the day of and the day after Dudley's murder. "Do any people move out because they don't like it here?"

"Our residents tend to stay put. All of our floors are secure and handicap accessible." Dr. Brinkley gestured towards a framed picture hanging on the wall. The picture was a schematic drawing of the facility floor plan with names penned in each apartment.

I stood and perused the wall schematic with great interest. Sure enough, Denise's mother, Louise Wagner, lived in a first-floor apartment. There were only two vacancies in the entire facility. "How much do these suites go for?"

Dr. Brinkley stood and motioned me towards the door. "The fee schedule is outlined in the folder I gave you. Why don't I show you around and you can get a feel for Montclair?"

By the time the tour was over, I wanted to sign myself in and never move out. I thanked Dr. Brinkley for the tour, "accidentally" knocked the logbook off the wooden stand, then quickly bent to retrieve it.

I flipped through the pages until I saw Denise's squiggly signature. She'd signed in at seven p.m. the evening of Dudley's murder and signed out at seven a.m. the next day. Disappointment bit me hard on the butt. I'd hoped to snoop around and find something to incriminate Denise and all I'd done was wasted my Wednesday morning.

I lifted the logbook to its stand. "I'm so sorry. I'm not usually so clumsy."

"No problem, Mrs. Jones," Dr. Brinkley said with practiced ease. "Come back, and bring your mother with you. She'll love it here."

Fat chance of that. Mama wanted to live at home and nowhere else. It wouldn't matter if this place was the Taj Mahal or some other wonder of the world.

When I returned to my office, I tossed the glossy Montclair packet on my desk and got back to work. I didn't give the retirement home another thought until Mama fanned the colorful pages past my face that afternoon.

"What's this?" Mama waved the packet like a matador signaling a bull. "Are you trying to get rid of me? I won't go in an old folks home. I'm not old." Mama made a big show of dropping the information into the trash can. The packet hit bottom with a loud thwack.

Which should have tipped me off that she was seriously pissed. Mama lives to recycle. Ordinarily, she would no more toss a piece of paper directly in the trash than she would purposefully dismember her grandchildren.

Her refusal to consider Montclair annoyed me. Those wide carpeted hallways, the soothing music, the oversize watercolors on the walls, and the yummy smells from the cafeteria made a nice package. "It's a wonderful place, Mama. You should take a look at it so you know what's available."

Mama got down in my face and snarled at me. "What's out there is a bunch of old folks waiting to die. There's nothing at Montclair that I want. All I need is right here in this house."

I had no plans to stick Mama anywhere, but it irked me that she wouldn't even look at the materials. I grabbed the packet out of the trash and showed her the glossy pictures inside. "See how lovely this is? Activities. A pool. Great food."

Mama rolled her eyes and tapped her foot impatiently. "If I added one more activity to my life I couldn't think straight. Why would I want to live thirty minutes away when my life is here in Hogan's Glen? Besides, I don't have any intention of moving into an old folks home."

"It's not an old folks home." It was my turn to roll my eyes. "Montclair is a Retirement Center. That means there are all kinds of fun programs out there and I bet it's affordable too." I thumbed through the pages until I found the price list, tucked way in the back of the stack.

I skimmed the info until I found the bottom line. My mouth fell open. The price for the living quarters started at two thousand dollars a month. Holy cow.

If we sold this house and the girls and I lived in the Gray Beast, I could keep Mama at Montclair for a few years, but that would be it.

"What?" Mama asked, her brown eyes smoldering embers of coal.

"This place is expensive. How do people afford it?"

"Who cares?" Mama said. "I won't be stuck in the middle of nowhere with someone else thinking up make-work for me to do. My life is here, and I'll thank you to quit interfering in it."

I pointed to the price list. "When folks buy into this community, they don't get their money back. In addition, they pay a monthly rent to live there. This is not a good investment. Who would throw such massive amounts of money away?"

"Lots of folks," Mama said. "Particularly if it got unwanted relatives off their hands."

Mama's caustic tone ate at my heart. Did she think I didn't want her? I rushed around my desk and hugged her. "You're not unwanted, Mama. The girls and I need you here. Montclair appealed to me. If it weren't for the expense, I wouldn't mind living there."

Mama looked at me like I'd lost my mind, but then she held me close. "These places don't take children. Are you gonna hand your girls over to Charlie while you make potholders for the rest of your days?"

"Hell no. If I can't afford Montclair for you, I sure can't afford it for me, even if I met the minimum age requirements, which I don't. The concept just appealed to me. Solitude with comradery, exercise without athleticism, meals without having to cook, that sort of thing."

Mama soothed the hair back from my face and kissed my

forehead. "Honey, you don't need to move into a retirement home for that, you just need a vacation. That's all."

"Right." A vacation wasn't likely, not when I was trying to keep Jonette, Bitsy, and Charlie out of jail, not to mention trying to build up my client base. Who would do my work if I took time off?

"I mean it. A vacation would do you a world of good. You ought to take Jonette and go up to Berkley Springs. Soaking in that mineral water and getting a massage or two would do wonders for you."

So would getting laid, but I didn't see any help for that either. I wasn't about to run off and leave Mama in charge of the girls for a long weekend. You had to stay right on top of teenagers or they ran all over you.

I wasn't sure Mama still had the right stuff anymore. I had visions of her being tied to a kitchen chair and stuffed in the coat closet as Charla and Lexy's friends drank all the booze in the house, played Russian Roulette with the guns under my bed, and tore up the furniture.

"I'll think about it," I said to placate her.

Britt Radcliff dropped by my office the next day. His sour expression could have sucked the joy out of an amusement park.

"We've got to stop meeting this way," I teased, but Britt didn't crack a smile. So much for trying to lighten his mood.

Britt flipped open a small notebook pad. "I've got Charlie Jones down at the station. He says he was here the night bank guard Bennett Glazier was killed. Is that true?"

I wasn't keen on it getting around that Charlie had slept over. "It was a one-time thing."

Did Britt think I was sleeping with Charlie? I flushed with heat. It shouldn't matter what Britt thought but it did. I wished

I could come right out and say that I wasn't sleeping with my ex, but I didn't want to broach such a humiliating subject.

"Charlie's been arrested for Glazier's murder," Britt explained. His rigid posture and curt tone implied that this was serious business indeed. "What time did he arrive and depart on the evening of the murder?"

My heart skipped a beat. Charlie, arrested for the bank guard's murder? I leapt to my feet so that Britt wasn't looking down at me.

Charlie needed my help. I wasn't going to spend the next few years taking the girls to prison to visit their father. "He arrived between ten and ten-thirty p.m. I was watching that TV drama where half the program is devoted to cops and the other half is devoted to lawyers. I'd been watching the show for a while, but I wasn't to the lawyer part yet. Charlie spent the night and he left the next morning to take the girls to school. That time I know for certain. It was a quarter of eight."

"Any chance he slipped out during the night?"

"It's possible but extremely unlikely. Dudley's dog would have heard him moving about the house. If Charlie had been up after we went to our separate beds, I would have known about it." It was extremely clever of me to have worked the fact that I didn't sleep with Charlie into the conversation.

Britt scribbled down a few notes on his pad. His stern features were inscrutable. Was my recollection of the evening the same as Charlie's? "What time did Bennett Glazier die?"

"The medical examiner believes it was after midnight, but there are a few hours' variance."

So Charlie might not be off the hook. It was possible he murdered the guard first and then came over to my house. "Do you have any other suspects for Glazier's murder?"

Britt sighed heavily. "A whole bank full, but the evidence points to Charlie. He accessed files on his bank computer the night of the bank guard's murder. He didn't have an alibi for either murder. We have a ballistics match. The same gun was used for both murders."

My skin prickled. Charlie was in big trouble here. "But you said the evidence pointed to Jonette not so long ago."

Britt sighed. "Jonette has a solid alibi for the second murder."

"I can't believe Charlie killed anyone."

"Reliable sources confirmed Charlie and Dudley had a heated discussion at the bank on the afternoon of Dudley's murder. This information didn't come out until we questioned the bank employees after the second murder."

Discussion? I doubted it was that civil. Charlie was used to being king in his own domain. Dudley had clearly encroached on Charlie's territory. "What about?"

Britt looked pained. "Stay out of this. Charlie Jones wasn't right for you, and it always boggled my mind that you couldn't see it. Don't get sucked into his problems."

I exhaled slowly. Britt didn't trust Charlie. Unless new evidence came to light, Britt would lock him up and throw away the key. "Charlie used people, but he could be generous and charming." Why didn't Britt see that?

"He's a long way from that person now. Rumor has it his wife's been sleeping around on him and he's unhappy about that."

Who wouldn't be?

"We have a cold-blooded killer on the loose," Britt said. "Lock your doors and stay in at night."

He couldn't scare me off so easily. "You're concentrating on the wrong people. What about Robert Joy?"

"What about him?"

"He blames Dudley for that White Rock boondoggle. I bet he lost a lot of money because of Dudley's wink and promise business philosophy."

"You think these killings are related to Old Man Wingate's farm? Isn't that far-fetched?"

"If you don't like Robert Joy for the murders, what about my oddball neighbor? Ed Monday hides out in his house and he has a problem with the bank." I took a deep breath. "Right before Dudley's death, Ed was escorted from the bank by the security guard. The same guard who is now dead."

Britt scribbled a few words in his notepad, then flipped it shut. "Do you suspect everyone in Hogan's Glen?"

"All I know for sure is who isn't the killer. It's not Charlie or Jonette or Bitsy or Violet Cooper."

Britt visibly started. "Violet Cooper? How does she fit into this?"

Did he think I was making all of this up? "She blames Dudley for the schoolteacher pension fund swindle. He was on the board when all that went down. But I spoke with her and she's legally blind. She couldn't do it, although her son Jasper is certainly angry and hotheaded enough to have killed Dudley."

"I don't like you snooping into everyone's business."

"That's the beauty of this. Accountants get paid for snooping through dirty laundry."

"You know anything about these murders, you jolly well better tell me."

"I told you everything I know."

"Investigating homicides is dangerous. Stay out of this." Britt stormed out of my office without waiting for my reply.

I ground my back teeth together and ignored the resulting jaw pain. Wasn't it obvious that I was doing his job? My friends and family weren't killers.

If Britt didn't see that, how was he going to solve these murders? No matter what he said, he needed my help. I was clearly better at detecting than he was. Britt should have stuck to teaching Sunday School.

CHAPTER 21

Lexy had a twenty-four hour vomiting bug and I did the Mom thing for the next few days. By the time I got my life back I was in desperate need of golf therapy. It had been two weeks since I'd swung a golf club and that was unacceptable.

My phone rang Wednesday morning as I headed out to my golf league. I didn't want to be late. But what if the call was one of my girls with an emergency? I walked back into the kitchen and grabbed the phone. "Hello."

"Cleo, it's Charlie."

Did he think I wouldn't recognize his voice? "Yes?"

"I need to talk to you."

I glanced at my watch. If I were late checking in at the course, I would lose my preassigned tee time in the first group. And since the tee times rotated, I didn't often get the chance to be in the group that went first. "I'm in a hurry. Can't this wait?"

"This won't take but a minute. I looked into that bank loan of your sketchy neighbor. All the paperwork is here. Ed Monday took out a loan, all right. And he hasn't paid a penny back to the bank."

Ed took out a loan? "I don't get it. I saw the man almost have a heart attack when he opened his statement. He swears he didn't take out a loan."

"Believe me, Ed Monday took out a loan."

The sarcasm in Charlie's voice wasn't lost on me. I well knew that tone. It implied that I'd wasted his valuable time.

"All the paperwork is in order," Charlie said. "Dudley was always very thorough about that sort of thing."

The hair on the back of my neck snapped to attention. "Dudley?"

"Dudley was the Loan Origination Officer for this loan. Why do you find that strange?"

"My neighbor said he'd talked to Dudley and that Dudley promised him he'd get it straightened out. Why would Ed lie to me?"

"I've never felt good about Ed Monday living next door to you and Charla and Lexy. He probably killed Dudley over this loan. I want you and the girls out of that house today."

I glanced up at the clock, aware that my morning was ticking away. What a time for Charlie to be concerned for our safety. "Oh, for heaven's sake. Ed's my neighbor, not a career criminal."

"How much do we know about him, Clee?" Charlie asked. "He hasn't lived here very long. He's a stranger, really."

It didn't matter that I'd had the exact same thoughts myself. The fact that Charlie believed my neighbor was guilty automatically pushed my buttons to defend Ed. I gazed at the shuttered house next door and it didn't appear threatening to me. Sleeping maybe, but not threatening. "I've lived next door to the man for over a year. He doesn't stay outside long enough to murder anyone."

"I don't know, Cleo. What causes a person to snap? How do you know he got upset over a bank statement? What if it was something else?"

What was he implying now? That I didn't know what I was talking about? "I saw the statement, you blockhead," I shouted into the phone. "What if it happened just as Ed said? That he didn't take out a loan and when Dudley looked into it and discovered Ed was right, what if the real killer took Dudley out of the game? For that matter, what if Dudley and the killer were in league together?"

"Dammit, Cleo. Dudley was my best friend. He was not a crook. He wouldn't have killed for the fifty thousand this loan is worth. Not when he routinely administered million-dollar trust funds. Fifty thousand would have been small change to Dudley."

How could Charlie remain so loyal to a man who'd had an affair with his wife? "Look. I don't have time to discuss this right now. I'm late for an appointment." I took a deep breath. "Thanks for looking into Ed Monday's banking problem. I appreciate your help." The conversation I had with Britt Radcliff came back to me. Was Charlie out on bail or had the charges against him been dropped? "Are you out on bail?"

"Yes, that Britt Radcliff has it in for me. I'd still be rotting behind bars if you hadn't corroborated my story." He paused for a moment before adding, "Thanks for saying I slept over."

His intimate tone irked me. Did he think we were a team now that we were being civil to each other? He'd better think again. "I'm surprised you told anyone."

"When faced with jail or an upset wife, I'll take an upset wife any day. By the way, Denise is furious with me. She's sure I slept with you and she accused me of cheating on her. That's rich."

I rolled my eyes at the phone. I didn't want to hear about Charlie's sex life or lack thereof. I had enough problems of my own in that area. "I would rather not have this discussion with you. Thanks for looking into Ed's loan. Bye."

I clicked the phone off before he could say another word. If he was having trouble with Denise, he'd have to work that out on his own. I was no longer his sounding board. I was his ex-sounding board and I didn't have to do it any longer.

I breezed into the golf course parking lot, and Christine Strand fairly spit at me. "We were ready to give your tee time away, Cleo. If you need to warm up, I'm moving someone else in your slot. Your foursome is ready to go and the next one is on deck."

I managed a tight smile. "Sorry, I got hung up at the last minute. I'll be right back."

I bopped into the pro shop and was instantly blindsided by a beaming Rafe Golden in a crimson polo and dark slacks. Had he greeted everyone with that gigawatt smile this morning? "I need to sign in for the Ladies League," I mumbled, steering clear of the golf club display.

"Walking or riding?" he asked. His bedroom eyes swept my length. I could feel myself warming under his perusal. This was lust. A biological reaction. I wasn't responsible for the way I responded to him. My brain chimed in to remind me that I was taking this slowly. Rafe flirted outrageously with every woman in the club.

"Riding." Who would walk when they could ride? I had never figured that part of the sport out. Driving those little golf carts around was more than half of the fun. A better question would have been, are you going to drive the cart or entrust your life to someone else?

"Morning, Cleo." Jonette sauntered in behind me. Her skintight matching lavender top and shorts looked like a breath of leftover Easter in the pro shop. "Morning, Rafe."

Oh goody. Jonette was here to watch me melt under the hot gaze of the golf pro. "Morning, Jonette," I said. "You in the first group?" I tore my gaze from Rafe.

"I am now. I offered Betty a two for one deal at the tavern if she'd swap times with me."

"Great. Are we riding together?"

Jonette appeared to think for a moment. "Gosh, I don't know. It's so hard to choose between you and Christine."

I flicked a quick glance to Rafe, who'd given up the pretense of working the cash register. He leaned over the counter to catch our every syllable. "I was looking forward to riding with Alveeta, myself," I said.

"You do that, sweetie. You take Alveeta and I'll take Christine. We can dump them both deep in the woods and they'll never find their way back to civilization. Rafe wouldn't mind, would you?"

Rafe grinned at Jonette. "Anything you ladies want is fine with me. Although it would be best if you didn't discover more dead bodies. That's bad for business."

That thought was sobering. Had it only been two weeks ago that I'd found Dudley? It seemed like a lifetime ago. So much had happened that I didn't feel like the same person.

I snatched a cart key from the plastic bin next to the cash register. "I believe it's my turn to drive."

Jonette held out her hand. "Think again. It's my turn until you beat me. Hand it over, sister."

I hated when she was right. At this rate, I'd be a hundred years old before I was driving the cart again. Before leaving, I exchanged another one of those earth-moving glances with Rafe.

Jonette must have been singed with the afterburn. As I strapped my clubs in her cart she asked, "Are you sleeping with him?"

I arched my eyebrows at her. "No commitment, no sex with Cleo."

Rafe Golden was in the same category as chocolate cake, ice cream, and strawberry daiquiris. Bad news. I could devour a whole tub of ice cream when I was feeling needy.

Jonette punched me in the shoulder. "That man is after you, mark my words."

The new and improved Cleo was okay with his pursuit, but I didn't know how to respond. As soon as sex entered my romantic equation, additional variables came into play.

Logistics, performance anxiety, old lingerie, countless fears, personal hygiene. The obstacles multiplied as I thought more about having sex with Rafe. Better not to think about it.

We worked our way down the number one fairway under the disapproving glares of Tweedledee and Tweedledum. I'd already used six strokes to get my ball to the fringe of the first green, including one short tour through the woods. I selected my nine iron for a little pitch and run shot, hoping for solid contact so that I'd have a short putt to hole out.

Christine's ball lay in the lower sand trap, Alveeta's ball balanced on the downhill slope behind the green. Jonette's third shot cackled gleefully on the green.

At this rate, Jonette would drive the cart for the rest of the season. There was no way I could beat her today without asking for extra strokes and even that wasn't a sure thing.

I took dead aim at the pin and struck the ball firmly. My ball rolled right into the cup like it was supposed to. I gave a yippee squeal and danced up to the pin to pull my ball out.

Celebration. Now this was something I hadn't done in a while. I'd missed it. The new Cleo wanted to have more moments like this. I threw my ball high in the air and caught it on the fly.

"Lucky duck," Jonette said.

My success went right to my head. "How about we switch to match play for the remainder of the round?"

"Get serious," Jonette said. "One chip in and you think you can take me? Your luck isn't that good."

"This is going to be my day. I just know it."

Jonette laughed at my cockiness. "I'll spot you two strokes a hole. What am I going to win?"

"I'm going to win a home-cooked meal."

Jonette's eyes twinkled. "Dinner and a dare."

"What kind of dare?"

"Winner's choice."

We'd played this game a lot as teens. A shiver of reckless anticipation sped down my spine. "Definitely."

With three holes to go, we were even in the match. That's when disaster struck. Alveeta casually mentioned something about the bank. I wasn't so swept up in my golf game that I had forgotten all about the murders of two bank employees. What else was going on at that bank?

"Excuse me," I interrupted. "Did you say your daughter was having trouble at the bank?"

Alveeta nodded. Her luminous brown eyes glowed with motherly pride. "Shaquell works in credit-card collections down at the bank. Folks swear they're all paid up but Shaquell has unpaid invoices that prove they're lying."

I knew some people didn't keep up with their credit-card payments, but to have many complaints that something was amiss with their accounts was unusual. Best of all, this new bank problem supported my theory that the murders were related to money.

Dudley and Charlie were bank vice-presidents. Were they aware of what had been going on? My instincts had been wrong about Charlie's personal life. What if the police were right to suspect him of the murders?

Charlie and Dudley, masterminds or dupes? At this point I didn't know. I had no trouble believing that they'd each been caught up in their own worlds and not paid attention to things at the bank. Conversely, Dudley liked to flash money around and Charlie's new wife was very high maintenance. I could also see Charlie and Dudley helping themselves to a little something extra without much remorse.

With those thoughts circling viciously in my brain, was it any wonder I lost the golf match to Jonette?

"What time should I come for dinner?" Jonette asked with a smirk.

I beamed the smirk right back at her. "Your colorful dinner will be served at half past six."

"Colorful?" Jonette looked worried.

"Mama and Charla are cooking tonight," I said. "I'd hoped to avoid another rainbow-colored meal, but now you have to suffer alongside of me."

"In that case, I'm going to be merciless with my dare," Jonette crowed. Her eyes sparkled with mischief. "You have to kiss Rafe in front of Christine."

"That's not fair," I complained even as excitement thundered through my veins. "I don't like public displays of affection, and the last thing I'd do is to put on a show for Christine."

"Hey, I have to eat Rainbow Dinner," Jonette pointed out. "It's only fair that you do something equally nerve-wracking." Jonette zipped up the cart path towards the pro shop. "And I expect to collect right now." She nodded towards the concrete pad outside the pro shop entrance where Rafe stood conversing with Christine and Alveeta.

"Hell," I grumped. What would Rafe think of such brazen behavior? He wasn't irresistible, and I wasn't desperate. But I wasn't one to back down from a dare. My pride was at stake.

Jonette glanced at her watch. "You've got ten minutes to kiss the pro on the lips, starting right now. If you choose not to, you owe me a seafood dinner tonight at the Boar's Head."

The Boar's Head was outrageously expensive. I had griped about their price gouging for years. "Don't be thinking you're dining on lobster, stuffed mushrooms, and swordfish tonight. You're eating Rainbow Surprise at my house."

"Tick, tock." Jonette pointed to her watch. "Ten minutes or I'm digging out my Sunday best for a nice evening on the town."

I squeezed past Christine and Alveeta. Rafe's masculine scent made my blood vibrate with need. "About that lesson." My voice trailed off so that he'd lean closer. "I decided to reschedule."

"Reschedule?" His sandpaper voice caressed my ear with heat and lust.

"Yes." A lightning bolt of excitement raced through my hand as I touched his arm, setting my nether parts on fire.

Rafe clamped his hand on my arm and propelled me towards the pro shop. "My calendar's inside." Panic joined the other dangerous emotions zooming through my veins. If I didn't do something, I'd be paying through the nose for a formal dinner with Jonette.

I stumbled over nothing, but it stopped our forward momentum and got me square in his arms. Exactly where I wanted to be, dare or not. All thoughts of murderers and logistics and twenty-year-old lingerie winked out of my head.

His brown eyes darkened with desire, then his lips covered mine. A familiar light storm took hold of me and bathed me with radiant masculine heat. Passion gripped me in a way I hadn't known was possible.

Carnal and wickedly seductive, his kiss fried every nerve ending I possessed. I was lucky I remembered my name, and even more surprised to find that I was still fully clothed, when we came up for air.

Silent expectation warmed my skin. I knew we'd finish this. Not here, not now. Later. The new Cleo was ready to take on the world, or at least, this one man.

With self-control I hadn't known I possessed I stepped out of his embrace, ignoring the shell shocked expressions on Alveeta and Christine's faces. Sauntering past Jonette, I mumbled, "Rainbow Dinner. Six-thirty."

CHAPTER 22

"Hey, Aunt Jonette!" Charla said. "I heard you won dinner at our house today at the golf course."

I put down the folder I'd been reviewing in the living room and rushed to intercept Jonette. I wasn't exactly keeping my activities with Rafe a secret, but I wasn't broadcasting them either. I was just in time to see Jonette give Charla a warm hug.

"But did you hear how I won, Beautiful?" Jonette's amber-flecked eyes sparkled. "On a dare. Your mother kissed the pro in broad daylight in front of God and everybody."

My heart sunk. I wanted to chide Jonette for mentioning the kiss, but she only reported the truth. Worse, she looked thrilled to be sharing the news. I wasn't sure how Mama or Charla would react. Lexy was in the backyard with the dog so I didn't have to worry about her reaction just yet.

"Mom!" Charla stomped her foot loudly. Her wonderfully expressive face darkened with anger. "How could you do this to me?"

I wasn't the type to sit idly by when accused. The first words out of my mouth were unfiltered. "I don't recall you being involved. This was between me and Rafe and Jonette."

As soon as I heard what I'd said, I felt heat rush to my face. Hell. I'd made an innocent kiss sound like a hot love triangle.

Well, maybe not an innocent kiss. I'd been fairly captivated by that kiss and Jonette darn well knew it, which was why she was crowing now. She hadn't really wanted that dinner at the

Boar's Head. What she wanted was for me to admit that I had desires, that I was still human after Charlie.

I was human, all right. And if I was eighteen, I'd be sneaking out my window tonight to meet Rafe somewhere to do more kissing and whatever else it might lead to. However, I had spent the afternoon thinking things through and sneaking around wasn't the wisest course of action for a mother of two.

"Do, Jesus!" Mama exclaimed, one hand over her heart. "Are you so hard-up for a man that you have to throw yourself at the first one to come sniffing around?"

I had behaved shamelessly, but I wasn't ashamed of my behavior. There was a difference. "I'm not desperate, Mama, just exploring my options. I don't quite have the hang of dating just yet."

"But Mama," Charla wailed. "He's kissed you two times now and you haven't been on the first date with him. If I did that, I'd be under house arrest for a month."

Damn straight. Maybe even grounded for life.

No wonder the double standard had been invented. Ah, the thrills of parenthood.

How did Mama survive me and Jonette growing up? Not that I wanted her advice, then or now, it's just that there was more to parenting than I'd given her credit for over the years. "It's not the same thing, Charla, and you know it. I'm single, but I'm not dead. You make it sound like it's my fault the guy is interested in me."

Lexy walked in with Madonna. She embraced Jonette and Madonna went crazy licking Jonette's ankles.

Charla waved a wooden spoon at Lexy. "You're never going to believe what Mom did today. She kissed that golf guy. Again. I'm never going to be able to hold my head up after this."

Lexy eyed me sharply. "Are you serious about this guy, Mom?"

Trust Lexy to cut right to the chase. "I don't know that it's serious per se, but it's fun. Seriously fun kissing Rafe. There. I said it. Are you happy, Jonette?"

Jonette laughed aloud as she hugged Madonna. "Yes. I'm seriously happy. Deliriously happy. Couldn't be happier."

Mama pursed her lips momentarily and set the table in pointed silence. I could tell she had a lot on her mind, but thankfully she didn't burden me with it. And she stopped clutching her heart, which was a good thing.

Lexy seemed okay with the news I was interested in someone. Charla wasn't. I'd have to sit down with Charla and make sure she understood that her Mom and Dad weren't getting back together. Maybe then she would accept that I was moving on.

Jonette sniffed appreciatively as she took a seat at the cozy kitchen table. "What smells so good?"

"Pork Chops in Paradise, better known as Green Night," Charla said as she brought over the three bean salad.

How much food coloring were we going through these days? Thank God it wasn't toxic. Surprisingly, green pork chops were edible. After dinner, I talked Jonette into walking the dog with me. We turned left out of my driveway and walked up Main Street to Elm.

Madonna didn't bound playfully ahead the way she did when I normally walked her. Instead, she remained in Jonette's path, obviously wanting Jonette to pay attention to her. Jonette obliged the dog. Madonna's tail waved in broad strokes. "She likes you a lot," I said.

"Madonna and I are good friends," Jonette said. "I'm surprised you still have her. I meant to ask you about her at the bank the other day. I thought Bitsy was taking Madonna home with them after the funeral."

"So did I, but Bitsy is having trouble handling the Saint Bernard she's got. The two dogs together are like an X-rated circus act. We had to go to heroic measures to keep them apart. Every chance they got together, her dog would be on Madonna."

"Hot damn," Jonette said. "Is Madonna still in heat?"

Who knew these things? I hadn't paid attention to the dog's hormonal cycle. In a house with three menstruating females, what was one more? But wouldn't I have noticed something messy like that? Wouldn't there have been spots left around? "I don't have any idea. I must be a bad dog mother."

Wait a minute. Jonette had never owned a pet in her life. How did Jonette know more about Dudley's dog than I did? "What's going on here?"

"I spent some time with Dudley and Madonna." Jonette shot me an enigmatic look and rubbed Madonna's chin. "That's why the two of us are such good friends, aren't we, girl?"

At the intersection, we crossed Schoolhouse Road and entered Hogan's Glen Park. I needed the additional distance of the park to walk off the calories from that heavy green dinner I just ate.

It occurred to me that Jonette's friendship with Madonna was a solid link between her and Dudley. Was this why Jonette's fingerprints were in Dudley's house and car? "Did you and Madonna hang out together a lot?"

Maybe it was all very innocent. Dudley could have hired Jonette to be his dog sitter.

"You could say that," Jonette said.

"I could, but why would I?" Getting information about Dudley out of Jonette was like pulling teeth. Her secretiveness irritated me to no end. "What's this all about, Jonette? I know you're holding out on me."

"Don't get all snippy with me," Jonette warned. "We hung out. That's all. Took a few day trips together."

I hated it when she did this to me. What was she trying so hard not to say? "You traveled with Dudley and his dog? Is that why the police consider you a suspect in Dudley's murder?"

Jonette gazed over at the deserted swing sets. Why wouldn't she just come right out and say whatever it was she was trying so hard not to say? I had no choice but to grill her. I started with a zinger. "Were you sleeping with Dudley?"

Jonette's color paled. "Absolutely not."

That seemed like a truthful response. I tried again. "Were you sleeping with his dog?"

She almost smiled at that question. "No."

"Well then, what were you doing with the two of them? Wasn't your life complicated enough without adding Dudley and his dog to the mix? What are you too chicken to tell me?"

I didn't think Jonette would answer me. She was walking so fast I had to run to stay up with her.

"I'm not chicken about anything," Jonette said. "I didn't want to tell you this because you're the only person who's ever believed in me one hundred percent. I didn't want you to know I'm such a loser. The truth is, I'm lonely. So lonely it hurts. You've got everything, Clee. I've always wanted to be you, even when you were married to that gigundo loser Charlie. You've always had people who cared about you. When I saw how attentive Dudley's dog was to him, I decided I needed a dog like Madonna. Is that so bad?"

I dug my heels in and dragged the dog to a stop. "You want Madonna?" Did Jonette kill Dudley for his dog? I clenched my teeth so that question wouldn't slip out.

Jonette shook her head in denial. "I don't want Dudley's dog. I want a puppy. I worked out a deal with Dudley. If I helped him with Madonna during her pregnancy and when the puppies were little, then I could have a puppy for free. I didn't want a little yippy dog like my mother has. I want a big kick-ass dog that will eat any bad people that knock on my door."

I sighed with relief. Her explanation rang true. Why didn't

she say something before about being lonely? I could have made more time for her. Not that I'd been much fun recently, but, hey, I would have made an effort if only I'd known. "Saint Bernards aren't kick-ass dogs. Madonna has been friendly with everyone who's come to our house."

"So what?" Jonette squatted down and hugged Madonna. "She's big and that's enough to put most people off."

Poor Jonette. It must have cost her plenty to confess her loneliness. I couldn't believe that she wanted to be me. My life had been just as screwed up as hers, but at least my mother had never thrown me out and disowned me. Even when I got pregnant in college and married Charlie instead of finishing my education, Mama was always there for me. "Do you want Madonna?"

"Thanks, but no." Jonette sniffed. "I love this dog, but she's settled in with your family. Would you let me have one of her puppies? Please?"

"Puppies?" My knees went weak, almost as if one of my daughters had come home from school and announced she was pregnant. I stumbled over to the nearest park bench and sat.

"She should be pregnant," Jonette said. "Dudley and I took her to be serviced by a stud dog three separate times, one day at lunchtime. If that didn't do the trick, Bitsy's dog might have closed the deal. I'd help you just like I was going to help Dudley. What do you say?"

Puppies. I just couldn't get past that part. It appeared that I now owned a dog and puppies were in my future. I wasn't ready for labor and delivery. I had assumed Charla and Lexy's husbands would attend them when their times came. I planned to sweep in and be the devoted grandmother every other Friday evening.

Hell. I didn't even know if the dog was pregnant. How did one determine such a thing? "Do I have to get her to pee on one of those little home pregnancy kits?"

"I have no idea," Jonette said. "Dudley was taking care of that part. What does her vet say?"

I blinked. "She has a vet?"

"Of course she has a vet. Grady Murphy over at the Animal Clinic. You should take her in for a check-up and get your name on her file. Dudley had an electronic ID tag inserted under her skin in case she was ever stolen or lost. You'd need to get that record updated too."

"Puppies. Ohmigod. Does that make me a step mom or a grandmother?"

"You're taking this rather hard, Cleo," Jonette said. "She might not be pregnant. I mean, what if she's barren like me? Maybe she can't conceive."

Jonette sat down beside me and Madonna promptly put her head in Jonette's lap. I felt as if I were nine months pregnant again and it was too much to take in. Was I so close to the edge that a little unexpected news would push me into the loony bin? "I hardly know what to say. I'll have her checked out. But please, don't mention puppies to the girls until we know if she's pregnant."

"I'd never do anything to hurt those girls," Jonette said. "I love them as if they were my own. Although I have to say, your Mama and Charla in the kitchen are a little scary."

"Hey, I warned you it was going to be a crazy meal. I've eaten orange eggs, blue pancakes, red grits, and God only knows what all else recently. Mama says I was stifling her creativity by not letting her cook. I hope that the color thing wears off soon."

"My dinners are always straight out of the freezer case," Jonette mused. "It's a treat to eat green pork chops. I'm relieved you can appreciate their need for creativity. I was pretty worried about you."

"Me too," I said. "I don't know how long I've been operating on automatic pilot, but now I feel like I'm in an 'all systems go' mode. I can't thank you enough for not giving up on me this past year or so."

Jonette reached over and squeezed my shoulder. "That's what friends are for. You've always been there for me."

This was getting entirely too sappy for me. Time for some sarcasm. "Yeah, but you're still six months older than me."

"And I got to experience everything first," Jonette bragged. "I got my driver's license first, I got to vote first, and I got to drink legally first. You can't beat that."

Jonette stood and stretched. "Time to go. I've got to pee."

Some things never changed.

We headed home at a fast pace. The things Jonette had experienced first hadn't been all good. Even so, I was glad she had known what to do after my divorce. I never knew she had experienced all this numbness and anger and grief as part of her divorces, at least, not until I experienced it for myself.

All I'd ever done was to make sure she was still a part of my life, no matter what. I hoped that was enough. It would truly suck to be a bad dog mother and a bad best friend.

Jonette and I told each other everything, but Charlie and Dudley had never operated that way. How had Dudley reacted to Charlie's accusation that he was sleeping with Denise? I knew they had argued.

Would they have arranged to meet later and settle their differences? I'd seen them go at it before, in jest, of course. Charlie had out-muscled Dudley every time.

No amount of wheeling and dealing would have saved Dudley from Charlie's wrath. I could see why Britt thought Charlie was guilty. I could even believe that Charlie had been driven by rage to kill his best friend. The hole he'd dug for himself tugged at my feet.

Chapter 23

Madonna woke me up when she stood up on our bed. She whimpered softly in her throat. I groaned unhappily at my sleep being interrupted.

"If you weren't cute and quite possibly pregnant I would be very angry with you right now," I said without opening my eyes. Madonna huffed dog breath on my face and licked my nose.

Yikes. That was a little too personal for me. Nose-licking violated my own personal buffer I kept between me and the rest of the world, and it wasn't hygienic.

Groggily I opened my eyes, mentally preparing myself to walk down the stairs and let her out in the backyard, but my bedroom didn't look like my room. Like a carnival sideshow, my walls were awash in a sea of flashing red and blue lights. I sat up quickly, trying to get my bearings. Madonna rested her head on my shoulder and my nightgown dampened under her drooling mouth.

I was used to being drooled on now, but it had been a long time since I'd been abruptly awakened in the middle of the night. Adrenaline pumped through me like a fire hose. Someone was out there. And the police were after that someone.

Self-preservation demanded that I burrow back into the safe world under my covers, but I had my family's safety to consider. If something bad was happening, I had to protect Mama and my daughters.

There was a good chance the police had made progress on

their murder investigation. This house was on the main through-way. They must have pulled someone over. Who was it? I had to know.

I darted over to the window and stared unblinkingly at the scene below. Cops with drawn guns huddled behind parked vehicles on my lawn. My breath hitched in my throat. My heart hammered under my thin cotton nightgown.

I shivered. This was no routine traffic stop. This was more. So much more, but what was it? Madonna whimpered beside me.

I held my breath as the cops entered Ed Monday's house. Holy cow. It was an invasion. I had to tell someone.

I speed-dialed Jonette on my bedside phone. "This better be an emergency," Jonette grumbled into the receiver.

"Jonette, wake up," I whispered anxiously. "Some weird commando stuff is going down over here. I've got a yard full of cops."

"What?"

"You heard me. Cops. They're everywhere."

"Did Lexy set the bathroom on fire again?" Jonette asked.

"Not funny." Lexy had experimented with matches not long after my divorce. She'd been sure she could contain a fire built in the tub, but she'd forgotten about the shower curtain which incinerated quickly.

"What are they doing in my neighbor's house at four-thirty in the morning?" I asked.

Jonette yawned into the phone. "That's what they do on TV. Go after notorious criminals when they're sleeping. Less resistance that way."

I groaned aloud. "Ed Monday is not a notorious criminal."

"They're not waking him up to give him a citizenship award," Jonette said. "What's happening now?"

I edged the dog's head out of the way and stuck my head close to the screen. "I can't see a damn thing. Oh. They've got the street blocked with police cars too. I can't believe this is happening. Wait a minute. There he is."

"We're on the phone," Jonette griped. "I'm not getting a video transmission."

"They're stuffing Ed in a squad car and leaving."

Just then, I spotted Britt Radcliff down in the knot of cops on my lawn. "Hey. I see our favorite detective. I'm going down there to see what's going on."

"I will kick your butt big time if you don't call me right back," Jonette said. "Better yet, I can be there in five minutes."

"Forget it. The street's blocked. I'll call you back."

I slipped on my sneakers and a robe, then darted outside. "Britt. What's going on?"

Britt blocked my way. "You don't want to be involved with this, Cleo. Go back inside."

"I saw you haul Ed Monday off in handcuffs. Will my family be next?"

"This was a special circumstance."

I wasn't reassured. Bad thoughts swirled in my head. What had Ed done? "Did Ed kill Dudley and the bank guard?"

Britt escorted me up my steps. "Ed Monday's arrest has to do with an outstanding federal warrant. So far the evidence doesn't tie him to the murders."

"Other than his yelling at Dudley and being forcibly escorted from the bank?"

"Stop poking your nose around in police work. You are unnecessarily endangering yourself. If Ed looks good for the murders, I'll add that to the charges against him."

Why was everyone picking on my poor nose tonight? I covered it protectively with my hand. "Are you sure you've got the right man? Ed Monday couldn't fix a bank error by himself."

"Ed Monday is a fugitive. He'll be taking up a new residence, courtesy of the government."

I didn't have any trouble imagining Ed having a secret life, but I didn't want him to be a rotten person. Especially since Charlie had called it from the start. That meant my intuition still wasn't worth a damn.

My shoulders slumped. How could I expect to solve Dudley's murder when I couldn't tell the good guys from the bad guys?

Britt held my screen door open for me. "Go back to bed. We want to get out of here before the entire town wakes up."

I wasn't ready to be thrust aside like a discarded toy. "What about the mass murderer on the loose?"

Britt ruffled my unruly hair and his eyes warmed. "I would be closer to solving my cases if you'd quit providing alibis and character references for everyone I try to arrest."

My mouth opened and an exasperated gasp came out. "But my friends didn't kill anyone. I know them."

Britt squeezed my shoulder. "In my line of work I see everything. It isn't unusual for the murderer to be well acquainted with the victim."

"Why don't you suspect me?"

Britt choked out a short laugh. "I can read you like a book, Cleopatra Jones. Every emotion you're feeling flashes across your face. If you'd killed Dudley, I would have arrested you that day on the golf course. I brought Jonette in for questioning because she was the last person seen with the victim. And Charlie didn't get anything that wasn't coming to him."

I felt heat rushing to my cheeks. "Charlie isn't perfect, but adultery isn't in the same league as killing your best friend."

Britt scowled. "The jury's still out on Charlie's innocence. I like him for the murders. I just don't have any solid proof that he did it. Yet."

"Charlie isn't the only one who could have done it. This town is full of people who hated Dudley."

Britt's expression grew stormy. "Stay out of this. You've got kids that depend on you. You're not expendable."

My lips pressed tightly together. Britt didn't scare me, but I got what he was saying. "I promise not to do anything stupid."

I said good night and went inside. Stupid was a matter of perspective. It wasn't stupid in my book to do everything possible to flush the serial killer out of our town. My family's safety depended on it.

Charlie called to gloat after I returned from driving the girls to school. "I was right about Ed Monday, wasn't I?"

"What did you hear?"

"The big arrest is all over town. Ed Monday bombed some building as a college student then changed his name and hid out for the last thirty years."

I sat down hard on the living room sofa to digest this news. "That is a surprise. Britt wouldn't tell me what Ed had done this morning."

"*He* was over there? Damn. I always knew he had a thing for you."

I blinked. Charlie sounded jealous. Of Britt Radcliff. My intuition wasn't the only thing on the blink around here. "Britt was here to arrest Ed Monday."

"I never liked Radcliff. He was always sniffing around, always standing too close to you."

I toed off my shoes and swung my feet up on the sofa. Once I finished this call, a nap was my top priority. "If it makes you feel any better, he doesn't like you either."

"I have some rights here," Charlie said. "My children live in that house. They're too impressionable to have their mother dating anyone."

My blood boiled at his pronouncement. "You weren't concerned about the girls mental well-being when you committed adultery. You scratched your itch and didn't give a damn about any of us. Grow up, Charlie. I am seeing someone and they're dealing with it just fine."

"I don't like it," Charlie snarled into the phone.

"You don't have a choice." I hung up on him. My blood seethed. No way was I calm enough to sleep now. Might as well go to my office and get some work done.

For sixteen years Charlie Jones told me what I could and couldn't do. Not anymore. I was my own woman now.

I wouldn't readily relinquish the freedom I'd discovered. Been there. Done that.

My newfound freedom had come at a terrible price. I wouldn't get myself in another situation where someone else called all the shots. I could look out for myself and my family. I definitely did not need any man telling me what to do.

Empowerment. I could do anything with it. I could ask Rafe out on a date. I could spend my entire discretionary budget on frills or truffles or a hot-air-balloon ride if I so desired. I could golf every day of the week.

But the most important thing to the new me was keeping my family safe. I couldn't assure their safety with a serial killer on the loose. I'd like nothing better than to see my ex rot in jail for years, but I wasn't convinced he'd killed anyone. The timing of the White Rock development derailment seemed entirely too coincidental. It was time for me to learn more about Robert Joy.

The mobile office parked on the recently flattened Wingate farm did nothing to shore up my flagging courage. I drove past the development three times before the Gray Beast would stop. This place had a forgotten melancholy air that was enhanced by all the abandoned equipment dotting the land.

It didn't take an accountant to add up the facts. This place was dead in the water. I was onto something here.

I knocked on the door. "Anybody home?"

Someone better be here. I'd parked next to a pickup with Robert Joy Construction emblazoned on the door panel.

I didn't have much of a plan other than to sound out the developer. If he was the killer, I didn't want to alarm him. My story was that I was interested in moving out here. Anyone who knew me wouldn't believe it, but Robert Joy didn't know me.

The door opened. Robert Joy wore jeans, a T-shirt, and a navy-blue windbreaker. Not the well-dressed executive of an up and coming venture. More like a bum in hiding. My skin prickled with excitement.

His eyes gave me the once over as he asked, "What can I do for you, ma'am?"

I swallowed my last minute reservations. Finding the killer would make Hogan's Glen safe for my family. "I'm Cleo Jones. We met at the funeral the other day. I was hoping you might have some information about this development."

"You interested in building out here?"

"I've been living with my mother since my divorce and it's time to move out. If I build out here, what sort of time frame are we talking about?"

His eyes gleamed when I mentioned the word divorce. Maybe I should have worn torn sweats so that he wouldn't think I was on the make. This was not the occasion for panty hose and a flattering dress.

"For a pretty little thing like you, I'd do a rush job. Four to six months from when we break ground, weather permitting."

If he wanted to assume I was a stupid female, maybe I should play along. I wasn't doing too well in the role of brainy sleuth. "Ooh. Six months is a long time. I was hoping there might be a model home or something I could purchase and move in right away."

"There's nothing here, except for the old farmhouse, and there are other plans for the farm house. It's going to be a community center."

His gaze swept my length again, lingering on my boobs and ass. I shivered. Not because I was interested, because I felt like I was being slimed. I would need a shower after this. "Six months. I don't know if I can wait that long. I was interested in living here because I heard it was going to be part of the city. I want sidewalks and curbs and a quiet residential neighborhood. Mama's house is on the main road."

"Not a problem, sweet thing. This development has annexation written all over it. You'll have as many city amenities as you desire."

Including tawdry sex with the developer if I didn't watch my step. I couldn't think of a worse fate. Nausea rose in my throat.

Forget acting stupid. I wanted real answers. Not some condescending pat on my head by the male in charge. "Doesn't that have to be approved by the town council?"

Robert Joy winked at me and handed me some glossy brochures. "I've been assured the approval process is a mere formality. It's greased."

"Greased? Like a brownie pan?"

"Sure thing. Look those papers over. We have something for every budget. If a single-family home is too pricey for you, we've got several styles of town homes planned as well."

I stuffed the brochures in my purse, glad not to be holding what he'd just touched. I'd decontaminate my purse as soon as I got home. This guy was so sleazy, he had to be guilty of something. "It's the six months wait that bothers me."

"Six months goes fast when you're building your dream home."

"I'll think about it."

"Drop over anytime. I'll give you a guided tour once we start breaking ground."

"You've already sold some parcels?"

He nodded. "Sales are brisk. You definitely want to jump in on Phase I. The prices increase next month. White Rock is the deal of a lifetime."

I'd had enough of his leering at me. Nothing could be as good as the deal I had right now. Room and board and all I was out was the cost of groceries and utilities.

I backed out of there and sped off. Robert Joy was a hustling salesman. What I didn't know was how far he would go to do his job. Had he killed Dudley when he found out that Dudley's promises weren't within his realm?

I needed to know more about Robert Joy's background. He didn't arrive in Hogan's Glen without a history. If I worked at the bank I could run his credit report. If I was a cop I could check his arrest record. Only I wasn't a banker or a policeman. I was an accountant.

I had a computer. I could search for previous Robert Joy developments. Those places probably had Homeowners Associations. It wouldn't be out of the ordinary for me to contact them, offer them my services, and inquire about the developer.

I didn't like men talking down to me. I didn't like men who leered at me. So Robert Joy already had two strikes against him.

I didn't want the murderer to be someone I knew. I wanted it to be a stranger like Robert Joy and I wanted him to go directly to jail.

The developer had been right about one thing. Six months wasn't a long time. I'd been with Mama for much longer than that and we hadn't killed each other yet.

Maybe I'd been going about this sleuthing all wrong. What if it wasn't a money angle? I hadn't considered revenge or passion as motives.

Most of the town had a grievance against Dudley, but the

bank guard hadn't been overtly rude to anyone. Since I didn't know much about the bank guard, I had to focus my investigation on Dudley's murder.

Who had hated Dudley enough to lure him out on the golf course when no one else was around? If I knew that, then I'd know who killed him. My thoughts were logical, but my growing uneasiness was not.

Identifying the killer would put me right in his path. I didn't know the first thing about killers, but I would willingly give my life to protect my family. I hoped it didn't come to that.

CHAPTER 24

After calling Homeowners Associations for three Robert Joy developments I found on-line, I felt like Goldilocks. Greenbrook Farms curtly informed me they had a big gun CPA firm on retainer, Jackson Meadows might consider replacing their current CPA if my price was cheaper, and Fox Hills was desperate for a CPA.

I seized the opportunity and tootled down the road to meet the frantic treasurer of Fox Hills. Kamikaze interstate traffic kept my full attention on the way there. I wasn't sure why people tolerated this congestion all the time. Even with our recent crime wave, I'd be glad to get back to Hogan's Glen.

"How lucky for me that you called this morning," Geraldine Young said as she showed me into her two-story brick home, a shy toddler riding her hip. Geraldine was a vibrant brunette in her late twenties. She wore a white blouse, designer jeans, and a toe ring. "I phoned ten CPA's in the last twenty four hours and none of them could do this audit right away."

"Homeowners Association Audits are a growing part of my accounting business," I said, handing her my business card. The slate floor in her spacious two-story foyer told me a lot about the quality of the houses Robert Joy built. He might be a sleaze bag, but he knew how to put a house together.

"I'm glad to work you in this time, but I don't routinely do things last minute." Over the years, I'd found the need to be firm with new clients. If you let them walk all over you at the start, then your relationship was doomed to a series of disappointments. I wanted to learn about Robert Joy, but not at the expense of gaining a bad client.

"This is a one-time emergency, I assure you," Geraldine said. "Our previous Association treasurer died in an auto accident six weeks ago. I just got the books and his records last week. It took me a few days to go through everything, and I was horrified that we were overdue for the yearly audit."

"Your Financial Report is completed?"

"Yes. I have everything set out for you in the kitchen. Can I get you a cup of coffee?"

"Sure." I sat down at an oak table in a room painted the rich red hue of Arizona rock formations. While she strapped her baby in a high chair, I flipped through the records.

The Financial Report for the three-hundred-member association showed that this group had a good start on their Capital Reserve Fund. Bank statements, a copy of the association checkbook register, invoices, assorted receipts, and the General Ledger were included in the expandable folder. Everything looked relatively straightforward.

All right. I had myself a legitimate client. Now for the digging part. "Is there anything I should know about your Association?"

Geraldine handed her baby boy something that looked like a pretzel but smelled like a graham cracker. "What do you mean?"

I sipped my coffee and remembered I was being subtle here. "Are there any outstanding issues that don't appear in past years' records?"

"You mean stuff like did the developer mismanage the Association fund before we took it over?"

"Something like that."

"There was a problem with timely snow removal the first winter, but Chad Browning, our judge in residence, got that problem straightened out right away."

Delinquent snow removal wasn't particularly heinous. If I wanted real dirt on the man, I needed to ask more pointed questions. "One of the reasons I called you is that your developer is building up in my area now and I had some questions about Robert Joy's integrity. Did you know him?"

Geraldine caught the baby's cookie on the fly. She looked like she might bust out laughing. "He hit on you, too?"

I nodded. Satisfaction zoomed through me. This was what I'd navigated through death-defying traffic to learn.

Geraldine's brown eyes twinkled. "Robert Joy thinks he's God's gift to women, but don't hold that against him. He's all talk in that department. Fortunately, he builds a great house."

I chewed my bottom lip. I'd wanted the man to be guilty of something that might indicate deviant tendencies. If she didn't want to talk about the personal stuff, maybe she'd talk about his professional abilities. "You haven't had any trouble with inferior products being substituted in your home or things not being as specified in your contract?"

"No. I wouldn't be here if I had. What's the bottom line here?"

Through the doorway I could see the adjacent room cluttered with toys. Geraldine splurged on her kid but she didn't own one piece of dining room furniture. She didn't look like a person who would be easily swayed from her path in life.

My best bet was to lay my cards on the table. "His current development is dead in the water. He doesn't have the approval he needs from the town council to annex White Rock into the city. Without that approval, the number of dwellings he can build on that parcel of land is limited. Since his arrival, we've had two murders in our small town. I thought if I asked around, I might find out more about the man behind the development."

Alarmed, Geraldine picked up her son and hugged him close. "You think Robert Joy is a murderer?"

I hadn't meant to upset her. The baby cried and Geraldine looked as if she might join him. Okay. Maybe there was such a thing as too much honesty. I scurried to do some damage control. "I don't think anything. He's a stranger to our town, someone I don't know much about. It's easy to point fingers at people you don't know."

"Who died?"

"The banker who brokered the deal for the development and a bank security guard. Do you think that if Robert Joy got mad he might act aggressively towards a man who thwarted his plans?"

Geraldine pulled her son's hands from her mouth. "My husband and I came out here a lot while our house was being built. Robert Joy was very hands-on and kept close tabs on his work crews. I never once saw him do anything violent."

I could just imagine the phone calls Geraldine would make when I left her house. There would be a slander suit on my desk before I returned to my office. "I never said he did anything violent. All I said was that I didn't know him very well. If you say he's nonviolent, I believe you."

"Do you have kids?" Geraldine asked.

"Two daughters."

"No wonder you're worried. If anything happened to my little guy, I'd be devastated."

Worry united mothers around the world. I thanked Geraldine for her coffee, her information, and her business, then headed home. If the sleazy developer wasn't the killer, who was? The field narrowed back down to folks I knew well. Bummer.

A handwritten note addressed to me was in the Gray Beast that afternoon when I went to pick the girls up from school. I don't normally get notes in my car, but I didn't have time to read more than the envelope because I was running late. Whatever was in the note could wait. I shoved the unopened envelope in my purse and sped off.

With all the police activity in my yard two days ago, I was uncomfortable with my daughters walking the four blocks to and from school. Our neighborhood was probably the safest it had ever been, but I had reached emotional overload. No amount of my kids telling me how uncool it was for them to be picked up by their mother reached me.

I needed to know that my girls were safe. The world was not a nice place and I couldn't just sit back and trust in the goodness of my fellow human beings. Not when my babies were at risk.

As I waited in the queue of minivans and SUVs, Lexy walked with her friends over to the car, bubbling all the while about the middle-school yearbooks that had just been distributed. Charla strolled by alone, looking for all the world like she didn't know us. In my rearview mirror I saw her stop to fool with her purse, check out the parking lot in her compact mirror, and then duck in the backseat. She hunched down low and said, "Drive."

I drove, but only because they were both in the car. "This isn't a bank heist, Charla. And hello to you too."

"Mom." Charla drew my name out into two irate syllables. "Don't do this to me. It's so embarrassing to be seen in this ugly car. Why are you still driving the same car you drove in high school? Why can't you be a normal mom and drive a minivan?"

When I was her age, I'd thought the Gray Beast wasn't cool either. However, this perpetual motion machine never broke down, and best of all, it was paid for. I couldn't in good conscience trade it in just because it wasn't what the cool moms were driving.

And I couldn't idly stand by while she badmouthed our reliable car. Someone had to speak up for the Gray Beast. "Hey, this car is practically a vintage automobile."

Charla shoved on her sunglasses and scrunched down below window level. "Practically vintage doesn't count. It means this car is old as dirt." She gestured towards the line of cars exiting the parking lot. "Look. Even the nerdy kids drive newer cars than this old dinosaur."

"This car is one of the safest on the road if there's an accident," I said. "Besides, it's transportation. A ride is a ride."

Charla turned sixteen next year. Maybe I would get another car for me and teach her to drive the Gray Beast. I didn't want her to be driving around in a car that would collapse like an accordion at the slightest nudge. The Gray Beast was solid. "You'll feel differently in a year or so."

"No way. I will never like this car. You're ruining my life by forcing me to be seen in this rust bucket."

There wasn't an ounce of rust on this car. Even though we'd bought it secondhand, Daddy had religiously insisted the car be washed and waxed with regularity. He would be shocked at how I'd let the car's appearance decline. It no longer gleamed from frequent hand waxing, but the dull patina suited its personality much better.

With a flash, I realized I had just repeated a conversation I'd had with my father when I was about Charla's age. He'd bought the Gray Beast through the newspaper when I was fifteen.

"Cars like this don't come along every day," he'd said.

I'd been just as horrified as Charla, but then I'd realized that driving gave me freedom from parental oversight, and I'd changed my tune. Driving this sturdy car hadn't hurt me one bit. Charla would just have to adjust that attitude of hers.

Lexy piped in about the yearbooks again, and then we were home and doing the homework and supper and watching TV thing. It wasn't until my bedtime that I remembered that note I'd found in my car. What was that all about?

I padded down to the kitchen and retrieved the plain white envelope from my purse. Everyone else had gone to bed and it seemed as if I was all alone in the dark house. Was the note from Jonette? She hadn't called today. Maybe she'd written a quick thank you for her rainbow dinner and tucked it in the car.

Or maybe it was a card from Rafe. A man with such luscious bedroom eyes surely had poetry lurking in his soul. It wouldn't be beyond him to slip over here on his way to work and leave a romantic poem in my car.

With those warm and fuzzy thoughts in mind, I ripped open the envelope. Warm and fuzzy flew right out the window. My blood chilled as I unfolded the single sheet of white copy paper inside.

This was no love note. The page was dotted with glued on letters cut from glossy magazines, the kind of thing a serial killer might send to a victim.

Dear God. What had I gotten myself into? Had the other two murder victims gotten similar notes prior to their death? Had my fact-finding trip to Far Hills this morning rubbed someone the wrong way?

I couldn't quite catch my breath.

Britt Radcliff's words came back to haunt me. He'd warned me to stay out of this because I wasn't expendable. I couldn't imagine what my daughters would do if something happened to me. Worse, I wouldn't get to see them grow up, to see them dress up for prom, graduate from high school and college, get married and have my grandbabies.

My hand shook so bad I had to put the sheet of paper down on the counter before I could read it. The very first word was misspelled and that made me wonder about the intelligence of the person sending the note.

Cum to the maintenance shed at the golf course tomorrow morning at dawn to find out who killed Dudley. Don't tell anyone or the meet's off.

I read the note twice to be sure I understood. I was to go to the golf course, alone, at a time when no one else would be there. My first reaction was—hell no. Not in a million years.

Letters like this one weren't written with the recipient's best interests at heart.

Who sent it? I had no idea.

Was this someone's idea of a sick joke? I looked at the words again, studying them separately and individually, as if they were pieces of a jigsaw puzzle. Surely, if I could just calm down, I could figure this out. The instructions were direct, but some words were misspelled.

How could a person misspell "come" but get "maintenance" right? That didn't make any sense. Was this someone with legitimate information? Or was this a trap to lure me into an unsafe place and kill me?

So much for thinking the note might be from Jonette, even though her spelling had always been problematic. She would have called or come over if she had something important to tell me. And, she hadn't sent me notes since high school geometry class.

Charlie would have spelled every word correctly and added a few extra sentences to make himself sound more important. I couldn't imagine him leaving me a note unless he thought my phone line was tapped or there were electronic bugs in my house. Not that I had any experience with either of those things, but I'd watched my fair share of detective shows and read plenty of thrillers.

Shit. Was my house bugged? There had been plenty of cops here two days ago. They might have bugged my house trying to find out if I knew anything about Ed Monday.

I looked around my familiar kitchen, and every shadowy nook

and cranny seemed like a great hiding place for a listening device. I pawed through stacks of junk mail before I realized I had no idea what I was looking for.

I shoved the hair back from my face and took a deep breath. I needed a reality break here. The likelihood of my house being bugged by the authorities or Dudley's killer wasn't very high. I was jumping to conclusions because of that note.

That note. I picked it up again by its corners and reread it. The words hadn't changed any in the last five minutes. Hell. If I called Britt or anyone else, the person wouldn't show up. Questions shot through my head like bullets.

Why me?

Why a private meeting?

What the hell time was dawn anyway?

I sat down hard in a kitchen chair. Was I really going to do what the note said? The killer had already struck twice, and I could be facing certain death. If the killer had sent this, he'd been standing in my yard. He'd sat in my car. He'd been close to my family.

My fists clenched reflexively. I was never letting my daughters out of my sight again. Hogan's Glen was a dangerous place. Bad things happened here.

The chances of me being able to keep my daughters locked in the house for the rest of their lives were slim to none. There had to be a better way, because if I restricted our freedom of motion due to someone else's activity, hadn't they won? I didn't want to spend the next forty or so years being afraid of my shadow.

I wasn't completely defenseless. I had Daddy's guns under my bed. If I decided to do as the note said, I could take Daddy's pistol with me, for protection. I knew which end of a gun was which, even though I wasn't a great marksman.

Maybe I should call Rafe to go with me. Only, the meet was

221

set for the golf course, Rafe's home turf. Was Rafe the one who sent me the note? Athletes weren't usually star students. He might be a lousy speller.

What if I called him and he was the killer? Would he kill me and my entire family?

Shit.

I couldn't trust anyone.

I shouldn't go.

It was crazy to go, but I needed to go because I had absolutely no idea who killed Dudley. It could have been Robert Joy the sleazy developer. I thought I'd ruled him out, but the note had appeared right after I visited his last development.

Darnell had plenty of reason to kill Dudley, and he was mean enough to do it. Jasper's mother, the blind sharpshooter couldn't have done it. Jasper and Rafe worked at the golf course so they had plenty of opportunity. Jasper had guns in his house. Did Rafe?

Britt believed the killer might be Charlie or Jonette or Bitsy. All of them had reason to hate Dudley. Charlie thought my neighbor, Ed Monday the fugitive bomber, had done it. I wanted Denise to burn in hell for breaking up my marriage, but she had a solid alibi for Dudley's murder. I knew Mama, the girls and I didn't kill anyone, but I didn't know much else for certain.

If I didn't go and this was a "Deep Throat" source that for some reason couldn't go to the authorities and who trusted only me, this case might never get solved. And I really wanted to end this reign of terror. I'd like to show the world that in spite of being set aside by my husband, I still had some value. That what I did mattered.

Madonna must have gotten lonely up in my bed because she came down to see what was keeping me. I patted her big head and a plan began to form. While Madonna wasn't a pit bull or a rottweiler, she had the advantage of being huge. Her size was intimidating if you didn't know her or know much about the friendliness of Saint Bernards in general. I could take her with me. With Madonna and a gun I should be safe.

I could also take my cell phone, punch in the emergency number, and hold my thumb poised on the send button while I waited at the maintenance shed. That might work.

I reached over and picked up today's paper from the hutch where Mama had left it after she'd done the crossword puzzle. Sunrise was at six a.m. If I got to the course early, I would have the advantage of knowing the lay of the land ahead of time.

This was starting to sound like a very viable, very safe plan. I'd take my cell phone, Daddy's pistol, the dog, and a flashlight. That sounded good. And dark clothing to blend into the shadows.

I exhaled slowly.

I must be nuts.

I was going to do this.

Meet with an unknown person in a secluded area.

Alone.

Not exactly smart when you looked at it that way. But I could leave a note for Mama and the girls telling them where I was.

Yeah. That was good. I tucked a small flashlight in my shoulder bag and went upstairs to set my alarm clock for five a.m. I didn't want to oversleep and miss the meeting. I wanted to solve these murders. And I wanted the killer to pay for what he'd done.

I found a pair of dark slacks, an old black turtleneck, dark socks, and black slip-on loafers. Too bad I didn't have black sneakers.

That done, the only thing left to find was Daddy's pistol. I'd kept his guns hidden under my bed in hopes that would keep Mama and the girls from finding them. I'd seen the guns under there from time to time when I declared war on dust bunnies, but for the most part, the taupe dust ruffle on my bed covered up a multitude of sins.

Getting down on my knees and leaning over was all the invitation Madonna needed. She lay down next to me and thumped her tail happily, expecting me to wrestle with her. I lifted the ruffle and made a chilling discovery. There were only two guns under my bed.

Daddy's pistol was missing.

Where was it?

Had Mama come in and retrieved the gun as soon as people in town started being murdered? Or, even more worrisome, did one of the girls have it?

I would find out just as soon as I got back from my early-morning meeting. Neither the twenty two rifle nor the shotgun was small enough to fit in my purse, so I couldn't take either of them.

But now I had no weapon. There went half of my security plan.

It was probably better that way. I might have hurt myself or someone else if I had a gun. A "loaded" cell phone and a giant dog should be enough for an early morning meeting, right?

I could be careful. What were the chances the note was left by a homicidal maniac? Few things in life were certain. If I had to believe something, I was going to believe that the person who left the note had information, nothing more.

No problem.

As I got ready for bed I repeated those words over and over again so that I would believe them. I stared at the ceiling of my room, sure that I would never fall asleep.

So it was something of a shock to hear the alarm clock ring in the dark. I quickly hit the off button and slipped into my stealth outfit. Madonna groaned and lowered her big head back on my spare pillow. "No you don't," I said. "Get up. You're my first line of defense if this meeting turns ugly."

She must have thought I was talking to myself because she didn't move. It was only when I tugged on her collar that she stirred herself to grudgingly descend her throne.

I only had the smallest of qualms about taking a quite possibly pregnant dog into the line of fire. Would the dogcatcher come and take Madonna from me if he knew I was endangering her life?

I couldn't worry about animal welfare now. I had a killer to apprehend and I could only do that if I got to this meeting without alerting anyone else. I had no intention of Animal Control or my family members knowing that we'd left this house.

Fortifying myself with coffee was a necessity. In the kitchen, I scribbled off a quick note to Mama and the girls giving them specific instructions to call the police if I wasn't home before it was time to leave for school.

The dog seemed to catch my nervousness because she kept pacing around the kitchen. I double-checked to make sure that the flashlight worked, then drove to the golf course.

There were no cars on the road, no cars in the parking lot. Everyone who had any sense was still home in their beds, where they should be.

The closer I got to the maintenance shed, the more I questioned my sanity. This was not a smart thing to do. I should have disregarded the note and called someone.

If I was a cigarette smoker, I'd be chain-smoking right now. As it was, I craved chocolate and wished I kept a supply of candy bars in my car for emergencies. The closest thing I could find to chocolate in the Gray Beast was a used gum wrapper. Ugh.

I grasped Madonna's leash and steered her in the direction of the maintenance shed. Birds were making rustling sounds in the dark trees lining the parking lot. My nerves shouted, "Go home." But I couldn't. I was a woman on a mission.

The person who sent me that note had information I needed. I had to keep believing that. If I didn't, then the only other possibility was that I was going to my own funeral.

CHAPTER 25

There was a chill in my bones that had nothing to do with the brisk pre-dawn air. My plan to hold my cell phone in one hand with the emergency number already punched in was a no-go. I needed the flashlight because it was pitch black out here and I had the dog leash in my other hand.

I hoped like hell this wasn't a trap. I didn't relish being the killer's next victim. No one was lurking outside the maintenance shed, but the acrid smell of gasoline wafting out of the building puckered my nose.

Madonna was my weathervane. She wasn't agitated or off balance in any way and I felt relieved. So far, everything was going according to my plan. I stood outside the windowless building and waited. Was someone hiding inside the shed? I'd feel safer if I knew that no one was in there.

I entered the maintenance shed, stepping over the path of straw that led out the door. Madonna pulled me along on her leash.

Everything seemed to be in a semblance of order. There was no evidence of vandalism, no big white envelopes with my name on them sitting around. There were no people lurking behind the large grass-cutting machines in the darkest corners of the building.

Shovels and rakes lined the walls. You never knew what might come in handy in a situation like this. I was admiring a motorized sand trap rake when Madonna nudged me and I stumbled.

As I went down on my knees, a gun roared in my ears and the shed door swung shut.

I cowered beside Madonna on the floor. I was too scared to move, too scared to stay put. I took a shaky breath of the gasoline-scented air. This was bad. I had to get out of here.

No more shots rang out. I concluded I was alone in the shed. I grabbed my light and rushed to the door. It was locked.

Madonna barked incessantly at the door. Shit. Why hadn't Madonna barked before we were locked in? What kind of reject guard dog was she?

My stomach fell to my knees.

I wanted out of this building, fast.

Okay, Cleo. You've got a brain. Use it.

Why would someone shoot at you and then lock you in this aluminum frame building?

The pungent odor of gasoline permeated the air. With the quivering beam of my flashlight I traced the straw path on the floor. I'd assumed that the straw was used to cushion the concrete floor, but now that I thought about it, having straw around a place that spilled a lot of gasoline wasn't a good thing. All it would take was one spark and this place would go up like a matchbox.

The line of straw ended in a big heap, as if someone had been carrying straw away from the pile and lots had dropped on the way out of the building. Still, the pile worried me.

I darted over to investigate it. The closer I got, the stronger the smell of gasoline became. Whoever spilled the gas must have tried to cover it up with the straw. Rafe's occupational safety program needed a serious overhaul.

Red metal glinted at me from the pile. I pushed the straw aside and discovered three open gasoline cans and several bags of fertilizer. A cold chill raced down my spine.

This was not good. This pile of flammables and combustibles

were a disaster in the making. I hurriedly sealed the cans and dragged them away from the straw.

Madonna pawed the door. Her incensed barks reverberated through the metallic building. I tugged the heavy fertilizer bags in the other direction from the gas.

That's when I smelled smoke. My breath caught in my throat. Smoke. The straw. Fire.

What if I hadn't discovered that pile of gasoline and fertilizer? I wouldn't be long for this world.

A high pitched cackle sounded outside, scaring the breath back in me. I had to get out of here. Right now. Or I would be toast.

This building wasn't ventilated. Even if the shed didn't go up in flames, smoke inhalation could be fatal. I ran a quick lap of the building perimeter, Madonna barking at my heels, urging me faster and faster.

My lungs burned.

My hamstrings ached.

Why hadn't I kept in shape?

I couldn't budge the big bay doors. They must be padlocked from the outside. Shit. No windows and all the doors were locked.

But this place was filled with tools and machines. I huffed my way over to the biggest mower and climbed up on it. I'd seen the guy cutting the fairways with this big gang-style mower. The engine was in front, tractor style, and that gave me hope that it was powerful enough to get me out of here.

Flames licked under the doorway. I was running out of time. The fire would be in the building in seconds. Madonna barked unceasingly.

I turned the key.

Click.

Nothing happened.

The engine didn't turn over.

Ohgod. Ohgod. Ohgod.

I was too young to die. I wanted to see my girls grow up, to hold my grandbabies.

Think, Cleo.

If the motor didn't start automatically, then there must be a combination of things to do. I'd never driven a tractor like this before, but once on vacation I'd ridden Uncle George's field tractor. That one had a clutch which had to be engaged and a manual choke mechanism.

I looked frantically at the knobs and pedals and began pulling and pushing things in various combinations. One knob activated headlights on the tractor.

I turned the key again and heard the engine whir until it caught. The room brightened as the fire caught in the straw near the door. I pushed a ball-headed lever by the seat forward and maneuvered towards the nearest wall.

I didn't know if this would work but I wasn't waiting around for help to find me. I was getting out of here right now. Please, please, let this work.

Metal grated and groaned when the mower struck the wall. I crouched down and covered my head as rivets popped and the wall failed. Fresh air wafted in my face. I gulped untainted air as if I'd been underwater too long.

Bizarre questions flickered through my brain. Would my auto insurance cover this accident? And, how would I explain to Rafe that I'd destroyed his maintenance shed? How much did a maintenance shed cost, anyway?

Madonna surged through the hole I'd made in the wall and bounded around the building, barking as she ran. I couldn't worry about the shed now. Madonna was on the trail of someone.

I followed her on the tractor, the headlights picking up the twin trails of paw prints and human footprints on the dew-covered grass of the number two fairway.

I lost sight of Madonna but I honed in on her barking over the rumble of the tractor. In the faint pink light of daybreak, I drove down the center of the fairway of this par five. It doglegged left and once I rounded the bend, I visually picked up Madonna about one hundred yards ahead of me.

She'd stopped running and was standing on someone.

Good girl.

The person under Madonna wore dark clothing and was not very large. A metallic object gleamed in the grass about five feet from the dog. I drove up, stopped the tractor, and jumped down. I investigated the metallic object first. In the tractor's headlights, I recognized the initials engraved in the handle plate.

J. A. S.

Daddy's initials. Joseph Anthony Sampson. This was Daddy's pistol. My heart caught in my throat. How had this person ended up with my father's gun? Had the killer been in my house like Charles Manson's creepy crawly people?

Had Dudley and the bank guard been shot with Daddy's gun? I picked up the gun and pointed it at the person under my dog.

A person who was sneezing her head off. I saw traces of bleached blonde hair trailing from her stocking cap and I suddenly knew who Madonna had taken down.

Denise.

Charlie's wife.

Hell. I should have trusted my instincts.

Denise had everything. Why did she have to kill people? Wasn't it enough that she'd ruined my life? How much destruction was enough for this woman?

Why? That question hammered through my brain, and I couldn't begin to answer it.

But I did remember I had my cell phone in my purse which was miraculously still slung across my chest, bandolier style. I dialed the emergency number and requested assistance. I didn't call Madonna off Denise or encourage Madonna to stop barking.

That barking was the sweetest sound I'd ever heard, second only to the wail of the approaching sirens. That day when Denise lay down on my bed flashed into my head. She must have stolen Daddy's gun then. Did she hear I'd burned the bedding she touched? Was that why she tried to burn me to a crisp?

Over all the racket, I asked her, "Why Denise? Why did you try to kill me?"

In between sneezes, she screamed at me. "You ruined everything. All my plans. I had to kill you."

My fingers tightened reflexively on the pistol grip. "In case you haven't noticed, I'm very much alive, and you're going to jail. That is if you don't die from sneezing to death."

"Damn you, Cleo. I was so close. Why did you give Charlie an alibi for the night of the bank guard shooting? I almost had it all."

"You're wrong, Denise. You had it all, only you didn't place any value on what you had."

"Can't you get this dog off of me?" she whined.

"Nope." I smiled bitterly. "I figure that's the least I can do to repay you for almost torching me."

"Damn it. You must be part cat. How the hell did you get out of there?"

"I used my head, which is something you should have done before you became a murderer. What did I ever do to you? Why did you have to go and kill Dudley? He was just getting his life back together. And the bank guard. What did he ever do to you?"

"Go to hell. I don't owe you any explanations."

The sirens were closer now. I saw the flashing lights in the distance. The cops and firemen would be here any minute now. I wanted to kick the shit out of Denise. And puncture her inflatable boobs. And rip every strand of bleached hair out of her head.

Instead I stood there aiming the loaded pistol at her, watching Madonna drool incessantly as she barked. Slime trails of doggie spittle decorated Denise's stocking cap and black shirt like strands of gleaming tinsel on a Christmas tree.

Denise wiggled and Madonna closed her massive jaws around Denise's neck. My eyebrows shot up. Remind me never to cross this dog. When Madonna got pissed, she meant business.

But she was definitely on my team. She wasn't the type to transfer her loyalty to a bleached blonde with inflatable boobs.

After helping me catch Dudley's killer, Madonna could sleep in my bed for as long as she liked. So what if I smelled like a dog for the rest of my life? Madonna had saved me from being shot between the eyes. I'd saved us from being toasted. We were a great team.

CHAPTER 26

I had just given my story to the police and the mayor when Rafe arrived. His penetrating gaze never left mine as he strode to my side. "What are you doing here?" I asked, shivering.

"I work here, remember?" He gave Madonna a quick pat on the head. "What are you doing here? The cops say the course is closed again today while they investigate the fire. I can't make any money if the golf course is closed."

"Sorry about that," I said. "It wasn't my choice to meet at the course."

"Tell me what happened."

I didn't much care for his imperious tone, but I had ruined his shed. Would he hold that against me? As I repeated the events for him, he grew agitated. He grabbed me by the shoulders and shook me. "Why didn't you call me? Did you think you could take on a killer by yourself?"

I struggled to get away from him, but he held me fast. Why didn't my wonder dog attack him? "Dammit, Rafe," I said. "I don't need this. I have to get home to my kids and explain what happened to them."

He glared at me again, and then he kissed me. Hard. My head started to spin and I think the earth may have moved a time or two.

I'm pretty sure I melted against him, the kiss was so hot. Maybe my clothes incinerated. I couldn't tell.

I opened my eyes when I realized he'd stopped kissing me.

Catcalls from the assembled police officers rang in my ears. I said the first thing that popped into my head. "That was no first-date kiss."

He grinned and my toes curled. Again. "This isn't our first date. We may never have one if you keep doing harebrained things like meeting serial killers at daybreak."

I waved him away. "Don't start on me. Britt has already fussed and read me the riot act. I want to go home."

He pinned me with a look. I may not have known him very well, but I recognized that look. It was the "we'll talk about it later look." Daddy had perfected that look on Mama. That look said "you're not off the hook," but most of all it said he cared.

Was I ready for a relationship with Rafe? I was still emotionally vulnerable from Charlie's betrayal. Letting this physical attraction flame out without ever indulging our apparently very mutual passion was a good idea.

Fortunately this wasn't a game show and I didn't have to choose door number one, two or three.

With trembling hands, I rooted through my purse for my keys. I couldn't make my hands stop shaking. Madonna nudged me with her head, and I would have toppled over except for the tight grip Rafe had on me.

"I'll take you home, Cleo," Rafe said.

"You don't have to do that. My car is over at the maintenance shed."

"So are about twenty other vehicles. It will be tomorrow before you can get the Beast out of there."

"I've got to take the girls to school," I said.

"The golf course is closed for the day. I can help you out there."

Britt winked at me as Rafe led me back down number two. I could just imagine what he'd be telling his wife about that hot kiss Rafe gave me. It'd be all over the grocery store before lunchtime. It would be headline news by evening.

I envisioned the kiss taking on such legendary proportions, that folks would forget to give me credit for flushing out the killer. They wouldn't even bat an eyelash at my detecting skills or give me an ounce of credit for saving myself.

On the other hand, maybe they'd remember that I'd been a pillar of the community for years. That I did their taxes on time and that not one of my clients had ever been audited by the IRS.

One could only hope.

Madonna and I were just starting in on our second cup of coffee that afternoon when Jonette walked in. After reassuring Mama and the girls that everything was all right, then sending the girls off to school with Rafe—in a cool car, no less—I'd slept for a couple of hours.

The excitement had been too much for Mama. After she fixed me a bowl of chicken soup for breakfast, she popped a sleeping pill and went to bed for the day. When she came to, I expected to be blasted for my reckless behavior.

Work was out of the question. I'd declared today a holiday, but the truth was I couldn't get any work done because I still didn't understand *why* Denise had killed Dudley and the bank guard. I should have pressed her for more answers this morning.

"There you are." Jonette greeted me with a warm hug and then joined me at the table. "You're the topic of conversation all over town. Joan at the beauty shop couldn't stop talking about your flaming affair with Rafe this morning, Buck over at the gas station thought you and Madonna ought to get some kind of award for getting that killer off our streets, and Edna at the grocery store says your problem is that there's too much sex on TV. Edna says it's no wonder that you're sex starved."

My coffee went down the wrong way and I coughed it out. "Sex starved?"

Jonette's grin was so smug I wanted to wipe it off her face. Trouble is she had a right to grin and she knew it. She had insisted adamantly that it wasn't natural for a woman of my age and previous sexual proclivities to have such a long period of abstinence.

"Yup. Sex starved. She said you wouldn't be jumping men in public if you weren't all revved up by those racy TV programs. Doesn't that make you wonder which programs she's watching? Doesn't sound like they're the family programs."

I smirked. If I didn't laugh about this, I was going to spend too much time thinking about being sex starved. Which I most certainly was. "My guess is that she's jealous. She wishes she could lure a man like Rafe Golden into her bed."

Charlie and the girls came in just then. The girls swirled through the kitchen for a few minutes foraging like locusts, then swept out to watch TV. Charlie fixed himself a cup of coffee and joined Jonette and me at the kitchen table. "What's this I hear about Rafe Golden taking the girls to school this morning?" Charlie asked.

"He brought me home from the golf course because my car was blocked in. It was very nice of him to help out," I added defensively. I didn't know if Charlie had heard about this morning's kiss or not, but I didn't need him doing any macho stuff in my kitchen right now. I had just been through a terrible horrible rotten no-good day.

Charlie crossed his arms and scowled at me. "I don't like him hanging around here, especially in the mornings. People might think he slept over or something."

"That's not really your concern," I murmured into my coffee. It occurred to me that Charlie's wife had just been arrested for murder and that she'd tried to frame him to take the blame.

His day hadn't been that much better than mine. "About Denise. Why did she do it?"

"You'll have to narrow it down a bit, Clee," Charlie said. "Denise did a lot of things, and none of them were good. I found out today that she's been playing me from the get-go. I was her ticket to computer access to unlimited funds at the bank. What my computer passwords couldn't get for her, she used Dudley's to obtain."

"I thought her alibi for Dudley's murder was solid. I saw that logbook myself."

"Her mother lives on the first floor. Once her mother went to bed, Denise went out the window and no one was the wiser."

I ran my finger around the rim of my daisy-splashed coffee mug. I wasn't surprised that Denise didn't have any love in her heart for Charlie. She hadn't minded sleeping with him and taking him away from me because that furthered her own interests.

How did Charlie feel about being used in such a callous manner? I'd never liked her and now I felt completely vindicated about my distrust of her.

"Was that what this was all about then? She killed Dudley because of money?"

"Not just some money. Millions of dollars. Dudley found out what she was doing when he checked into Ed Monday's bank problem. She'd been authorizing loans in Dudley's name and siphoning the funds to an offshore account in her mother's name. I've spent the day combing through our records for the police. The bank guard could place Denise at the bank the night of my supposed fishing trip, so that's why she killed him."

Charlie's hand reached out to cover mine. "She'd have killed you too if you weren't so quick on your feet. I'm still in shock over what she tried to do."

I edged my hand out from under his. I felt sorry for Charlie.

His life had been turned upside down by Denise. But if he'd been content in our marriage, he never would have strayed in the first place. I was absolutely positively certain I didn't want him back.

Charlie cleared his throat. "I was wondering if I might speak to you for a moment, privately."

His tone of voice was carefully calculated. He and I both knew that I had always melted whenever he lowered his voice and put that sort of heat in his eyes. But it wasn't happening today.

Hallelujah!

I had finally exorcised the man from my thoughts and desires. I was a free woman. "Anything you have to say to me can be said in front of Jonette."

"Dammit, Clee," Charlie said. "I wanted to do this right. The thing is, I hardly know what to say. I've used some really bad judgment these past two years. I should have listened to you in the beginning. You said Denise was a two-bit hustler when Dudley hired her as a bank teller. You were right. I was wrong, so wrong that it almost cost you your life. Can you ever forgive me?"

Forgiveness was cheap, and surprisingly, I didn't want to snap Charlie's head off any longer. He'd made some whopper mistakes, but he'd paid for them too. "No problem."

Charlie shot an imploring look at Jonette to leave the room, but Jonette sat as if her butt was glued to the chair. I didn't mind Jonette hearing this conversation. We'd shared so many private conversations over the years, she knew Charlie as well as I did, better even because of her objectivity.

Charlie leaned closer to me. I was glad the dog lay on the floor between us so that he couldn't scoot his chair next to mine. "I want you and the girls to move back home, Clee. I want us to try again."

His ludicrous suggestion made me laugh out loud. "You're joking, right?"

Unfortunately he didn't crack a smile. "I'm serious. This whole thing made me realize that there's no substitute for family, and you and the girls are my family. I need you, Cleo."

This was what I'd been secretly hoping for over the last year and a half, to have Charlie beg me to come back to him. But now that he'd come to his senses, I wasn't the least bit interested in his offer.

Denise may have led Charlie out of the rose garden, but he'd gone under his own power. What Charlie and I had had in our marriage, though it had been enough for me, it obviously hadn't been enough for him.

And even if I had a brain seizure right here and now and actually thought moving back in with him was a good idea, I'd always be wondering where he was when he was out of my sight. Every month, I would be scouring the charge card bills for evidence that he'd been cheating on me again.

No, the situation we had right now was best for all concerned. Charlie was here on the rebound. Once his wife was sentenced he could move on with his life and he'd forget that he'd been over here groveling.

My silence must have unnerved him. "I swear I'd never so much as look at another woman," Charlie pleaded. "Please, Cleo. I've missed you."

It took me about three seconds to formulate my reply. "I'm sorry, Charlie. I'm moving on with my life. I'm seeing someone now and I don't know if I'll ever marry again."

"You can't mean that." From his dark expression you'd have thought I wanted to leap off the cliff at Hogan's Glen Overlook Park.

"I do mean it." I held his gaze so that he'd know I was firm in my decision.

He leaned back in his chair and didn't say anything for a few long moments. Then he grinned his special sexy grin. The one he always flashed when he had sex on the brain and about ten minutes until blast off. The one that used to curl my toes.

I noticed right away that my toes weren't curling. I was absolutely impervious to "the look." No matter what was in my future, it wasn't being Mrs. Charlie Jones again.

He rose from his chair. "I can see you just need a little more time. I'll be back."

Unexpectedly, he leaned down to kiss me on the mouth. I turned my head so that his lips brushed my cheek. I rejoiced because I wasn't awash in gooseflesh.

I stood with him. "What we had is over, Charlie. Get that through that thick melon head of yours. The entire police force witnessed another man kissing me this morning, and you want to know what? I was kissing him back. Right there in broad daylight."

"So what? I got married. But I still think of you all the time. We were meant to be together, Cleo. Just like the original Cleopatra and Julius Caesar."

I ushered him to the door. "Now you're scaring me, Charlie. Since when do you know anything about ancient history?"

His eyes twinkled. "I'll do whatever it takes to get my woman back."

"I'm not your woman," I hollered to his back.

He grinned from his Beemer. Charlie Jones always rose to a challenge and my refusal to take him back had awakened his competitive instincts. I might as well have lit the Olympic torch and proclaimed, "Let the games begin."

Jonette put the empty coffee mugs in the sink. "Well that was entertaining. Who would have thought he'd be here begging for you to take him back?"

"It's not going to happen. I'm so over him."

241

Jonette eyed me dimly. "Don't forget who you're talking to here. I know how sex starved you are and how lonely you've been. If you mess this thing up with Rafe, you'll be thinking of pulling Charlie up from the injured reserve list."

"I've never thought of men as interchangeable. I can barely handle them one at a time. I can't imagine stringing Charlie along while I date Rafe."

"Honey, you're not going to have to string him along. Charlie finally wised up. He was a better man when the two of you were together. Now that he knows that, he's gonna try to get you back."

"Thank you, Doctor Ruth. I kind of got that on my own."

There was another knock at my kitchen door. I peered out the window and recognized a now familiar red convertible. Rafe's car. "Hell. When it rains, it pours."

Jonette headed for the front door. "This is my cue to leave. I wouldn't be complaining too loud if I were you. Most women would kill to have it raining men."

Raining men. Did that mean I could reach up and catch the one I wanted? Interesting concept. I opened the back door and stepped into Rafe's embrace. "I thought you'd never get here," I murmured in his ear.

ABOUT THE AUTHOR

Maggie Toussaint is a scientist by training, a romanticist at heart. She's fascinated by how things work, whether it's complex machinery, a Sudoku puzzle, or the subtext of a conversation. She's married to a PGA Certified Golf Instructor, has two daughters, and lives in coastal Georgia. She writes features for *The Darien News*.

She received an MA in Environmental Science from Hood College in Frederick, Maryland. She's a member of Mystery Writers of America, Sisters in Crime, and Romance Writers of America. Whether she's writing cozy mystery or romantic suspense, you can count on a page-turner of a story and vivid characters. Visit her at www.maggietoussaint.com.